ELK DREAMS

Written by: Glenda and David Clemens

Narrated by: David Clemens

Copyright and Disclaimers

This is a work of fiction. Names, characters, organizations, places, events, and incidents are either products of the author's imagination or are used fictitiously.

Text copyright 2021 by Glenda and David Clemens
Cover art copyright 2021 by Glenda J Clemens
Cover photo copyright 2021 by Don Detrick
All Rights Reserved

No part of this book may be reproduced, or stored in a retrieval system, or transmitted in any form or by any means, electronic, mechanical, photocopying, recording or otherwise, without express written permission of the author and publisher.

Special Thanks

To Don Detrick

For the amazing photo of
A goofball elk for the cover.
Nelson really appreciates it!

To Proof Readers:
They make all our books much better
David Rains
Christie Carlson
Desi Hart
Cindi Bowles
Briana Faria

DEDICATION

This book is dedicated to:

Ray Clemens—
He is one of the men
In Old Man Coffee
And a great help
In all the dilemmas.
(AND there were a lot
Of dilemmas!)

On the Horns of a Moral Dilemma

Genesis 22, verse 5-10

(from the King James Version of the Bible)

And Abraham said unto his young men, "Abide ye here with the ass; and I and the lad will go yonder and worship, and come again to you"

And Abraham took the wood for the burnt offering, and laid it upon Isaac his son and he took the fire in his hand, and a knife; and they went both of them together.

And Isaac spake unto Abraham his father, and said, "My father here am I." And he said, "Behold the fire and the wood: but where is the lamb for a burnt offering?"

And Abraham said, "My son, God will provide himself a lamb for a burnt offering." So they went both of them together.

And they came to the place which God had told him of; and Abraham built an altar there, and laid the wood in order, and bound Isaac his son, and laid him on the altar upon the wood.

And Abraham stretched forth his hand and took the knife to slay his son.

Some Everyday Thoughts

"We are tamed animals
(some with kind, some with cruel, masters)
And should probably starve if we got out of our cage.
That is one horn of the dilemma.
But in an increasingly planned society,
How much of what I value can survive?
That is the other horn."
— **C.S. Lewis,**

CHAPTER ONE

Intentions were important to Simon Chowdhury. Simon did not intend to die today, the last day of the year.

He was a man who set intentions for his day-to-day life. Others might call them to-do lists, but he called them intentions. His mother teased him about his intentions, then one day she told him, "You can play Simon Says with your intentions until the sun rises in the west, son. But intentions always require action and attention to be of any use. Don't tell me what you intend, Simon, show me what you attend to."

His grandparents had come to the Seattle area from India, long before he was born. Thinking of his mother, who he called Amma, he tried to smile, but blood trickling from his mouth and neck made smiling impossible. He felt a tear trickle across his face and down to his nose and mouth, adding more salt to the blood.

I love you, Amma. I wasn't paying enough attention. I really didn't intend to die today.

To further his pain in dying, he didn't understand his sister, Tamal, a tall, elegant woman with striking features and a brilliant mind. She was the smartest woman he'd ever known. She worked in Edmonds, Washington at The Pacific Arts Gallery and made a big impact there. He had only one question: Why was she so determined to destroy him?

No point in worrying about her now. I wish she had talked with me, or at least explained why.

He struggled to breathe. He couldn't speak and trying to speak increased his pain. His current predicament confused him. His intention this morning was to take a quick hike up Little Si to watch the sunrise over Mount Si. He loved when the morning light shone on mountainsides and crept slowly into the valley below.

Sunny days were uncommon at this time of year, and he wanted to take advantage of the opportunity. He loved standing on the small mountain watching the sunlight appear on the Cascade mountains in Washington State. He wanted to begin the last day of the old year with the sun on his face.

He'd planned to come back tomorrow morning and greet the sun for the new year, if the clear weather held for another day. After sunrise today, his intention was to head back home and get ready for Old Man Coffee tomorrow. He'd even remembered to buy coffee and donuts.

He'd climbed to the top of Little Si, watched the sunrise, then turned to make his way down the mountain. It had surprised him to hear his sister's voice calling for help. It was not like her to be outside the city, especially out hiking alone. Yesterday, he had invited her to join him today in welcoming the sun on the last day of the year, but she had declined.

Now he knew, she didn't really need help. She just wanted him deeper in the woods and off the beaten trail. Her anger confused him. W*hy Tamal? I don't understand.*

He wished he had not told his sister of his plans for this morning. Simon was grateful he'd welcomed the sun before all hell broke loose. Seeing the sun rise one more day was something he now counted as the best, last blessing of his life on Earth.

He couldn't see much now, but he could see the ground where he was lying on his right side. He could see the sunlight casting dappled patterns through the tree branches. The damp earth on which he lay smelled good, but it was cold and getting colder with each painful breath.

He felt the clumps of dirt, twigs, and leaves tossed on his body. *I always wanted a natural burial. I will be fine, but I'd rather not have died today. That's a moot point now. I'm supposed to host Old Man Coffee tomorrow. Sorry, fellas.*

He could hear his sister's heavy breathing as she worked to cover his body. Throughout the entire incident, the only words she'd said were, "I've heard enough from you, Simon. I never want you to say another word to me, brother. I'm well and truly fed up with Simon Says."

It surprised him she was strong enough to overwhelm him with such efficiency. Her strike was so sudden and unexpected, he'd not been able to put up a defense. She stabbed him over and over in the neck. Then she'd cut out his tongue. The indignity of her cutting out his tongue was nearly as humiliating as dying, murdered by his sister, on his favorite mountain.

Tamal looked at the antique knife in her hand. "You're such a sap, Simon. You kept this old Hindu bichwa dagger as if it were something important. It's nothing more than the dregs of our ancestors." She didn't notice she was crying until her nose began to run. She pulled off her ski mask, blew her nose and forced herself to quit crying. She didn't notice the tear drops or mucus from her nose on the knife. She tossed the dagger on top of her brother and buried it with him.

She tossed the larger branches and rocks on top of his body. To Simon, they felt heavy, but not crushing. He couldn't hold his eyes open any longer. The grit from the debris hurt his eyes, but the pain of his wounds no longer bothered him.

He sighed as he closed his eyes.

Dying isn't as hard to do as I'd thought it would be.

Then Simon had no thoughts or intentions to attend to.

CHAPTER TWO

Tamal Chowdhury picked up her ski mask and tucked it into her back pocket. She walked a few steps away from her brother's grave, turned her back to the grave, and closed her eyes for a few moments. She took a deep breath. When she was sure she was calm, she opened her eyes and turned to look where she knew her brother's body lay. She smiled to herself and thought, *no human will easily find you, brother, although I think the animals will find you quicker than I'd like.*

Regardless of her skill at burying her brother, she knew she had limited time to vacate the premises before other humans were hiking to this peak. She piled a few more big rocks and heavy branches over the grave, then picked up armful after armful of leaves and debris. She tossed the rotting leaves over the top of the whole grave until it looked much like the rest of the floor of the surrounding forest. It would have to do.

She quickly hiked away from the site of the murder and to the trail her brother had used. She took a minute or two to scan the trail and brushed evidence of Simon's and her footprints from the trail. She then jogged down Little Si where the trail allowed and walked where the trail was too steep with lose rocks. Once at the parking area where morning hikers were arriving, she quickly went to the cars.

She ignored the hikers and her car, but drove her brother's car to the Sallal Grange, close by in North Bend. She parked the vehicle behind the building, under some trees away from the major traffic areas. She did not notice the ski mask had slipped out of her back pocket and lodged itself under the seat belt.

Tamal got out of the car, tossed the keys on the dashboard, and locked the car doors. She doubted anyone would even notice the small black SUV. Even if they did, it wouldn't happen soon. With the holiday weekend festivities, nothing seemed to go on in the sleepy little town of North Bend, Washington.

Tamal smiled and walked away between the trees, where she paused for a few minutes, watching her brother's car just to be sure no one had seen her. She thought of her father's death in his old Volvo. She'd thought she would miss her father, but she never did. He was just another bossy man. She'd had more than enough of bossy men in her life. First her father, then Simon. Now Roger, her husband, was beginning to sound like yet another bossy man.

Once she was certain no one noticed her, she walked out of the trees to the sidewalk on North Bend Way. She stretched as she looked around. Cars passed. Others were walking or jogging and not paying attention to her. *Good. I'm ready to get back to my car and head home.* She walked a few seconds and then sped up her walking until she was jogging.

She jogged nearly a mile back to the Little Si trailhead. It took just over ten minutes, which was a relief. She was tired. She'd had a busy physical morning. Burying her brother took more effort than she'd expected. After the adrenaline rush of the killing, the work of burial was a genuine struggle.

She got in her car, drove to the McDonald's, and bought a breakfast sandwich and iced coffee. She deserved the treat after how hard she'd worked this morning. It was nearly eight o'clock. She had a full day ahead of her.

She drove on I-90 heading west with Gustav Holst blasting through her car. The Planets were epic and to her mind the score of her life. By the time she was nearing the turnoff for the Issaquah Highlands, she was feeling better, more herself. The completion of her task for the day, then the music lifted her spirits, reinforcing her belief that she was a woman beyond mere mortal women. She felt she was an elemental force, a powerful woman.

She drove to the apartment she was renting between the Sammamish Highlands and Redmond. The apartment was nice enough and cheaper than it would have been in West Seattle, but she hated it. Doing something about her living arrangements was next on her agenda.

Her recalcitrant husband thought they should stay together in West Seattle. She'd hated the thought of living with Roger even one more day. His desires for children and sex more frequently than she cared for were part of the problem. She wanted sex only when the urge for climax couldn't be accomplished any other way.

The final straw, on her birthday, was his agreement with the family: she should stop talking about her deceased twin Taman. She knew they thought she'd murdered him in the womb. What if she did? It wasn't for them to fuss at her, especially Roger. She was through with marriage to Roger, but not through with the house she felt should be hers. She deserved much more, of course, but the house was an adequate beginning. Roger would come around or she'd find a more permanent way to have him out of the picture of her life.

In her apartment, she cleaned up after the hike and the elimination and disposal of another competing sibling. She laundered all her clothes to be sure all traces of her brother and Little Si were completely gone. She vacuumed the floors, scrubbed herself in the shower and wiped every surface in the apartment clean.

Hunger gnawed. She had worked hard today and needed more sustenance. She reheated pizza from the night before for her lunch. She tried to make plans for the future, but she was exhausted and yet jittery with anxiety. Restless energy drove her. She gave up working on plans for her next steps in life and instead watched a movie. She could not remember a single scene and kept rewinding the movie.

When the movie didn't work, she opened her computer and the on-line art galleries from around the World. She flipped through each art piece, stopping only for a few minutes at the ones she loved.

Her favorite artist, Artemisia, helped calm her mind a little. The bold women she portrayed spoke to Tamal. These women were her sisters. Especially Judith. She did what needed to be done in life. Tamal would willingly pay much for one painting by Artemisia. Judith was always a reminder that men never failed to underestimate women. The heroine brought an important man to his knees and took his head as her reward. Women of strength and power could always bring a man down.

She smiled and whispered, "Someday, Tamal. Someday, Artemisia will be hanging on the walls of my home."

When she turned away from the computer, she knew the beginning would be to build up the Pacific Arts Gallery to real glory. She wanted real art by actual artists. Not the splashes and dullness created by local wanna be artists. One more painting of Mt. Rainier or Puget Sound and she would choke the artist with her bare hands.

Her head ached a little. Her fatigue was overwhelming her. It was only seven in the evening, but it felt like midnight. She sighed and shook her head.

Finally, she gave up and went to bed early.

She tried to read an art theft mystery by her favorite author Estelle Ryan, but the words blurred and the plot was something she couldn't comprehend. Finally, she gave up, turned off the bedside lamp and closed her eyes.

She didn't hear the New Year's Eve fireworks. One day was much like another to her. She'd never understood celebrating just because the calendar flipped another page. The only celebrations she enjoyed were those for her personal accomplishments and for art exhibits.

She slept long and hard that New Year's Eve night, not dreaming of anything in particular. A few silly animals such as a blue butterfly, a goofy, grinning elk, and a bobcat hunting for mice and baby birds whispered to her in her dreams. Chameleons paraded around, taunting her, their tongues flicking, tasting her skin. She ignored them all. Except for one chameleon that reminded her of the reclusive billionaire, Hadar Hamal.

Now there was a man she'd love to know better, especially about his money. With a man who looked like Hadar standing beside her, Tamal would be glorious. She could see the headlines now. They would be the talk of the artistic elite around the World. Now there's a man worth killing for.

She smiled in her dreams and told herself, *this new year will be the making of my dreams come true.* Sadly, it would mean other obstructions would need to be removed, but none of them would really affect Tamal.

CHAPTER THREE

Near White Center in West Seattle, people were stirring, getting ready for their day. It was New Year's Day and very few people had to be up early for work. One household was welcoming this day of no school, no work, and an entire day to continue working on their new home. It was the first home they'd ever owned and though it was small, and nearly one hundred years old, it was theirs. They planned to celebrate the New Year by making donuts.

Donut Friday had become a family tradition. Today was both Friday and their first New Year's Day in their new home. This Friday was more special than usual. It was the New Year, and they all looked forward to what the year would bring.

The father and husband of the happy family, Stan Dalton, pulled his journal out of the bedside table and wrote out his dream. Dreams had been much more common for him since starting the practice of shamanic journeying, a form of meditation taught as core shamanism. He found that his dreams and his journeywork were often related. Part of the practice was to write down the dreams and journeys as soon as possible. His Power Animal, Nelson, a young bull elk who had a propensity to grin nearly all the time, had been active in his dreams last night. When he finished writing he turned to his wife, Renee and said, I'll get the donut dough started before I go to Old Man Coffee.

She reached up and said, "You seem a little down, sweetie."

"Just a dream I had about Old Man Coffee."

"Not a good one?"

"Not a bad one, really, just one that has left me uneasy. I'll head out to the garage studio and do a journey after I get the dough started. I want to be sure I remembered everything Nelson had to say, and try to get a little more clarification."

She smiled and said, "I'm going to give myself a few more minutes of lazy snoozing before Nina wakes up."

"Great. No need to be up and at 'em early today. I'll see you ladies after Old Man Coffee."

A few blocks away, another couple rolled out of bed, glad for the day off from work. The man, Harvey Marlow, groaned a bit with arthritis as he rolled out of bed. His wife, Sharla, patted him on the back and said, "Get up, old man. We're starting a new year today."

He grinned. "Hey, forty-eight isn't old."

"No, it isn't but I bet your achy joints are telling you something different."

He looked over his shoulder. "If you really loved me, you'd warm up these old man bones."

She chuckled. "I'm going to the bathroom. When I come back, we'll see what we can do. It's our anniversary so we should have sex at least once today."

He laughed, leaned over and kissed his wife. "Making love with you on this day or any other is fine by me. I'll use the hall bathroom and meet you right back here to celebrate another year together."

Sharla smiled, remembering their wedding twenty years ago today. They'd married in Cozumel on New Year's Day. They'd gone there on a whim and married without a lot of fanfare, but a lot of joy and love. They counted their week there as their honeymoon. It didn't seem possible they'd been together for twenty years, but she was happy in their life and marriage. She supposed such happiness made the years go by quickly.

Sharla wanted to go back to the island where they started their lives together and celebrate their twenty years of marriage. What Harvey didn't know was that she'd arranged for a weeklong stay at a Cozumel high-end resort starting tomorrow. They had a private cabana with a private beach in front of the cabana. She'd been going to the gym every day for months to tone up her body to look good in her new, bright pink, polka dot bikini.

Today, she knew Harvey would head a few blocks away to join his buddies for Old Man Coffee at Simon Chowdhury's home. The day was going to be sunny and not too cold, so each man would bring his folding chair and a go-cup or thermos of coffee. All the men were within walking distance of each other, and they all played musical instruments of one sort or another. Harvey played guitar, both acoustic and electric. The men would sit and gab for an hour or two in Simon's driveway.

She'd asked once why they sat in the driveway. He'd said, "We wanted it to feel like we were just taking a break together. We want to talk about serious things but not have it be a part of our routine family lives. We also didn't want any fuss or bother. Stan, Roger, and I, have wives. Jack has a husband. Stan has a kid. We wanted this to be just us, old men, hanging out, chatting, and having coffee. Besides, with wives and kids around, we couldn't curse or talk about the finer aspects of life."

She'd chuckled and asked, "So you sit around saying 'shit' 'fuck' and 'damn straight?'"

He'd grinned and nodded. "More or less. But we also talk about music, life and our inner demons. Just old man shit."

"Well, although none of you qualify as old, I think it's great."

While Harvey was hanging with his friends, she would finish the last preparations for their journey. She'd tell Harvey his plans for the coming week as soon as he finished confabbing with the fellas of Old Man Coffee. Before Old Man Coffee with Simon and their buddies, she'd warm his bones up a bit to wish him Happy Anniversary.

Of course, what Sharla and the Old Man Coffee gang didn't know, was that Simon was communing in a deep and abiding way with Mother Earth. He'd not had a chance to cancel the plans for the morning Old Man Coffee session.

CHAPTER FOUR

Simon had a nice home he loved. His flat driveway was unusual in the Seattle area, but made for easy sitting and talking. Most of the time they all walked to Old Man Coffee, but today, Roger showed up in his pickup. He planned to go buy flowers and candy for his wife as soon as they finished Old Man Coffee.

All the Old Man Coffee buddies showed up except for Simon. He didn't answer the door and Stan said, "I bet he had to go get coffee."

Harvey laughed. "Yep, last time it was his turn to host Old Man Coffee, he had to drink hot tea. Tea isn't what Old Man Coffee is all about. After all, this isn't Old Man Tea."

Jack, Roger, and Stan all laughed with Harvey. They knew their friend Simon was a forgetful sort of fella, but a great friend to them all. They sat in their lawn chairs in Simon's driveway, chatting. After about ten minutes Roger said, "I'm calling the son-of-a-bitch and see if he's forgotten what day it is or who's supposed to be hosting."

Simon's phone buzzed, but he didn't hear or feel a thing. Not feeling anything was a blessing for him. The forest carnivores were busy digging up his body. The rats and mice hadn't bothered with digging him up but burrowed down and started munching as soon as the other human left. Before long, a large yellow cougar who intended to enjoy the fine feast, chased away the small rodents.

By the time Simon's phone was buzzing, it was no longer in his pocket but tossed aside in the feeding frenzy. Bobcats, foxes, and coyotes had feasted after the cougar had eaten his fill. Then the smaller animals came back to enjoy the buffet. Insects were busy partaking of the bounty and laying eggs as well. Simon's desire for a natural burial and returning to the land was fast becoming a reality.

Roger shook his head and said, "It went to voice mail. He's probably busy with something and can't answer."

"Maybe," Stan said, "But, I've got an uneasy feeling. I'm going to go around back and take a peek through the patio door."

Jack stood up and said, "I'll go with you, buddy. Just in case."

"Just in case what?"

Jack grinned. "Well, in case there's a drop or two of blood. I wouldn't want you to pass out or get frightened."

The other men laughed, knowing Stan was a great bass player but could have never been a doctor or nurse. The sight of blood or sometimes just a scratch and he'd keel over.

Stan shook his head. "Hardy, har, har. That's ripe, coming from a drummer."

Jack laughed and said, "Kaboom, Ching," mimicking playing the drums.

They opened the fence gate and went around back to peek in the patio door. Simon's dog Pavlov, a big yellow lab, was whining and scratching at the door. They could see the water dish and food bowls were empty. Stan said, "I don't like this. Simon would never leave Pavlov alone for a long enough for the water and food bowls to be empty."

Jack jiggled the door, but it was locked. "Do you have a key to his house?"

"No. Let's go ask Roger if he does. Simon is his brother-in-law."

"Right. Good idea."

The two men went back to the driveway and told Roger and Harvey what they'd found. Stan asked, "Do you have a key to his place, Roger?"

"No," he sighed. "And the last thing I want to do is phone his sister, but I'll do it."

"Things still not going well with you two?" Jack asked.

He shook his head. "Don't ask. She gets weirder every day. I've enjoyed being separated for a couple of weeks, but I'll call her. We can't leave Pavlov like that."

He pulled his phone out of his pocket, dialed his wife's phone number, and put it on speakerphone. After the fourth ring, it went to voicemail. "If your name is Roger, hang up and leave me the fuck alone. Everyone else leave a message and I'll get back to you."

Roger blushed and sighed but left a message. "Hey, Tamal. Sorry to bother you, but I'm at Simon's house. Me and some friends were meeting him today. He's not home and Pavlov is begging to be let out. I don't have a key. If you could come let us in, it would be great." He ended the call and looked up at his friends.

Harvey said, "I don't know who pissed in her Post Toasties, but I'm sorry as hell things aren't going well with you two."

"Me too. I can't seem to help myself. I still love her, but she is in an angry and vindictive frame of mind."

"What's changed?" Jack asked.

Stan watched his friend, struggling to explain what was going on in his marriage. They had a rule they didn't talk about their wives or husbands, but eventually they all did.

Roger shook his head and shrugged. "Nothing, really. She gets this way every year about this time. Her birthday is December 19th and for weeks and weeks she's been talking about her twin brother, Taman."

Stan shook his head. "I didn't know she had a twin brother."

"He died during birth with his umbilical cord twisted around his neck. Every year she seems to get worse and worse. She says shit like, 'I used to talk to my brother. We'd talk about Amma and her heart beating and what we were going to do when we got out of Amma's belly.' Stuff like that, over and over again, talking about her twin brother while they were in her mom's uterus. It freaked us all out."

"That is a little weird," Harvey said, "But maybe she just feels his loss even though it's been years and years."

"That's what I thought too. A few days before her birthday party, I'd asked her when we might have some kids of our own. She said she wasn't ready. I let it go, although she's been delaying having a child for our entire five-year marriage."

"After her birthday party at her mom's house, she was more angry than usual. I tried to calm her down, and she said, 'I wasn't born yet, and neither was Taman. It was him playing with his umbilical cord. It wasn't my fault he died!' So, I tried to reassure her nobody thought she had anything to do with his death."

Stan asked, "Did that help?"

"No. She slapped me, called me a two-faced idiot, which I still haven't figured out, and left the house. I haven't seen her since. She's called a few times screaming and yelling at me but that's it."

"So, you've talked with her?"

"After her last tirade, I told her not to call again until she was ready to get help. So now, I talk only through her lawyer. She says she doesn't want a divorce, but she wants me to move out of the house and pay the mortgage and let her live in our house. Even if I could afford to do that, I'm not sure I would. I love our house. You guys know I'm a builder. I've done a lot of upgrades and special treatments at our home. Now, I can't imagine living in any other house or neighborhood."

Harvey clapped him on the shoulder. "Your house is a showcase, all right. I'm sorry this is happening to you. Let's see if we can help Pavlov."

"How?"

"First, I need something from my truck. I'm a mechanic, but I have some ordinary builder's tools too. Then, you young bucks just follow me around back. I'll show you how to break into a house without damaging the property." He went to his pickup and unlocked the toolbox in the back. He pulled out a large flathead screwdriver and said, "Follow me, boys."

In less than a minute, he had the sliding patio door open and Pavlov came racing out of the house and loped around the yard a bit before stopping to pee and poop. Then the dog raced up to Roger, jumped up, put both feet on Roger's shoulders, and licked his face with joy.

Roger grinned and asked the dog, "Hey fella, what's going on? Where's your daddy?"

The dog raced back into the house, and the men followed. The smell of dog urine and feces assaulted the men. Roger followed the dog who raced into the main bathroom where the puddles of dog urine and a couple of piles of feces were on the bathroom floor. The dog whined and Roger rubbed Pavlov's head. "It's okay, Pavlov.

What a good dog you are. Let's get you some water and food."

Back in the kitchen Stan said, "I checked the garage and his SUV is gone. I bet you money he went on a hike. Maybe he is injured or lost or something like that. I've told him over and over he shouldn't hike alone. He always says, 'I'm careful. I'll be fine'."

Harvey said, "Maybe he just went on a short trip and had problems. I'm sure he wouldn't have left Pavlov to fend for himself."

Roger nodded. "I'll take Pavlov home with me, but if I don't hear from Simon by this afternoon, I'll call the police."

Jack said, "Let me help clean up the dog mess. No reason Simon should have to come home to the stench. If he hasn't come home to care for Pavlov, it means he can't get home."

Stan nodded. "I agree. I just wish he'd called. Anyone of us would have come over and taken care of Pavlov."

"After I opened the door for you," Harvey said.

The friends laughed at his jest, but none of them were comfortable with how things stood. Once they'd cleaned up the mess and locked the patio door again, they stood in the driveway with Pavlov sitting on Roger's feet. Stan said, "I'm going to drive to a few trailheads I've heard him talk about and see if I can find his car. That would give us a starting place."

"Good idea," Harvey said. "Today is my 20th wedding anniversary. I don't know what Sharla has planned, but I'm sure she has something in mind. I'll be out of pocket for the rest of the weekend but call me if you need me."

Jack said, "I'm working this evening through midnight. The hospital is busier than usual and lots of the nursing staff are out with the flu. I won't be available for the next few days."

"No problem," Roger said. "If Stan and I don't find him in the next few hours, we'll get the police involved."

CHAPTER FIVE

New Year's Day Tamal woke feeling refreshed and lighter than she had in a long time. She showered and dressed in a comfortable pair of dark purple cotton and linen trousers and a warm, red, and purple long-sleeved tunic that fell nearly to her knees. It was embroidered with various paisley patterns in soft reds, pinks, yellow and gold. She brushed her hair and used tortoise-shell combs to pull her hair a little away from her face.

Tamal loved her deep brown skin and long, waving black hair that fell nearly to her waist. Her eyes were black as shining coal and at nearly six feet tall she was a striking woman. She dressed in more traditional Indian fashion than American fashions, not in homage to her heritage, but rather because it helped her stand out in the crowd. Her way of dressing and natural beauty created some mystery around her. Clearly, she wasn't just another pretty face in the crowd.

Her father was of mixed East Indian and American descent. He was much taller than most Indian men at nearly seven feet tall. Her brother was tall and her husband, at six foot plus an inch or two, was only slightly taller than Tamal. She liked being as a tall as a man nearly as much as she enjoyed being as strong as a man, although she kept this tiny fact to herself.

Her phone rang, and she saw it was Roger calling. She frowned and let it go to voice mail. After a few minutes, her phone alerted her to the voice mail she knew was there. She listened to Roger's voice asking for help for Simon's damned dog. She said, "I don't give a tinker's damn about Simon's dog." She deleted the voice mail and fixed her usual breakfast of granola, yogurt and fruit.

After breakfast she wandered around in her small apartment,

feeling unsettled. Living in this small apartment, alone, rather than her home in West Seattle with Roger, made her angry. She fumed at the injustice of Roger not letting her live in their house. Yes, she'd been the one to leave, but only to keep from killing her husband. She treasured their home more than their marriage. She'd spent many hours and much effort creating a home that was artistically appealing yet modern and functional. Roger had built every upgrade she asked for and had helped her create special places in the home that lifted her spirits.

She didn't want to divorce Roger, but she didn't want him around either. Having a husband was a mere convenience for her, but she did want the house he had remodeled for her. He told her he loved her, but love wasn't what she was after. She sure as hell didn't want any children for everyone to fawn over. *Besides,* she told herself, *West Seattle is a little too common and crowded for my tastes.*

She really wanted to live in Edmonds near the art gallery, Pacific Arts, where she worked as an assistant curator, salesperson, and event planner. It was just herself and her boss, the owner of the gallery, Heather Aldersen. Sort of. Heather was in Paris right now, riding around and around in a circle. She would stink up the Paris baggage claim before long.

Tamal's mother lived in Edmonds in a nice big Craftsman style house all by herself. Her home faced Puget Sound and had glorious views of the area. Tamal couldn't afford an apartment near the art gallery. Apartments there were nearly as expensive as in downtown Seattle or Bellevue. But her mother's home was a few short blocks away from the gallery.

She wasn't sure what her next step in life would be, but it relieved her to have no brothers or father now. Her father's death a few years ago wasn't really her fault, at least not completely. If he hadn't been driving faster than the speed limit, he wouldn't have crashed into the bridge abutment. Maybe. He could have downshifted his older than sin Volvo, even without the brakes working. *Too bad, so sad, Daddy.*

She sure as hell didn't miss her father or his provincial ideas about women's roles in life. She'd tired long ago of his pushing her to a career in engineering when all she was interested in was beauty. Art filled that need nicely. Besides, with her artistic instincts, she was a valuable employee and well paid for her efforts.

Tamal wasn't sure how she felt about Simon's death. She didn't exactly regret it, but was a little sad all the same. If their mother hadn't always doted on him and expected her to adore him too, she might have let him live. He was the Golden Child of the family. He played the big brother role to the highest degree, and it had only gotten worse since her father's death. Simon was constantly telling her how she should be as a wife and daughter. *Simon says! Simon says!* And whatever Simon says, Amma, their mother, agreed she must do. Tamal hated him. Yet a part of her loved him, too.

She felt herself building up a head of steam. She was soon livid with rage. She stomped around her apartment shouting, "Simon, you sack of shit! Simon says, take care of Amma. Simon says, clean Amma's home. Well, Simon with the big mouth full of orders, I'm not a fucking maid, asshole. You could have cleaned Amma's house as easy as I could. Hell, she could hire a damned maid if she weren't so cheap. It's not my fault you're dead!"

She shouted a bit longer, then ran out of steam.

She muttered, "I'm not cleaning any house I don't live in. I deserve a nice house like Amma has."

She went to the fridge and pulled out a diet soda. In her bedroom, she turned on the computer. Once online, she checked her joint banking account with Roger and saw there was more money there than she'd realized. "You've been holding out on me, husband." She transferred a few thousand dollars into her personal checking account at another bank. Roger was not a signatory on that account. No one knew about the account other than herself. Then she opened her own bank account and transferred most of the money into another account at yet another bank.

Next, she went to her mother's checking account. No one in the family, including her mother and the bank, knew Tamal had learned the password to be able to access the account. Even the bank thought it was her mother, the blessed Basanti Chowdhury, mother of Simon, Tamal and the never born Taman, who accessed the account.

She smiled, thinking of her mother's Indian heritage and how her mother's parents had immigrated from India in the 1940s. They were blessedly deceased. Tamal appreciated she did not have to deal with sending them on their way.

In her mother's account, she saw the many thousands of dollars. She didn't take any of the money but began to formulate a plan to have her mother's house be her home. She would do what every loving daughter should do and care for her elderly mother. She was sixty already. Tamal thought it an appropriate age to think about leaving this planet. Not right away, of course, but soon.

She wished she'd gotten Simon's banking details before she killed him. Now, she might be too late. Soon, she knew one of his loser friends would miss him and call the police. She must lie low and avoid any suspicions police or Simon's friends might have.

She picked up her phone and called her mother. "Hi, Amma." Tamal knew her mother, Basanti Chowdhury, loved when she used the endearment 'Amma'. It felt silly and childish to Tamal, but she needed her mother's support right now. "How are you doing, Amma?"

"Fine. I'm happy you called. I've been missing you."

"I've missed you too, Amma. Could I come visit you today? I'll bring you a treat. How about Gulab Jamun?"

Her mother laughed but was pleased Tamal remembered her favorite Indian treat. It was a little like the American donut, but round and tasted much better than anything at regular bakeries. "You don't have to bring me anything, but I wouldn't turn down such a treat. It's to die for."

Tamal smiled and thought, *if only you knew, Amma*. She said, "Great. I'll be at your place in about an hour."

Her mother was delighted, and that was exactly how Tamal wanted her to be. Her mother had been talking about getting a roommate to keep her company in the big house. Tamal had better plans in mind.

At least better plans for Tamal.

CHAPTER SIX

Stan called his wife and told her what was going on. "I'm sorry about Donut Friday, but I think I should try to find Simon."

"I'll put the dough in the refrigerator to slow it down," Renee said. "You go see what you can learn. But you'd damn well better not go out on any trails alone."

He grinned. "I promise I won't. In fact, if I find his car, my plan is to call the police."

"Good, man. Nina and I need you home safe and sound."

"That's my plan, sweetie. Maybe we can have donuts for dinner?"

"Dream on, buddy."

He laughed as she ended the phone call.

He thought about his journey earlier this morning, but his Power Animal Nelson had said nothing about Simon. Nelson was worried about Roger. He related that Roger, and his wife Tamal were having serious problems. Listening to the phone message later and hearing what Roger had to say about their marriage, confirmed what the goofball elk had told him. Now Roger was taking care of Pavlov, Simon's dog, and Simon was AWOL. What Tamal's issues were concerning her birth, Stan didn't have a clue.

He shook his head, glad he had a wife who loved him and didn't go all bat-shit crazy when she had a birthday. He was even more glad that she cared about him and his wellbeing. She was a terrific wife and mother. He patted the steering wheel, turned on some jazz to listen to as he drove and said, "I'm a lucky man."

And he was.

Stan drove around the trail heads east of the Seattle area and out to the east edge of North Bend. There were more trails than he'd ever be able to canvas by himself, but he remembered a few trails Simon had talked about hiking. Mount Si, Little Si, Tenerife, Rattlesnake Ledge, and several along the Middle Fork Road. Stan drove through every trailhead parking area but found no sign of Simon's black Subaru SUV. Simon's distinctive collection of hiking stickers on his car, including Stan's favorite, 'Hike More, Worry Less,' was nowhere to be seen.

He simply couldn't think of anywhere else to look for his friend. Finally, Stan gave up and called his wife, Renee. "I've looked everywhere I can remember him talking about for his hikes. His car is at none of the usual trailheads. I don't know what to do next."

"What do you want to do next?"

"I want to find Simon alive and well, but I've lost hope of finding him this way. Since I'm totally clueless, I'm heading home as soon as I stop in North Bend to gas up. I'll call Roger when I get back home."

"Good. We'll have dinner ready when you get here."

"Donuts?"

"You'll see."

He grinned and hung up. Renee loved to make special meals, but more importantly, she loved making those meals fun and unusual. Stan thought for a few minutes about what she might have planned for dinner, but decided he'd rather be surprised. He hoped it wasn't ham and black-eyed peas. That's what his mother usually made for New Year's dinner. He liked ham but black-eyed peas were not his favorite.

He stopped at the Exit 31 Interchange on Interstate 90 for gas. While he was filling his tank, he looked up at the Outlet Mall across the road. He muttered, "I'll drive through the parking lot and see if his car is there."

After he finished with getting gas and driving through the Outlet Mall parking lot, Stan shook his head. "Buddy, I have a feeling things haven't gone well for you, but I'm damned if I know where to look now." Stan had no way of knowing that indeed Simon's car was in

North Bend but behind a building a few miles away from the Outlet Mall.

As he drove from North Bend back to West Seattle, he couldn't stop worrying about Simon. "Maybe I should have driven all the roads in North Bend." He shook his head. "That's just plain silly. I have no idea where he went. My effort to find him today was just a squirrel chase."

Simon was a good man and a great friend. He was quiet and loved living in his small house with Pavlov, his yellow lab. He loved playing his saxophone with Pavlov joining in from time-to-time. The dog would throw back his head and howl along with Simon and his sax until Simon's giggles put an end to their music. The dog and the man loved each other more than many people loved their friends, or families for that matter. Of all the men Stan had ever met, Simon seemed to be the one most at peace with his life.

Stan and he talked once about love and sex and Simon said, "I'm heterosexual for sure. I find women attractive and have dated a few that I thought might be long-term possibilities. But, I haven't ever really had a love relationship. I'm sure as hell open to the possibility but not really anxious about it."

"How old were your parents when they married?"

"In their early thirties. How about your parents?" Simon asked.

"They married very young. Momma was eighteen and Daddy was twenty-one. They got married as soon as it was legal without having their parents involved in their decision to marry."

Stan remembered Simon's mouth dropping open. "Damn. They were babies."

"Yep. But fifty years later they're still besotted with each other."

"That's cool. If I get married, it will only be for overwhelming love. It seems like too much work otherwise."

Stan thought about his parents and their lives. They'd worked hard and loved hard, and, against all odds, made a go of life. That's what he wanted too. He knew his life with Renee and Nina was love he could count on for the rest of his life. As a man living with bipolar disorder, their love helped him hold it together. Thinking of them and his talks with Simon helped him settle a little. But still he worried about his friend. He couldn't imagine not having Simon in his life. And he was sure Pavlov would struggle too. *Damn,* he thought, *I'm thinking Simon might never come home!*

As he passed Tiger Mountain heading west on Interstate 90, he said, "Simon my friend, I hope you are okay. We all need you in our lives."

It surprised him to have tears flowing down his cheeks. He brushed them away and said, "Nelson, you and I need to talk again, buddy." Later tonight, after dinner and Nina was in bed, he planned to journey and talk with Nelson about Simon.

"Nelson will have some answers. I hope."

CHAPTER SEVEN

Roger called Stan just as Stan was driving over the floating bridge on I-90 heading west for home. He pressed the button on his car to answer the phone. After greeting him, Roger asked, "Any luck on finding Simon?"

"No, not a thing. I've spent all this time driving through every trailhead I could think of between here and east of North Bend."

"Well, Pavlov and I went back to Simon's house to check and see if he was home. He's still not there. When I was looking in the windows, one neighbor came out and we talked a bit."

"What did you learn?"

"First, that the neighbor had a key to Simon's house, which she gave to me. Second, she said he was going to hike Little Si yesterday morning to watch the sunrise over Mount Si."

Stan shook his head. "Man, I drove through all the trailhead parking areas around Little Si and Mount Si. Simon's car simply wasn't there. I even drove through the Outlet Mall parking lot to no avail."

"Well, I'm going to call the police and wait with Pavlov at Simon's house."

"Good idea. I'm going home for dinner with Nina and Renee. If you learn anything, or need me, let me know."

"I will. I've got a bad feeling about all of this."

Stan shuddered. "Me too."

He ended the call, brushing away more tears.

Roger put Pavlov in the back of his Range Rover and lowered the backseat window a little for air. He turned, leaned against the back of the vehicle, pulled out his cell phone, looked up, and saw an unusual sight. There was a man in police uniform on a beautiful horse coming toward him. Pavlov was excited and barking at the vision as well.

Roger grinned and waved at the police officer on the horse's back. The rider pulled up close to the car and Roger. The horse ignored the dog barking but shook his head seeming to dismiss the yellow lab.

The police officer grinned. "Bart here thinks dogs are a fair bit down the ladder to him. Of course, that's what he thinks of me too. Can I help you?"

Roger nodded and reflexively reached out and petted the horse's nose. He loved horses. The horse let him and even pushed to be rubbed some more. Roger told the officer the events of the past 24 hours. "He's my brother-in-law and this just isn't like him."

The officer nodded. "I'm Marshall Cornish. I'm happy to help get the ball rolling."

"Your name is Marshall? Really?"

"Yeah, I'm just glad my last name isn't Dillion."

"I bet!"

"My momma named my baby brother Dillon though. He hates it, especially when mom introduces us as 'my boys Marshall and Dillon.'"

Roger laughed, then sobered quickly. "Me and my friends are really worried about Simon." He pointed to the house. "We can go inside if you'd like to look around."

"Let me just call this in. We are mostly a PR service and help with neighborhood watch and safety. But I can get the ball rolling for you. How long did you say your friend had been missing?"

"Over 24 hours. We were supposed to meet this morning for what we call Old Man Coffee."

"What's that?"

"We five friends sit in one or the other of our driveways or one of the fellas' garage if the weather is too foul. We drink coffee and gab for an hour or two. We make an effort to solve all of humankind's woes but barely keep up with our own."

The officer smiled. "That sounds great. When were you supposed to meet?"

"This morning here at Simon's house. The neighbor said he left early yesterday morning to hike Little Si and watch the sun come up over the Cascades, but he hasn't come home." Roger turned and pointed to the car. "Pavlov here was locked inside the house. We let him out and checked to be sure Simon wasn't home. I'm Simon's brother-in-law, so I've kept Pavlov with me until Simon comes back."

"I'll call this in and wait with you for the regular officers."

"Thanks. I really appreciate the help." Roger decided he would say nothing about having jimmied the patio sliding door earlier in the day. Now that he had the key to Simon's house, it seemed irrelevant. At least he hoped so.

Stan grinned, looking at the food on the table. There were maple bacon bars with gleaming maple frosting and chopped pecans on top. There were chunks of ham, pineapple, fried potatoes, and lots of bacon. There was a cheese platter and deviled eggs, too. There was also a small bowl of black-eyed peas, although none of them really cared much for them. This was New Year's Day, so they were good luck to eat. They'd each take a bite just to be on the safe side. Of course, there were several bottles of different flavors of hot sauce to top it all off.

"Holy smokes, Renee. This is some New Year's feast you have here."

Renee grinned. "It wasn't my idea." She pointed at their daughter.

Nina proudly said, "Momma asked me what I'd do if I were to make dinner with donuts and this is what we decided on."

"And Nina did most of the prep work and helped with all the cooking."

"Yeah, it was fun, but Momma really needed my help."

Stan shook his head in amazement. "I need to go driving all over King County more often. You ladies really went all out for dinner tonight."

They chatted and talked about which movie or shows to watch after they finished the feast. They had a long weekend ahead with no work or school. Nina begged to stay up a little late tonight. Stan said, "I don't know. You stayed up last night to see the fireworks bringing in the New Year."

"Okay, I get it," Nina said. "So, instead of staying up until midnight, how about I get to stay up until nine or ten o'clock?"

Stan smiled and looked up at Renee. "What do you think, Mom?"

"Well, I think we can swing staying up until nine tonight if we don't have any fussing about going to bed at 8 tomorrow evening."

Nina clapped her hands and hooted with glee. Then with a very sober voice said, "I promise. I won't beg to stay up late."

"Forever?" Stan asked.

She rolled her eyes. "Don't be silly, Daddy."

CHAPTER EIGHT

Tamal drove to Edmonds then to Sunset Avenue North where her mother's home faced out overlooking Puget Sound. The day was bright and clear, and the water was a brilliant blue in the sunshine. There was a bit of a breeze rippling the surface of the water, but for the first day of January it was a very pleasant day.

Tamal pulled into the driveway of her mother's home. Before she was completely out of the car, her mother was standing on the porch waving. Her mother's yard was filled with flower gardens and herb gardens. Most were mulched for the winter. Tamal had no intention of getting her hands dirty taking care of the garden beds. When her mother could no longer tend the gardens, a lawn would be planted instead. Of course, first she had to get into her mother's good graces and move in with her.

She pasted a loving smile on her face and went to her mother's embrace. Tamal allowed herself to melt a little into her mother's arms. She smelled of turmeric and cardamon with a hint of vanilla. Tears trickled down Tamal's face and she was shocked to find herself crying in her mother's arms.

"Oh, my precious Tamal," her mother said. "Come in and I'll fix you a nice cup of Darjeeling."

Tamal loved Darjeeling tea the way her mother made it, with a little honey spiced with cardamon and cloves. She handed her mother the box of sweet treats and allowed her mother to take her hand and lead her into the kitchen. Basanti motioned for her daughter to sit while she prepared the tea. She pulled out a beautiful platter trimmed in gold and painted with traditional yellow leaves and flowers. She placed the sweet treats on the platter and carried it to the table.

She handed her daughter a soft cotton handkerchief to wipe her tears and said, "Wait to tell me what is going on until we have our tea in our hands."

Tamal nodded and worked to control her emotions. *What's the matter with me? Why am I crying?* She took a few deep breaths and decided, *I've just been under a lot of stress.* She shuddered and waited quietly with her head tilted down while her mother prepared the tea. She lifted the hankie to her eyes and smelled the soft jasmine and rose cologne her mother always used. She felt herself calming a little.

Her mother brought the china teapot with matching teacups to the table. They had been in the family for many generations. The delicate bone china teacups and dessert plates with the pink, green and gold designs were as familiar to Tamal as her own skin. She smiled and looked up at her mother. "Thank you Amma for making this a special tea party."

Her mother patted her head and sat across from her at the small kitchen table. "Tell me Beti what is troubling you."

Tamal smiled at the Hindi endearment her mother used. It meant daughter, and it always made her feel special in her mother's eyes. "Roger and I are not living together."

"Why? Does he not love you?"

"He says he does, but I'm not sure. I do not think I love him anymore either."

"What are you going to do?"

Tamal shook her head. "I do not know, but I can't stay in the apartment I have in Redmond."

"Why are you living in an apartment?"

"Roger wouldn't go to an apartment, so I had to. I couldn't afford an apartment in Seattle. This apartment is the cheapest one I could find. I hate it. I feel alone and isolated. I can't think there."

"Could you think in your own house?"

Tamal shrugged and brought the handkerchief to her face again, relaxing a little with its fragrance. "I was so angry with Roger I couldn't think there either."

Basanti waited for her daughter to tell her at least a little of the truth. Her daughter had difficulty with knowing or speaking truth. When Tamal was upset, the truth was hard for her to tell. Simon had told her that the couple had separated shortly after Tamal's birthday. Basanti knew her daughter grieved over her twin brother who died in the womb and was stillborn.

So did Basanti, but she did not let it destroy her peace. She knew her stillborn son, Taman, resided in the Hindi heavenly realm of Swarg or might already have been reborn. Her daughter had always been obsessed with her twin. Far too obsessed, in Basanti's opinion. Tamal's constant talking of how she and Taman talked with each other in the womb made no sense to Basanti, a practical woman. Of course, they didn't talk together. They couldn't. It was physiologically impossible. So, she waited for her daughter to tell her the truth. Any truth. At least any truth that had nothing to do with the baby boy who had died during birth. *Perhaps if he'd been born first,* but Basanti quashed the thought as soon as it slipped into her mind.

Basanti took a sip of her tea and put a sweet treat on her plate. She delicately nibbled on the honeyed, crusty treat, loving the sweet feeling of her parents near her. The special treats were ones her mother taught her to make. Eating one, she felt the love of her mother surrounding her. She nibbled on the cardamon donut with a light drizzle of spicy honey crusting its golden surface. She watched her daughter, waiting and hoping for truth to come out of her mouth.

Finally, Tamal looked up at her mother. "Roger wants me to have a baby. I don't want to have a baby. Ever."

"Why not?"

"I know you don't like me to talk about Taman, but if I were to be pregnant, I know the baby would die. I don't want to take the chance. My heart cannot bear it."

Her mother nodded, not believing her daughter's words were the actual truth of the matter. Tamal didn't want a child because she knew the child would replace her in the level of love and affection for all her family. That was what her heart could not bear. She would have to kill the child at birth or even earlier.

Her mother said, "Regardless of what I think or believe, it is your body and you are the one to decide about how you use your body."

Tamal smiled. "That's far more modern than I would have thought coming from you, Amma."

"Well, just because I've been a traditional woman leading a traditional life doesn't mean my mind doesn't know how to think. I've loved my life most of the time, but sometimes I wished to be doing anything other than being a mother and a wife. Now it's too late."

"Of course, it's not too late. Right now, you can build your life however you want it to be, Amma."

Her mother shrugged. "Perhaps, but I'm an old woman now."

"You're healthy and vibrant. Ignore those numbers on the calendar, Amma. What would you like to do?"

"Bake."

"Well, you've been doing that all your life."

"No, I'd like to bake delicate sweets like these we are eating right now and sell them. I'd also like to make fancy treats from many cultures. I want to create a business sharing the joy of the sweetness I could make."

"Okay, so why don't you do that?"

"I don't know where or how to start. I've practiced making some treats already."

Tamal looked at her mother and smiled. She knew for certain she could help her mother and herself. Then later on, her mother could die and the house would be Tamal's. "Amma, if you will let me move in with you, I'll help take care of the house in exchange for rent and you can bake."

Her mother started to speak, but Tamal held up a hand and continued. "I hate being alone in that apartment. I don't want to have babies and I'm ready for a divorce. It's not fair to Roger to keep him hanging on to our marriage, hoping I'll have a baby. I won't. Ever. Anyway, I'd much rather live with you and help you. My career is here in Edmonds. It would save me a bundle of money not having to drive all the way up here several days a week."

"I'll agree only if you do nothing rash about the divorce. Give yourself some time to let that settle before you decide."

Tamal thought about it for a few minutes, or at least pretended to. Her mother quietly sipped her tea. Tamal took another sip of tea. "Okay, Amma. I'll wait on everything else if I can come home and live with you."

Her mother smiled and patted her daughter's hand. "Good. I have just one more request."

"What's that, Amma?"

"You help me figure out all the legalities and what I can do right here at home without having to spend a lot of money having a storefront. I want to bake at home and cater the treats from here."

Tamal nearly slipped and said her mother had plenty of money to support a small business for a few months, but she caught herself in time. "I'll be happy to help you, Amma."

"When do you want to move in?"

"Is tomorrow too soon."

"No, tomorrow is perfect."

Both women knew they couldn't fully trust each other, but Basanti knew her daughter better than her daughter knew her mother. Basanti had changed her bank account to alert her every time her account was accessed. Monday morning, she would go to the bank and change her accounts so Tamal didn't have access. She loved her daughter but knew from a lifetime of experience she could not trust her.

When Basanti died, her estate would go to Simon. Basanti left the house she'd lived in for most of her adult life to Tamal, but the considerable money and investments would go to Simon. If he were to die before Tamal, she would inherit the entire estate. Basanti wasn't sure, but perhaps she would have to make a different sort of will to keep Tamal from stealing everything from under Simon's nose.

His intentions were always good, but he also had a soft heart.

CHAPTER NINE

Detective Darren Jordan sat at Simon's kitchen table with Roger, Pavlov, and Officer Sally Quinn. He said, "I'd like to record our discussion if that's okay with you."

"Certainly. I wouldn't be able to do your job just taking notes."

"Thank you, but Officer Quinn will take notes too."

Roger nodded and shrugged. "That's fine. I want to find my brother-in-law as fast as we can. I'm worried about him."

"When did you see him last?"

"Three days after Christmas. We went to REI together to get new hiking boots and hiking equipment with gift cards Simon's mom gave us."

"Do you two hike together a lot?"

"Yes, we do, but we also hike with other people."

"Do you ever hike alone?"

"I don't, but Simon frequently does. When it is a short hike, he's done several times, he often doesn't even tell anyone where he is going. He just heads out and hikes. In fact, I'd only hiked a few times before I met Simon."

"Did you have any plans to hike this weekend?"

"Yeah, we were going to go up Tenerife on Sunday. I'd never been, and Simon wanted to take me up there."

"But you didn't have plans to hike this morning, right?"

Roger squirmed a little in his seat, thinking he should have already told the detective about the patio door and how he got the key to Simon's house. "Right. The next-door neighbor said Simon was going up to Little Si yesterday morning early for the sunrise."

Darren noted Roger's unease but let it pass for now. Instead, he asked, "Did he do that sort of thing frequently?"

Roger nodded. "He had a few favorite places he like to go to before sunrise and be up on the peak to watch the sun come up."

"Have you ever done that with him?"

"No, I'm not that much of a morning person and I haven't ever hiked in the dark. I'm a big a wimp in that regard."

The detective shook his head. "No, you're not a wimp. I'm a morning person, but I wouldn't go hiking in the dark. It's more risk than I'm willing to take with the wildlife, much less the trails."

"Simon said he wasn't afraid of the wildlife an hour before sunrise. They were generally heading back to their daytime hideouts by then."

"It would surely make me nervous. So, this morning, you and some friends were planning to meet him for coffee here, right?"

"Yes. We call ourselves Old Man Coffee. The five of us get together at least once a week in one or the other's driveway, have coffee and gab."

Detective Darren Jordan looked up and smiled. "I've never heard of such a thing. What if it rains?"

"Then we meet in Stan's garage. He has a music studio he's building in there and we can be dry and cozy. We are all into music and playing instruments so it is a perfect place for us. If it's bitterly cold, or raining we meet there. We thought we were pretty lucky to have these few days of sunshine and moderate temps."

"Have you checked with Simon's family?"

"I called his mom and said I'd missed a meeting with Simon, but he wasn't home now. I thought he might be with her."

"What did she say?"

"That he wasn't with her and she wasn't expecting to see him until his usual Sunday evening dinner. She gave me his phone number, and I told her I'd call him."

"She's your mother-in-law, right?"

"Right. Sometimes she forgets that I have his phone number. She's done that before."

"What about your wife, Simon's sister? Tamal, isn't it?"

Roger nodded and sighed. "I reached out to her, but she didn't reply."

"Are there problems between you two?"

"We are separated right now. I'm hoping we work it out, but I'd be surprised. We've separated before, but this is the longest we've been apart."

"Do you have her number?"

"Sure. I'll give it to you but if it goes to voice mail, you'll learn how angry she is with me."

Darren smiled. "I've heard some terrible voice mails. I can handle it. Have you tried to call her again?"

"No, but I will now if you want."

"Let's give that a try in case Simon is with her."

Roger pulled out his phone and dialed Tamal's number. He held it out for the Detective and Police Officer to hear. Once again, she did not answer the phone call, but he let the message play out. "If your name is Roger, hang up and leave me the fuck alone. Everyone else leave a message and I'll get back to you." He didn't leave a message but turned the phone off and laid it on the table.

Darren said, "I'm so sorry. If you give me her phone number, we'll try to reach out to her."

"Okay, I'm happy to do that. What else can you do?"

"It's too late today because of the darkness settling in to go up Little Si and look for him. Sally checked on our way here and there have been no sightings of injured folks on the trails."

Sally nodded and said, "Of course, that doesn't mean he isn't up there."

Roger nodded.

"We will get in touch with the search and rescue team right away though. They'll be on the trail as soon as it is getting light in the morning. It's not a big mountain but not one to hike in the dark."

"Thanks. I'll keep Pavlov with me at my house."

"Good idea. Now I need the names and phone numbers of the other men who were meeting this morning and your wife's phone number."

"Sure. I'm happy to help."

Sally looked up and said, "You told us one man drove out around North Bend and didn't find his car and it wasn't at any of the trailheads. Do you know Simon's tag number?"

"I could look in his desk and personal papers. It might be in there. I can tell you it is a Black Subaru SUV about a year old."

She said, "I'll do a quick search with his name and the car make. You may not need to go looking through his personal papers."

They sat quietly while she used her smart phone for the search. In less than a minute she smiled and said, "Got it."

Darren nodded. "Thanks, Sally." They stood up and Darren asked, "Is there anything else you should tell us that you haven't?"

Roger blushed. "Well, yeah. First, Simon almost always has his phone with him when he's hiking. Mainly to take photos but he usually has it with him. The other thing I hope's not a big deal. We sort of broke into Simon's house through the patio door to check on him and help Pavlov."

"You have a house key."

"Now I do. The neighbor next door gave it to me just before the equine officer called this in."

"Good. I thought there was something bothering you. Patio doors are super easy to get into without breaking them. I wish more folks used a bar in the track to make it harder to break in."

"Well, I'm for sure going to do that when I get home."

"Also, we'll see if we can ping Simon's phone. If it's turned on, I'm sure we can." Darren handed Roger his card, as did Sally. "Be sure you call us if you think of anything else. If we find him, either Sally or I will call you."

"Thanks. There is one more thing that might help. Simon bought a GPS device from REI. We were going to test it out on Tenerife on Sunday. I don't know how that works or how to tell you anything about it, but REI might help if we don't find him soon. He's my brother-in-law, but also my best friend. In fact, I met my wife after Simon, and I were friends for a couple of years. I need him in my life."

CHAPTER TEN

The police pinged Simon's phone and were sure the phone was on the top of Little Si or on the west face of Mt. Si. As the sky was getting lighter, though the sun wasn't quite up yet, the Eastside Fire and Rescue mobilized a team to search for Simon Chowdhury on Little Si. They were experienced hikers and rescue personnel. Their team today included Radar, a golden retriever who loved to find anything the team asked him to. Detective Darren Jordan met the team at the trailhead and gave them the pillowcase from Simon's pillow for Radar to have Simon's scent.

The detective stayed in the trailhead parking lot with a few other officers from the King County Sheriff's Department to keep hikers off the trail until the search was complete. The Sheriff's Deputies put up barriers at the entrance to the parking lot and trailheads, but hikers were not easily deterred from their beloved trails. The law enforcement officers stood around talking quietly and drinking coffee. Darren opened the back hatch and sat on the floor of his SUV, looking at the mountains as the sun began to highlight the shadows.

There had been a heavy frost with the overnight clear skies. As the sun began to warm the Earth, breezes picked up, making the air seem colder. All the officers were accustomed to the weather and had thermal undergarments, warm gloves, and hooded coats. The highest temperature today was forecast to be 38 degrees with clouds and rain moving in later tonight. As the sun was blotted out by the clouds, there would be heavy snow across the western portion of Washington State and the Cascade Mountains. By late afternoon they expected the passes would be closed and the North Bend area would have a minimum two to three inches of snow with six to eight inches possible during the night. It wasn't enough to stop the life of the valley, but it would slow things down and trails would be treacherous.

Darren didn't mind the cold, the wind or the snow that would soon be falling. He hated the feeling of dread that pervaded his thoughts. He had to deal with violent deaths on a near daily basis, but he never looked forward to the events surrounding the deaths. The pain and sorrow were difficult to watch in the lives of the people who loved the deceased. He was an empathetic man, but also an excellent detective. It was a great combination for the bereaved, but tough for him personally.

Officer Sally Quinn pulled up and parked beside Darren's SUV. She got out of her car, zipped up her coat, grabbed her go cup of coffee and went to stand beside Darren.

"Morning, boss," she said.

He smiled and nodded. He liked Sally. She was petite, barely five feet tall and weighed about a hundred pounds soaking wet. She was not a woman to trifle with, however. She had a black belt in karate, plus many other martial arts accomplishments. She nearly made the Olympic team a couple of years ago. Her short, dark brown curly hair and hazel eyes gave her a pixie sort of look. He knew from experience, underestimating her mind or physical skills was a mistake. He said, "You know you don't have to call me boss, right?"

"Yeah, but it feels right to me. Do you mind if I call you that?"

"No, just want to be clear. I'm the lead on this case, and a higher-grade officer, but I'm not your boss."

She smiled. "Got it, boss."

He chuckled and shook his head. Then his grim thoughts returned.

Sally watched his face change from light-hearted to quiet introspection. He was a foot taller than her, lean but muscular, with dark brown hair trimmed short and deep blue eyes. She respected him as a human being and as a detective. "So you think he's dead, don't you?"

"Yeah, Sally, I do. I don't have any deep insight, but that's what I'm feeling in my gut."

"Did the techies get a response on the cellphone?"

"Yeah. They pinged and his phone is probably on top of Little Si."

She nodded with grim, tight lips, then said, "If his phone is on Little Si, he probably is too."

"Yep. That's what I think. He could be lost, but I'd be surprised. This is a routine hike for him. My best guess is he is injured."

"What's your worst guess?"

"He is dead."

Sally shook her head. "Surely someone would have seen him if he was lying injured or dying on the trail."

"Well, he could have slipped on an edge of the mountain if he'd gone off trail a bit to have a better view. It would be hard to find him in all the brush and forest."

She nodded. "If he didn't go off an edge, then he'd be deeper into the woods."

"Yeah. It isn't a big mountain and looks tiny from the road, especially next to Mt Si, but once you're off the trail, it is rough as a cob and the forest is deep. It's easy to get lost even on Little Si if you're a novice."

"But he isn't a novice."

Darren nodded. "And that's why my thoughts are dark and foreboding. I think he is dead. Whether accidental or not, I don't have any feeling for."

Hikers were showing up and Darren said, "Let's go keep folks off the trail for now. The last thing we want, or need is a bunch of hikers tromping all over the evidence."

Sally shook her head. "IF he is up there, I'm surprised a hiker didn't find him yesterday. But, as you said, if he is off the trail, it wouldn't be obvious to a hiker."

"The only time a hiker would be off the trail is to relieve themselves," Darren answered.

"Unless they had evil intent," Sally added.

His nod was bleak. "Yeah."

Hikers were none too happy to be told they couldn't hike Little Si this morning, but most didn't fuss and wished the authorities luck in finding the lost hiker. They all knew it could be them someone had to look for some day. About two hours had passed when Radar, his dog handler, and a couple of other rescue people came down the trail toward the parking area.

Darren looked up and saw the dog handler put Radar in his car. He watched as the handler walked over to the detective and Sally. The handler said, "We found him, or at least what's left of him." He handed Darren a plastic evidence bag and said, "Here's his phone. I'll take you up to where he is if you're ready. The others are on their way down. We left his body as it is."

"Thanks," Darren said and turned to Sally. "Call this in and ask for the ME and forensic team. I'll check with the local folks here before we ask for more support. You wait here for our crew, then come up with them. We'll have the spot marked on the trail."

"Yes, sir. I'll start calling right now."

Darren pulled out shoe covers and nitrile gloves from his go bag and tucked them in his pocket. He turned to the dog handler. "I need to talk with the sheriff's gang and local police who are here, then I'll follow you up."

Darren followed the handler, Rick Wheaton up the trail. When they arrived at the spot where three orange flags and some orange tape were marking the trail, he stopped and pulled on his shoe covers and gloves. He followed Rick as they descended down a small path that was already becoming a trail. It took less than a minute to arrive at the spot where Simon's body was found. He squatted beside what was left of Simon Chowdhury. He looked up at Rick and asked, "Where was the phone?"

Rick pointed to another orange flag. "We marked it over there. It was several feet from the main part of his body. There are still pieces of clothing there too. My guess is whatever animal was digging in just tossed the phone and the clothing aside."

Darren nodded and looked around. "We're pretty far off the trail here and down in a deep depression." He pointed to a root ball in front of him. "I think when the tree fell, the roots lifting out of the ground caused this hole."

"I agree," Rick said, looking up at the root ball that was taller than his six-foot height. "I can't see the trail from here. I suppose we might hear hikers though."

"Why don't you go stand on the trail and talk in a normal voice? If I don't answer, talk louder until I do answer."

Rick nodded and walked back up to the trail from the depression where Simon's body lay. After about five minutes, Darren heard Rick and hollered back at him. Rick walked back down off the trail, using the same path they'd used in finding the body. Darren looked up and asked, "Well? Did you have to raise your voice or shout?"

"I didn't have to shout but raised my voice twice. Why did you want to know about the loudness of my voice?"

"I need to know if whoever killed him had to be really quiet during killing and burying."

Rick nodded. "Makes sense. Do you need me to stay with you?"

"No. Thanks for your help. You can go on down."

"I'd say no problem, but every time we find someone dead like this, it hurts. Much more than I ever thought it would."

"Me too. Every time is hard. I keep in mind though, that my job here is to bring him some justice if possible. It requires my human empathy for me to do a good job for him. If I lose that and stop feeling the pain, it will be time for me to find another job."

"Thanks for sharing with me, Detective. I'll remember your words. They are a good way to think about this all."

Rick walked away, and Darren turned back, looking over the field of the bloody remains of Simon Chowdhury.

CHAPTER ELEVEN

Tamal packed up her few belongings she'd taken with her to the apartment in Redmond, called the landlord, and left the keys to the partially furnished apartment on the kitchen table. It was a relief to be leaving the small apartment and moving on with her life.

She drove to West Seattle to see if Roger was home. His car was parked in front of the house and the lights were on. She decided against stopping to pick up the rest of her things. She drove to the nearest Starbucks, got a drive through latte, then parked in the parking lot. Using the Bluetooth device in her large luxury SUV, she called Roger.

When he answered, she asked, "Are you home right now?"

With a soft voice he said, "Hello to you too, darling. How are you doing?"

Tamal ignored his softness and efforts to connect with her. She said, "I'm doing fine, Roger, not that you really care. Save your endearments for a weaker woman. I want to come by and pick up the rest of my belongings. I was hoping you wouldn't be at home."

"Well, I am. It's Saturday morning. I'm usually home with you on Saturday mornings."

She held her emotions in check but really wanted to scream at him. "There is no more *usually* for us, Roger. I'm sure you know that by now."

He sighed. "I guess so, but it's not how I want things to be between us."

"We don't always get what we want, Roger. I want a different life than you want me to have."

"I want you to have the life you want and need."

"What I want is to live in the glorious home you've built for me.

What I want is to be the best damned art curator on the Western seaboard. What I want is to spend the rest of my life with you but without any children."

Roger held his temper back but really wanted to scream and yell at her. He'd never done that in their relationship. She'd always been the one who screamed and yelled.

Finally, he said, "I'm not leaving our home, Tamal. I want to live here with you. I hope you do become the best damned art curator on the Western seaboard. In fact, I think you probably already are. But I want you home with me and us having children and building a family together."

"I'll never have any children, Roger. I thought I made myself clear on that front. I just can't face the whole thing. Having children would bring us nothing but grief and I couldn't build the career I want with kids hanging on my skirt tails."

"How do you propose to solve our impasse, Tamal?"

"We don't *solve* anything, Roger. We move on in our separate ways. You give me the house, we divorce, and you get out of my life."

"Well, since that will not happen, do you have another idea?"

She snorted a derisive laugh. "No. And there will never be another idea, Roger. We bought the house together. I was the one who came up with all the ideas to improve the place. It's a showcase now because of me. It is only right that I get to keep the house. You've a lot of properties and could go live in one of them."

Roger shook his head. "I love you and will do what I can to help you in your life, but I won't just walk away from our marriage with nothing."

"Our marriage has always been nothing."

"I love you, Tamal. Our love isn't nothing. I want to keep our life together. If you don't want to have a baby, we can adopt."

"If you really loved me, you would know better than to make that suggestion Roger."

He took a deep breath, brushed away a tear from his cheek, and changed the subject. He asked, "Do you know where Simon is? He didn't come home. In fact, I don't think he has been home for nearly

48 hours now."

"Are you his mommy?"

"No, of course not. But I am his best friend. I called you yesterday morning to tell you he didn't show up at our weekly Old Man Coffee meeting."

"I ignored your voice mail purposefully. I don't even listen to your voicemails anymore."

"Nice, Tamal," Roger answered, feeling not only helpless in this situation but somehow abused, which made little sense to him. "Regardless, I'm worried about Simon. If you see him, please let him know I'm worried about him."

"Fuck you, Roger, and fuck Simon. Men are such a fucking drag! Even if I knew where he was, I wouldn't tell you. I want you out of my life. End of story!"

She disconnected the call and screamed at the top of her lungs. People passing by stopped and looked at her sitting in her car screaming, pounding on the steering wheel and stomping her feet on the floorboard.

A three-year-old boy looked up at his mother and said, "She needs a time out."

His mother tightened her grip on his hand and quickly pulled him away from the scene. "Come on, sweetie. Let's go get chocolate chip scones and not worry about her."

He had to skip a little to keep up with his mother but took a last glance over his shoulder at the woman continuing her temper-tantrum.

When Tamal noticed she was drawing a crowd, she lowered the windows and shouted, "Get the fuck away from me, you creeps." She started her SUV, revved it a few times, honked her horn, and backed up without looking. She rammed into a pickup truck behind her, then pulled forward. A man crossing the lot in front of her jumped out of her way as she sped past him.

The woman driving the pickup truck parked her truck, got out and looked at her bumper. It had a new dent among many. She decided her safest course of action was to ignore the bump and get a creamy mocha and cinnamon roll. Better to have the treat rather than invite the anger of the woman who'd added a dent to her collection of dents.

Tamal turned right onto 16th Avenue SW and then onto Delridge Way. By the time she got to the turn for the West Seattle Bridge, she finally remembered the bridge was closed for repairs. She cursed the bridge for being closed. The bridge did not notice or even care. Everything in the Universe was working against her, including the damned bridge. Everything in the Universe ignored her.

She followed the twists and turns of the nightmare that was Seattle streets and worked her way to Highway 99 to get onto Interstate 5. Once on the Interstate heading north to Edmonds and her mother's home, she began to calm down.

A plan formulated in her mind of how she could get rid of Roger. She hoped she could make him go away without damaging the beautiful home she'd designed, but if the house had to go with Roger, so be it. Divorce sure as hell would not happen now. She'd much rather be a widow. She was stunning in black.

Roger wiped tears from his face and shook his head. He stared out the window in their kitchen. "I can't believe I've gotten to this point in my life. I really thought we were the right man and woman to build a life together. I sure as hell wish I didn't love her."

He took a glass out of the cupboard and filled it with cold water from the faucet. The under-sink water filter and chiller was another luxury his wife had demanded. At first he thought it was a silly idea, but over time he'd concluded she was right. He never bought bottled water anymore since the water in their kitchen tasted as good or better than any in a bottle. He drank the water and looked around the beautiful chef's kitchen he'd built for Tamal, though she seldom cooked.

He leaned against the stone countertop, feeling his heart breaking as he looked at each beautiful detail his wife had requested. His mind, for the first time in many days, felt empty. He didn't know what to think or how to feel at this moment. He sat the glass in the sink and looked out the window. Clouds were moving in. As the clouds covered the sun, he felt gray despair drop over him like a shroud.

His phone rang, and he reflexively picked it up and answered. Later he would wish he had not. He had more than enough sorrow in his life, and it would only get worse today.

"Hello."

"Hi, Roger, this is Detective Darren Jordan."

Roger swallowed and said, "Your voice doesn't sound like you have good news for me."

"I'm so sorry. I do not have good news. We found Simon deep in the woods near the top of Little Si. It looks like homicide, but we won't know for sure until the Medical Examiner determines the cause of death."

Roger was quiet for several seconds that felt like an eternity. His face tingled and his hands were suddenly freezing.

The detective asked, "Are you still there, Roger?"

"Yes, I'm here."

"I was wondering if you would meet me at your mother-in-law's house in Edmonds. I need to talk with her and also think I should give her the news in person."

"Sure."

"Are you okay to drive, Roger?"

"I don't know." He wept with great shuddering sobs.

Darren said, "I'll come by and pick you up. I have your address. You shouldn't drive right now."

Roger nodded. He ended the call and went to the bedroom, laid on the bed and wept for his dear friend Simon, for his lost love, for his wife whose love had evaporated.

CHAPTER TWELVE

Tamal was driving on Interstate 5, almost to Interstate 90 when she changed her mind. "I'm going to turn around, go to our home and get my things. I'll just ignore Roger and anything he has to say. I want my things around me."

She got off the interstate at Rainier Avenue and worked her way back to West Seattle. When she turned on to the round-about at the intersection of the street where she and Roger lived, it surprised her to see a police car in front of their house. Roger was getting into the police car. She grinned and slowed down to allow the police car to pull away and drive down the street.

"Well, well, well. Mr. Perfect Roger is in trouble."

She drove slowly, hoping neither Roger nor the police would see her. She parked a few houses down and waited for several minutes to be sure they didn't circle around and come back to the house. When she felt the way was clear, she drove around the block and pulled into the driveway of their home. Once she was inside their house, it surprised her she didn't feel at home. She shrugged and got busy gathering her belongings and other items around the house she wanted for herself.

By the time Roger and Detective Jordan were nearly to Edmonds, Tamal was busy loading up her big SUV. She'd used all the laundry baskets and some boxes she'd found in the utility room to pack her things. She also used all the suitcases and backpacks in the house to load up more things. She laughed at the thought of Roger coming home and finding all the luggage and her belongings gone.

She looked at the enormous television in the den. Watching the 85-inch television was like being in a movie theatre right here at home. She shook her head, knowing she couldn't get the big screen television down from the wall. She carried the 50-inch television from their bedroom out to her SUV. She smiled, knowing Roger thought she was too weak to carry all these things by herself. He was constantly saying, "Here, let me help you with that," and she let him. She let him think she was too weak to do such things by herself.

She thought, *what you don't know, dear hubby, won't hurt me a bit. I've worked hard to build up my strength and muscles.* She smiled, knowing he often forgot she was nearly as tall as he was. She'd decided over a year ago that with her height she could be as strong as he was, and she worked to make it so. It had been several months since they'd made love, so he had not noticed her increased strength. She delighted at the thought of him trying to figure out how she carried all her belongings by herself.

Pavlov followed her through the house as she gathered things, whining now and again. She looked at the dog and said, "Your daddy is food for worms now, doggie. So sad for you. Roger will be your new daddy. At least until I decide what to do with him. Then it's off to the pound you go."

The dog cocked his head and went to his bed near Roger's side of the human bed. The woman made him feel uneasy, but he knew she belonged in this house. She exhausted him. He closed his eyes and dreamed of his friend Simon. An elk entered his dreams and lay beside Pavlov, comforting him and sharing with him the death of the human he loved.

When Tamal had all her things loaded up, she walked through the house to make sure she hadn't left anything behind other than every stick of furniture she wanted to keep but couldn't take with her. She shook her head and said, "I'll give it all some thought and next time I'll bring a big-assed truck."

She went to her SUV and pulled out of the driveway. She looked up to see Pavlov looking out the bedroom window. She had a moment of regret that Simon was gone, but only a moment. "Well, brother, if Amma is right and our souls are immortal, you surely are on a path to a new and better life. You've always been a better human than me."

She shook her head and chuckled. "What's the point in being a good human though if you don't have a good time?"

Detective Darren Jordan sat in a chair in Basanti Chowdhury's living room while Roger sat holding the old woman in his arms. She wept, and Darren knew in his gut Roger had nothing to do with Simon's murder. He had hoped that Tamal, Simon's sister and Roger's wife would be here, but no such luck.

He sighed and said, "Mrs. Chowdhury, when you are able, I've a few questions to ask you."

She nodded and pulled a muslin hankie from her pocket and wiped her tears and nose. She said, "A mother should never outlive her children. I'm sure you've heard that before, Detective."

"Yes, ma'am. It is a true sentiment in the hearts of all parents I've met."

She nodded again. "Go ahead and ask your questions."

"Do you know anyone who has a grudge against your son?"

She shook her head. "Simon was a truly good man. He was kind and loving to us all. He was the rock for our family. I can't imagine anyone purposefully killing him. Are you sure it wasn't an accident?"

"Yes ma'am, we're sure."

"Do you know how he was killed?"

Darren swallowed, knowing she deserved to know at least some details. He also needed her help with a particular detail. "It seems he was hit in the throat and unable to call out. He might not have been able to breathe well either. Also, whoever killed him used a strange knife to puncture his jugular vein and cut out his tongue."

She shook her head and paled at the description of what had been done to her beloved son. "Why would anyone do such a thing?"

"I don't know. I have a photo of the knife. It's cleaned up and if you are up to it. I was hoping you might have seen it before."

She nodded. "It is not likely. I only have the usual kitchen knives here and a letter opener. I'll look at your picture."

Darren handed the photo to Roger first, and he gasped. He

showed it to his mother-in-law. She screeched in a keening voice and rocked back and forth. "No, no, no. It cannot be."

Roger handed the photo back to the detective and said, "It looks remarkably like an old family heirloom."

"Where did you see it last?"

"Hanging over Simon's fireplace."

"Did he ever take it with him on his treks?"

"No. It was far too valuable for Simon to take in the woods. It was his great-great-grandfathers' knife. It's a 19th Century bichwa dagger from India. I don't know anything more about the knife itself other than he treasured it." He looked at his mother-in-law and asked, "Do you know anything about it, Amma?"

"It was my great-grandfather's prized possession. An uncle of his gave it to him on his twenty-first birthday. The knife was primarily used by brigands and robbers, though some in the military used it as well. His uncle used his dagger mainly in many of the uprisings and protests against the British rulers in the late 1800s and early 1900s."

Darren nodded. "I'll get a court order to search Simon's home unless you'd give me written consent here and now as his next of kin."

She looked at Roger and asked, "Will you go with him?"

"If you wish, Amma."

She patted his hand. "You are a good man, Roger. You've been a wonderful son to me and a brother to Simon. I'm sorry Tamal doesn't love you as she should."

He kissed her cheek. "Thank you, Amma. How Tamal loves is up to her. My heart breaks at the loss of her love, nearly as much as my heart breaks at the death of my dear friend, Simon."

"I know, my son. She will return here to live with me later this afternoon."

He was surprised but nodded. He looked closely at his mother-in-law and worried for her peace of mind living with Tamal. He said, "I hope that will be a loving experience for you both, Amma."

She shrugged her shoulders. "Don't worry too much, Roger. I've no unrealistic expectations regarding Tamal's behaviors and intentions. I love her dearly, but sometimes I feel she was never meant to be of this world." She sighed and shook her head. "Now enough of that. Are you busy Monday morning?"

"Not so busy I can't make time for you, Amma."

"I need to go to the bank and sign some papers. After that, I need to go to visit my lawyer. I cannot delay these needs. Please do not tell Tamal of my plans."

He nodded. "I understand. What time shall I pick you up?"

"Is 9:30 too early?"

"No, Amma. Will Tamal be here?"

"She will be at the gallery by 8:30. Her boss is gone all week on a European trip so Tamal is in charge of everything."

"I'll be here at 9:30."

CHAPTER THIRTEEN

Back in Darren's police cruiser, Roger asked, "Where's your sidekick, Sally?"

"Today is her son's third birthday. I sent her home to be with her family."

"I'm glad. No boy should be without his mother on his birthday. You are a good man, Detective."

"I try to be."

Roger let go of the thoughts of a three-year-old boy, knowing he would not have a son or daughter soon. Those thoughts added to his grief. He concentrated on what he could do. He remembered a saying of Simon's, "Control your controllables and let everything else take care of itself."

For now, he decided he would help find Simon's killer and help Amma. "So, what are your thoughts after talking with Amma?"

"Why do you call her Amma? I thought Basanti was her name."

"Basanti is her name but Amma is an endearment in the Indian culture. It is like calling my mother Mom or Momma."

"Ah. Now I understand. Their names are unusual to my American ear, but I want to honor all cultures I come in contact with."

Roger smiled. "See. You are a good man, Detective. Did Amma help your investigation?"

"I'm not sure. I know she was open and honest. However, I don't have any distinct thoughts about who killed your brother-in-law other than I do not think you or Basanti Chowdhury killed him."

Roger sighed and felt the heaviness of his grief. His wife was no longer in love with him, and his best friend was dead. The bleak, gray day fitted his emotions. He agreed. "No, I did not kill my friend and Amma would never kill anyone. However, Simon was her favorite child. She doted on him so much it was embarrassing for him."

"How did your wife feel about her brother?"

"It's hard to say. Sometimes she spoke of him with great love, but other times she complained bitterly about him."

"Why?"

"Well, within the Indian culture, the oldest male is, by default, the head of the family. Simon took that role seriously. Maybe too seriously. I loved him like a dear brother, but I could sometimes see Tamal's side of things. He would tell her 'you should do more to help Amma', or 'you must be a loving wife to Roger' or 'it's time for you to bear a child'. Things like that. Then she would scream and shout, 'Simon, says! Simon, says!' Although her words might have been seen from the outside of the family as a play on the words of a children's game, it was nothing like the game."

Darren nodded. "So was there a lot of animosity between the two."

Roger looked out the window and shook his head. "No. Maybe. Really, I don't know. She loved him. I thought she loved me, but perhaps I was wrong on both counts. I have trouble believing she would kill her brother. Then again, I have trouble believing she wants to dissolve our marriage."

"Could you be wrong about her feelings about Simon?"

Roger shrugged his shoulders. "That's my conundrum. I don't know, but I certainly can't see her killing him. At least I think I'm certain on that score. I especially can't see her killing him in such a brutal manner. She hated getting her hands dirty and would seldom go into the woods, much less hike up a mountain. The killing as you described it would take deft strength. I haven't seen that in my wife."

"In photos around your mother-in-law's home, she seems to be nearly as tall as you."

"Yes. I am one inch taller than Tamal. Simon is or was taller than me, though by a couple of inches."

"Is it possible you underestimate your wife's strength?"

"I don't think so. She is a stunning, elegant, girly, girl through and through. Beauty, not strength, is her forte. Even when we were relaxing around the house, just the two of us, she always was dressed and made up elegantly. I'd asked about it and she said, 'I am a proud woman. I want no one, including you, to see me less than perfect. A woman should always be beautiful no matter what disorder there is around her.' I don't want to make her sound like a snob, but in some ways, I suppose she was elitist."

Darren nodded but said nothing more. He wanted to read about Indian culture. His own mother had taught him, underestimating the power of a woman is a dangerous thing to do. She'd explained about foxglove, oleander, and lily of the valley flowers. They were her favorites, but they were also deadly. She'd said, "Sometimes beauty is there to warn us and other times to tempt us."

It seemed to the detective that this family of mixed generations and mixed social expectations and mixed inherited beliefs might be a pot of hot embers waiting to burst into flames. Certainly, the men in the family loved the women. The women were beautiful and alluring. Even Basanti, at age sixty, was elegant and beautiful. However, he suspected the men might have misjudged the strength and power of the women.

Roger continued looking out the window at Puget Sound, but for the first time he could remember it did not seem beautiful to him. The water reflected the grayness of the day. Mists covered the forests and islands in the sound. Bleak seemed to be the overriding feature of the day and also his emotions. He'd give a hearty sum of money for a sunny, crystalline clear day today without grief.

He looked at Darren and said, "I can't believe forty-eight hours ago the sun was shining and I was at least a little hopeful. Now, I feel as dreary as the weather."

Darren nodded. "I was thinking how hard this is for your family and the weather isn't helpful at all."

"Well, Simon would say, the weather doesn't give a damn about us mere mortals. Weather does what weather does. It's up to us to deal with it."

Darren smiled. "He sounds like he was a good human."

"He was. The best man I ever knew."

CHAPTER FOURTEEN

In West Seattle, Darren and Roger walked through Simon's home looking for evidence of a break-in or someone having taken items from the home. The only clue they found was the dagger above the fireplace. Although an artistic dagger of similar size, shape and color of the original, hung there, it obviously was not the family heirloom.

Darren asked, "Would Simon notice this dagger as differing from the original?"

"I don't know. Perhaps if he hadn't turned on all the lights before leaving the house."

"Let's try out your theory. Which lights do you remember being on when you first came in through the patio door?"

"Well, the light over the kitchen sink was on for sure."

"Okay, then you go turn that light on. Wait here while I turn off all the other lights."

When Darren returned to the kitchen, Roger said, "The front window blinds were closed."

Darren closed those blinds and returned to the kitchen. "Were the patio door blinds closed?"

"No. Simon leaves those open all the time so Pavlov can see out easily."

"What about when he's not at home? How does the dog go out to do his business?"

Roger grinned. "Well, until this episode it hasn't been a problem. Simon worked from home."

"Ah, so letting the dog in or out became an issue only when Simon was away too long."

"Yeah. Simon taught him to go to the bathroom to pee and poop if he had to go when Simon was gone."

Darren chuckled. "He must be a really smart dog."

"He is. What's next?"

"Okay, let's get back to the setting here. Were the breakfast dining area and dining room lights on?"

"No. The ambient light from the patio door was the only light in here, and the dining room light was off."

Darren walked to the opening between the breakfast area and the living room. "What lights were on in here?"

Roger pointed to two chairs across from the living room picture window. "There, on the table between the chairs, the lamp was on."

Darren turned on the lamp. "Any other lights on in this room?"

"No. The small hallway by the guest bathroom, that light was on and the bathroom door was open."

Darren flipped the switch in the small hallway. They turned and walked down the longer hallway to Simon's bedroom. Darren asked, "No lights on here?"

"None."

"What about his bedroom?"

"The bedside table lamp on the right side of the bed was on."

Darren turned on the bedside table lamp and turned to Roger. "Okay, what else?"

Roger shook his head. "No other lights were on as I recall."

Darren walked past Roger, leading the way back to the living room. "When we enter the living room, do *not* look up at the dagger just keep walking normally as if you were heading to the kitchen and garage."

Both men walked as if purposefully heading to the garage to go on a hike. Once they were at the garage door off the kitchen, Darren asked, "What do you think?"

"I think even if there had not been a fake dagger up there, Simon probably wouldn't have noticed its absence. There is more ambient light right now than there would have been an hour before sunrise. Sunrise would have been about seven."

"My thoughts exactly. I didn't see a television in the living room. Did Simon not watch television?"

Roger chuckled. "Oh, he watched television alright. He was

addicted to TV. This is a three-bedroom house. All the bedrooms are pretty big. One was his with the private bath, one was a guest bedroom with another bath between it and the third bedroom. Simon used the third bedroom as a combo study and den. He spent most of his time in that room. Come on, let me show you. One entire wall is television."

When they got to the study, Darren's mouth dropped open. "Never, ever tell my husband Martin about this."

Roger grinned. "It is a custom-built, very high-density smart television. It doesn't quite cover the whole wall, but almost. It's over ten feet wide."

Darren shook his head. "I've never seen any television this big."

Roger picked up the remote control and turned the television on to the PBS station. He chose one of the shows about America's national parks. He pointed to the recliners with drink holders. "Have a seat. After everything we've been through, we can get away with five minutes of wonder."

They sat with their feet up as Roger using a remote controller, turned off the room lights, turned on the surround sound and started the program. Darren clapped and said, "Okay. The first opportunity you have, tell my husband about this."

Roger laughed but was surprised to be crying while he watched the wonders of the country in which he lived. After several minutes he said, "I can't believe how much I've cried today."

Darren lowered his footrest and turned to the man beside him. "You've lost a dear friend, Roger. You should cry. Only a hardhearted man would do anything else."

Roger nodded, turned on the lights, turned off the television and stood up. "Thanks, Darren. What's next?"

"Well, we know that the fake dagger over the fireplace could have well been there for a few days and Simon might not have noticed it."

"I agree. In fact, if he had noticed it was a fake, I'm fairly sure he would have called me about it. He was very proud of his Indian heritage and the dagger was a part of that heritage."

"Next, we know you did not kill Simon. If we don't assume someone hated him and killed him in spite or anger, who stood to gain from his death?"

"I have no idea."

Darren asked, "Do you know where he kept important documents."

"Actually yes, I do. He and I exchanged information about where we keep private and important documents a few years ago." He walked over to the closet doors in the room and said, "His safe is in here."

"Do you have the combination?"

"Yes. I guess we should open the safe and have a look."

Darren watched Roger thinking about taking this big step. He waited quietly and said nothing. Finally, Roger sighed. "No matter how long I stand here he won't be coming back, will he?"

"No, he won't. But you may find clues in the safe that help us find his killer."

Roger nodded but didn't move or speak.

"I can get a court order if that would ease your mind."

"No," Roger said, shaking his head. "We exchanged information for exactly this sort of event. Since you can't put Simon back together and bring him home safe and sound, nothing about this will ease my mind." He pulled his smart phone out of his pocket, keyed in the password, and opened another app that required another password. Then he knelt and punched in the digital code to open Simon's safe.

As he opened the door of the safe, he felt he was opening a part of his friend's life he'd hoped he would never need to do. He sighed, opened the door fully, and reached for the documents inside.

CHAPTER FIFTEEN

Detective Darren Jordan sat and watched Roger's face go pale and then weep as he read his best friend's will. He waited while Roger read it again and then handed the will to the detective. Darren read the will and understood why Roger paled and wept. The two men sat quietly. They allowed the quiet to settle the emotions of a man who had lost the most important friend of his life. Now, he knew his friend had blessed him with his entire estate, which was very sizable and included this home.

Roger sighed. "Reading Simon's will has humbled me. I knew he loved me as a brother. I knew he trusted me implicitly. I never knew he intended to make me his prime beneficiary of his estate, or how little he trusted his sister to use his estate wisely. He said he expected I would be generous as I've always been, and he had no worries that I would take care of Tamal."

The detective said, "This is a lot of money and I think the implication is there may be more."

"There is. He holds several patents that bring in enough money he doesn't have to have a regular job. He wrote technical manuals, not because he needed the money but because he loved the detailed descriptions and instructions needed. He made a hefty bundle on those and on some he owns the copyright and gets regular income there as well."

The detective tapped the will and said, "This seems to be a very modest home for a man who had this sort of income."

Roger smiled. "Other than his electronic equipment and television addiction, he lived a modest life. Those he updated regularly and always bought the very best. He also always bought top gear for hiking, which was the most important thing to him besides Pavlov and his family. He also wrote blogs about his hikes and geology, which he loved. The blogs were on his own website. His technical manuals were mostly about geeky stuff, hiking and technical writing ins and outs. He wanted everyone who could walk to be out in the woods."

"His hiking is where the patents came in. He has designed several hiking apps and tech gadgets. One is a GPS alert system with flashing red light that is solar powered. If you're lost in the woods, turn the thing on and it helps rescuers find you, even at night. His income really took off when he marketed the device. For him personally, however, things, stuff, never meant much to him. He cared about hiking, his family, his friends and Pavlov."

"He sounds like he was a remarkable man and friend."

"He was." Roger looked out the window by Simon's desk and sighed. "These past few minutes, I've been thinking about my wife and our marriage and my attitude in the relationship."

Darren was a little surprised but remained quiet. There might be nothing Roger would say that would change the course of this murder investigation, but it might be helpful to Roger for him to listen. His husband Martin had told him once, "The thing I love most about you is your willingness to listen without giving advice or opinions. It is a true blessing, my dear."

He watched the man sitting across from him.

After a few moments of thought, Roger said, "I don't understand my wife. Although I love her, she doesn't want to be married to me anymore and doesn't want to have children. I long for children and to build a loving, rowdy family. She is right about our house. I built everything and remodeled everything in that home to suit her tastes and desires."

He looked at the detective. "It's not that I didn't like her choices, but mostly I did it for her. It is her house. I'm going to let her off the hook and let her have the house. I'll live here in this house my friend left me. His love and honor will be here with me."

Darren nodded. "I like the way you think, Roger."

Roger smiled. "Let's look at the rest of these papers and see if we can find anything that will help give Simon some justice."

Tamal unpacked enough of her things in her bedroom at her mother's home to get by for a few days. Not only did she not feel comfortable in her home in West Seattle, she didn't really feel comfortable here either. She knew where she belonged, but knew it was too soon. She would have to make do for now. Her house in West Seattle no longer felt like home. Her mother's home was her mother's home, and she felt like a visitor here.

A shadow of grief over Simon's death tweaked at the back of her mind. She hoped she'd been able to comfort Amma when her mother told her of Simon's death. Her personal grief now, was a surprise to her. She tried to tell herself it was what needed to happen, but, in this moment, the certainty of those thoughts was tenuous.

She had plans and once she set them in motion, she couldn't possibly stop her forward progress. The people in the world she lived in would be shocked at her planning and execution of her plan. She smiled, thinking of the word execution. It had a ring of virtue in her mind.

Her thoughts would make mere mortals shudder.

She left the bedroom and went to the kitchen to help her mother prepare dinner. The smell of jasmine rice with saffron and garam masala made Tamal's mouth water. "Amma, it smells delicious in here. What are you making?"

"Shrimp over saffron rice with tomatoes, carrots and peas. Plus, a creamy garam masala gravy to pour over it all with a little sour cream and chapati."

Tamal wrapped her arms around her mother. "Thank you, Amma. It's my favorite."

"I know. I want to pamper you and hold you close to my heart."

"And I you, Mommy."

Her mother smiled. "You usually call me Amma, but I remember when you were a very small girl how you called me Mommy when you wanted to cuddle."

"I'm feeling a little lost and need my mother near me."

"Because of Simon or Roger?"

"Both. I made a mistake marrying Roger. I never really loved him, at least not in the way I think married couples love each other. I'm sad Simon is gone too."

Basanti turned and looked at her daughter with eyebrows raised. "So, are you going to get a divorce?"

"I know you don't want me to, but it is the only fair thing I can do for me or for Roger. I want to devote my life to art and travel."

"Can you afford to do that, Beti?"

Tamal shook her head, noting the endearment for a daughter. "Not yet, but someday. I certainly can never afford my dreams if I have children. Besides, I'm not the mothering type."

"What type are you?"

"The Beti type. The beloved daughter."

Basanti patted Tamal's hand and returned to the stove. "You set the table. Dinner will be ready in a few minutes." She loved her daughter and knew her well enough to know, that although she felt loving intentions right now, her intentions could change at a moment's notice.

Tomorrow Basanti would change her will and her banking accounts. She would leave this house to Tamal. In fact, she planned to deed it to her immediately with the proviso that Basanti could live here until her natural death. There would be a small trust fund to pay the house insurance and annual taxes. Everything else she planned to leave to Roger with instructions to use as much of the estate as possible helping other people. Tamal needed and deserved the opportunity to become a responsible adult. After these chores were taken care of, she hoped Tamal would settle down and become more settled, more human.

CHAPTER SIXTEEN

Stan kissed his wife, Renee, and said, "I'm going out to the studio to journey. I want to talk with Nelson."

She smiled. "Tell your goofy, grinning Elk hello."

He chuckled and went out to his music studio. One of the first things he and his wife had done when they bought this home was to create a music studio. They built the large room in one half of the over-sized, two-car garage. For Stan, it was a place to play, practice with others, record, teach and just be himself. Here, he felt himself settle and was clearer of mind than anywhere else.

Stan had bipolar disorder but with the help of his incredible wife, a great psychiatrist, medications, and Old Man Coffee, he felt better now than any time in his life.

He appreciated, too, that his friend Mary Ellen was partnered with Helena Maloney. They were both from the Oklahoma and Texas areas of the nation. Helena had learned from family in Oklahoma about Core Shamanism. She'd taught Stan and Mary Ellen the basics. When he found the practice to be helpful, he went to a weekend retreat to hone his skills and understand at a deeper level the concepts of Core Shamanism.

Roger had called about an hour ago to let him know they'd found Simon and he was indeed dead. Stan had wept but felt he should have known Simon was gone from this planet. He'd been concerned about Roger and his marriage and thought that was the only problem with the group. He shook his head and snorted. "As if. We five men are wounded men in one way or another. All of us carry our wounds throughout life. I don't mind being wounded as much as I mind feeling I have little control in my life."

Then he smiled. The Core Shamanism was helping, and that was a good thing.

He unrolled his yoga mat on the floor, turned on the drumming app, lay down and covered his eyes.

In his mind he went to the Tooth of Time at Philmont Scout Ranch in New Mexico, where he'd gone as a young Boy Scout. It was a meaningful place of accomplishment for him. The sky was a brilliant blue and the craggy rocks were gray and brown. There, nearly to the top of the rock promontory, was another pile of rocks with a Bristlecone pine pushing its way up from the ground through the rocks. Beneath the pine, between the tree's roots and the rocks, was an opening Stan used for his journeys.

The drumming pulled him down, down, down the tunnel to the lush pine forest in the lower levels of Non-Ordinary Reality. Looking around, it looked much like the Pacific Northwest where Stan lived in Ordinary Reality. There, in the Lower World, stood Nelson grinning and munching on the grass with blades of green sustenance poking out between his smiling lips.

When Stan finished his journey, he waved goodbye to Nelson. He walked across the meadow to the opening, then up the tunnel beneath the roots at the base of the bristle cone pine, out to The Tooth of Time. He quickly made his way to his studio in his garage at the back of his home in Ordinary Reality. He sat up, drank some water from his water bottle and picked up his journal. He wrote for several minutes then stood up, picked up his journal and water bottle and went to sit at his desk.

He turned on a compilation of jazz standards he loved. He felt himself settle more into his body with the music settling and soothing his mind. He looked out the window of his studio, seeing the back of his house and the soft yellow glow of the light over the back door. The light always felt comforting to him. He smiled, seeing a bit of blue light flickering from his daughter's bedroom window. She had another fifteen minutes to read, but he was in no state of mind to fuss at anyone tonight, especially his ten-year-old daughter.

He looked down at the journal his mother had given him. She and his father both practiced Core Shamanism. He'd heard about Core Shamanism from them. He didn't start the practice himself until he helped his friend Mary Ellen, known by all as ME. ME did a regular podcast about the music scene in Seattle. She had attended several of his jazz gigs in the area. Her partner Lena, aka Helena, taught him the basics and he'd shared the experience with his mother. She sent him a journal that reminded her of her son. It looked like a fuzzy, not quite in focus, photo of the Milky Way at first sight. But, when it was tilted a little, the streaks of the galaxy were lines of music.

He touched the cover of the journal and said, "Thanks, Momma," and opened the book. He read what he'd written about the journey.

> When I got to the Lower World, I saw Nelson grinning at me with grass hanging out of his mouth. I went up to him and asked, "Why did Simon have to die?"
>
> "He didn't have to die, at least not yet, but someone decided he would."
>
> "Who?"
>
> "I don't know her name."
>
> "What did she look like?"
>
> "She had a black hood over her head and was dressed in all black."
>
> "How did you know she was a woman?"
>
> Nelson laughed and shook his head. "A man knows these things."
>
> I chuckled, shook my head. "Any objective evidence the killer was a woman?"
>
> "She had delicate hands, but they were powerful weapons."
>
> "What did she do?"
>
> "She hit Simon in the lump of his neck and poked him in the neck with an ugly sharp knife. Then she cut out his tongue, and he fell into the hole a tree dug. It was a really big hole. The root ball was taller than Simon by a lot."

I was shocked and shook my head. The sorrow was overwhelming in that moment, and I couldn't stop the tears. I sat on the ground weeping as Nelson continued quietly munching on the green grass. Finally, I asked, "What happened next?"

Nelson lay down beside me with his head in my lap. He sighed. "She covered him with leaves and dirt and rocks and branches, then she just walked away through the woods."

"She didn't get on the trail?"

"I don't know. Maybe after she left Simon, but I didn't see a trail."

"What else did you notice?"

"She was really tall and really mean. She was as tall as you, but not as nice as you."

"Thanks, I guess."

"You're welcome. You are a really good man, Stan."

"Can I help Simon?"

The elk shook his head. "He's moving to the next level of his being right now. I think he is moving up some ladder or something like that. He is sad about the woman but he is happy about the ladder."

"Is there anything else?"

"She used a bitchy knife."

I chuckled, thinking only a bitch would hurt a man like Simon. Then I answered the elk, "I'm sure she did."

Nelson raised his head, licked my face, stood up and said, "I'm going to go hang with the guys."

I stood up and asked, "You hang with other male elk?"

"Yep. It's sort of like your Old Man Coffee. But one of you isn't there anymore."

I patted the elk on the head and said, "Thanks, Nelson." I walked across the meadow to the opening of the tunnel. I went up through the tunnel and into Ordinary Reality back in my studio.

Stan closed the journal and laid his hand on the cover. He up and saw that his daughter's room was dark and there was no more flickering light. It relieved him to not have to deal with being a parent at this moment. He also rejoiced to have a loving wife and sweet daughter. All the important women in his life loved him too.

He knew he was a lucky man.

CHAPTER SEVENTEEN

Darren sat holding hands with his husband, Martin Daniels. He asked, "Do you think our television is too small?"

Martin grinned. "Well, it's fifty-inches wide. That seems pretty big to me. Why?"

"I think I'm just in lust."

"What's his name?"

"Samsung."

Martin laughed. "Ah. A good name."

Darren grinned and said, "I saw a television earlier today that is about ten-feet wide."

"Holy shit, Darren. We'd have to give it its own bedroom!"

"Yeah, that's pretty much how it was with the one I saw."

"Are you serious?"

Darren shrugged.

"You are! I never thought I'd see the day Mr. do-it-by-the-book and don't spend a penny you don't have to spend, is lusting after a television."

"They don't cost an awful lot."

"Does it have a job and bring home enough money for such a luxury?"

Darren furrowed his brow and smirked a little. "I don't know. I didn't think to ask."

"Well, Detective, you'd best ask. Detectives are supposed to ask questions as I recall."

Darren grinned.

Martin shook his head and said, "Okay. I'll give up and ask the question. How much is this going to set us back?"

"About 5 thousand. They're on sale right now."

"Yeah. Well, our bank balance is nowhere near that and I'm opposed to putting such a big, frivolous amount on a credit card."

Darren laughed and laid his head on his husband's shoulder. "I know and I agree. Although I'd never say no to such a television, I'm not serious about buying one."

"Good," Martin said and rolled his eyes. "We have other plans for our lives, including remodeling and upgrading our house."

Darren sat up straighter and turned to his husband. "I've got just the man for us."

"Is he a murder suspect?"

"No. At least not yet."

Martin laughed. "You are batting zero tonight, buddy. Once you are sure he isn't a murdering fiend, we'll talk. Until then, I need to head to bed. I have to be in early tomorrow morning for staff meeting to go over our new menu."

"Okay. Kiss me goodnight. I've got more research to do tonight."

Martin kissed him and said, "I'll put the television on the possibility list."

"I'd appreciate that."

"You'd better."

Darren smiled and went to his own bedroom. He and Martin had separate bedrooms but slept together from time-to-time. They were devoted to each other, and their devotion went much deeper than sex. Thinking of their love, he thought of the levels and types of love. He knew their love was eros, storge, and philia. They were sexually loving, a family of love, and brotherly loving friends too. He smiled and thought, *My guess is Old Man Coffee is a combination of storge, familial love, and philia, brotherhood love. Although each man has his own family, they felt to me like they were a band of brothers. I really like Roger a lot. He seems to be a good man. I sure as hell hope he isn't the murderer.* His instincts were clear that Roger was a good person, but he'd seen good people do terrible things.

He turned on the computer at his desk in the corner of his bedroom and started searching for records on the Chowdhury family. Most of what he found was routine and expected. When he got to the father of Simon and Tamal, however, his hackles rose. Paresh

Chowdhury had died in an automobile accident.

The cause of the accident was brake failure. The brake fluid line broke as he was driving about 80 miles an hour on a curve on Interstate 90. He was driving too fast, which according to his family was a usual state of affairs for him. However, the forensics team at the time couldn't say it wasn't just wear and tear. They also couldn't say the brake lines weren't tampered with. The lines were old and had surface stress cracks. They couldn't identify a specific spot that had been tampered with.

He pulled out his phone and made a note to talk with the forensics team first thing in the morning. He downloaded the PDF of the case reports of Paresh Chowdhury and saved them to his desktop file at the station. He then copied them all to Sally Quinn attached to an email. In the email he sent her, he wrote: *Please look at these documents. When we are together in the morning, let's talk about your impressions.*

If Paresh Chowdhury's death was not accidental, the entire case of Simon Chowdhury's death might become much more complex. Two family members dying in violent ways could not to be ignored. Darrell needed to interview Simon's sister. *Maybe the best way is to send Sally to talk with her first. Sally is petite and seems innocent and young on the surface. One minute in the gym with her, though, would set anyone's misconceptions of frailty to rest.* He grinned, remembering how she'd kicked his ass the first time they were in the gym practicing martial arts moves. After that encounter, he'd worked harder on his martial arts skills. It wouldn't do to have a tiny woman beat him more than once. He shook his head, grimaced, and thought, *Now that was sexist!*

He picked up his phone and sent another text message to Sally. *Why don't you stop by the Pacific Arts Gallery in Edmonds before you come in tomorrow? I'd like you to see if you can get an interview with Tamal Chowdhury. I want to hear your impressions of her. Be sure you record the interview.*

A few minutes later, his phone dinged with a message from Sally. *Sure thing, boss. I think there is a lot of hinky stuff going on with that family.*

He grinned at Sally's message, turned off his computer, picked up a Louise Penny book and laid it on his bedside table. He changed out of his clothes into pajamas, brushed his teeth and went to bed. He read about a drug ring Chief Inspector Gamache was after on the border between the USA and Quebec. Later, when he was asleep, he dreamed of Simon, Tamal, Roger, Basanti and her husband, Paresh. There was a lot of art in the dream. At a gala in an art gallery, there was exotic food and floral tea. A very tall, dark man seemed to hover at the edges. A bouquet of Lily of the Valley made a brief appearance surrounded by steam. The fragrance of the flowers permeated everything he saw and heard. There was an older than dirt Volvo too, smashed nearly beyond recognition as an automobile.

His dreams played out on the largest television in the Universe. His mind.

Sally was excited about her interview with Tamal Chowdhury tomorrow morning. No way was she going to sleep now. She needed to do some research.

She turned on her computer and Googled the Pacific Arts Gallery. She learned a lot about the gallery's history, including that Heather Aldersen was the owner and head curator.

Interviewing the sister of the victim tomorrow would be a big step forward. She also felt there must be a reason Detective Jordan wanted her to do a preliminary interview with what should be a really important part of the puzzle. As she researched Tamal Chowdhury and the gallery, she began to get an inkling of why he wanted her to interview Tamal. The woman seemed to be cloaked in elegant mystery.

When she saw a photo of Tamal at a gallery event standing beside a very tall black man, she smiled and said, "Aren't you a stunning beauty?" Tamal's skin was a lighter shade than the man's and seemed to glow. She wasn't nearly as tall as the man beside her, but by looking at others around them, she surmised Tamal might be as much as six feet tall. There was no one in the crowd as tall as the impressive black man. She muttered, "I might come up to his knees," and then giggled.

The most important clue to Sally's mind was the haughty, entitled smile on Tamal Chowdhury's face. It was as if she was saying to the elegant man, "You are lucky to be standing beside me."

The man's face showed less emotion, but he was clearly not enamored by the beautiful woman beside him. His look showed mild irritation, if anything at all. Mostly he was there to have his photo taken because he was the star of the show. Sally searched some more and learned that he was the enigmatic and reclusive billionaire, Hadar Hamal.

"Well, well, well," she muttered. "Now isn't that interesting. I wonder if Tamal knew who he was?" She shook her head and said, "Of course she knows who he is. A woman like Tamal would seek out a man of his stature, grace and especially wealth."

CHAPTER EIGHTEEN

Roger sat in the living room of his home making lists of things he wanted to take to Simon's house the next day. Pavlov lay beside him on the sofa, snoring shamelessly and drooling a little. He knew Tamal would hate that a dog was in their house, much less on their sofa and drooling to boot. It didn't matter now.

Roger was heartbroken Tamal had been here while he was visiting his mother-in-law, Basanti, with Detective Darrell Jordan. He knew it was probably best he had not been home when Tamal stopped by to pick up her belongings. Still, he felt overwhelming grief about the whole situation. He knew the only course for himself was to be as kind as possible to his wife while mourning not only the dissolution of his marriage with Tamal but losing his best friend Simon.

He composed an email telling her how sorry he was their marriage did not work out even though he still loved her. He wrote he will file for divorce or she could, or they could take a wait and see approach. He would honor her choices in the matter of their marriage. He then continued:

> You may have the house and all the furniture. I'll ask my lawyer to draw up a deed giving you full ownership of our house once the divorce is final. The insurance and taxes are paid up for the rest of this year. Starting next year, those costs will be yours to bear.
>
> I'll move my personal things from the house tomorrow. I will have no need of the dishes, pots and pans or kitchen appliances. I should be through moving out by early afternoon.
>
> I love you but agree our marriage is at an impasse. I want children and you do not. I want to create a family. I want a long

and abiding love which we seem unable to create together. Our marriage is no longer a tenable situation for either other of us. I promise to not challenge a divorce.

I'll be living in Simon's house. All my email addresses and phone numbers will remain the same, at least for the time being.

Also, tomorrow I'll take my name off our joint banking accounts. You may keep the money that is in there. I can take a draw from my business if I need to, but I will make no more deposits to those accounts.

Let me know if there is anything else I can do for you to help you through this troublesome and grief filled time.

All my love, Roger

He sighed, hit the send icon, and closed his computer. He was restless. He gathered his clothing and personal items on the bed. There were no suitcases left, so he went to the kitchen and pulled out large trash bags for his belongings. As each minute passed, he felt more and more uncomfortable in the house that had been his home for over four years.

Finally, he gave up and decided to go to Simon's house and take Pavlov with him. He finished shoving all his belongings from their bedroom and bathroom into the plastic bags. He then loaded them into his pickup truck. He and Pavlov took the brief trip to Simon's house. He'd return tomorrow to his old house to double check he'd cleared out all his belongings.

When he pulled up in the home's driveway where Simon had lived, Pavlov became very excited. He yelped and jumped up and down, eager to be out of the truck. Roger opened the garage door and pulled his truck inside. He let Pavlov into the house before he carried in all his belongings.

Once in the house, the dog raced from room-to-room looking for Simon. Roger felt bad and didn't know how to tell the dog what had happened to his buddy. The dog knew because Nelson, the elk, had told him, but still he looked for Simon with eager hope. *Nelson doesn't know everything.*

Roger sat down on the living room floor and waited for the dog to settle. After a few minutes, Pavlov came and sat in front of Roger and whined. Roger reached up and rubbed the dog's head. "I'm sorry, Pavlov. Simon is gone." The dog laid his head on Roger's lap and sighed.

Man, and dog sat as the man cried more tears than he'd ever imagined he had while the dog sighed and whined over and over.

Once Roger had all his belongings in Simon's bedroom, piled on the bed, he opened the drawers and closets. He gathered Simon's things and laid them on the bed in the guest bedroom. He would get Basanti and Tamal to go through Simon's things, then decide what to do with the rest.

In the bathroom, he took down Simon's bathrobe from the wall hook. Pavlov tugged on the robe and whined. Roger nodded and said, "Good idea, Pavlov. Let's put this on your bed, buddy. It might help you sleep a little better."

Pavlov followed Roger to his bed. When Roger laid the robe on the dog's bed, Pavlov immediately fluffed the robe a bit, then snuggled in his bed and closed his eyes. Roger patted Pavlov's head and said, "You're a fine friend."

Roger finished putting his clothes away and then went to the bathroom, pulled on pajamas, brushed his teeth and went into Simon's study. He turned on the television to watch Endeavor. He'd seen every episode of the young Morse as a fledgling detective, but was starting over, beginning with Episode One. He loved the character, a true wounded hero, who felt everything in his life deeply but worked hard to be the best man and detective he could be. He ruffled feathers but was a good detective. By the end of the first episode, Roger was too sleepy to stay awake any longer.

He checked all the doors and windows, then went to bed in Simon's bed. When he laid his head on the pillow, he smelled the scent that was unmistakably Simon. He cried some more, but before the last tear fell, Pavlov jumped on the bed and settled in beside him. Man, and dog fell asleep mourning their lost beloved friend.

Tamal sat in bed, in her childhood bedroom, with her laptop propped on a pillow. First, she checked all her social sites on the internet, then opened her email. When she saw there was an email from Roger, she started to delete it but decided instead to read it. As she read the email, she felt a huge burden lifted from her shoulders. She said, "I'll never make the mistake of marrying again. I for damned sure will never have a baby."

She had a tubal ligation a few months ago when Roger was out of town for a few days. The relief she felt at never having the risk of being pregnant was monumental. She felt liberated from her womb. The single act of making sure she'd never have a child boosted her ego and helped settle in her mind all she wanted to do in life.

She re-read the email and considered which way forward would be the best for her. She could make Roger file for divorce and her mother would be happier, but really, Tamal didn't care about anyone's happiness other than her own. The boon of course was that she could sell the house for a lot of money, maybe as much as a million dollars. *It's nearly as big as Amma's home and a lot nicer with many luxurious and modern upgrades. The money from the house plus what I'll get when Amma is gone will be enough to start my real life. I can sell her house for a big bundle, too. I can go anywhere I want and do anything I want with the money. I won't even have to get rid of Roger. Unless, of course, I can get Simon's house too. It'll bring in at least five hundred thousand.*

She smiled, thinking of all the things she could do with a few million dollars free and clear. Soon the elegant Pacific Arts Gallery would be hers too. Heather Aldersen wouldn't be coming back, and her altered will left everything to Tamal. Life, for Tamal at least, would turn out grand after all.

She smiled, thinking of how easy it was to get rid of the people who got in the way of her dreams. Before she took things in hand a few weeks ago, she'd believed it was hard to get away with murder.

Turned out to be much easier than she'd expected. She hadn't dared to murder anyone after her father. There were other murders, but no one could possibly blame her. Most looked like accidents.

She sighed. *I need to slow things down a bit, though. I shouldn't appear to be too delighted with how my life is becoming richer by the day.*

CHAPTER NINETEEN

Mary Ellen, better known as ME, an African American artist and Seattle area podcaster, turned on the propane heater on the patio of her home. She walked back into the kitchen, kissed Lena, her partner in life on the cheek. "Good morning, my dear. The sun is brilliant this morning. Let's eat breakfast on the patio."

Lena smiled, her blue eyes sparkling. "Sounds perfect. I have some new designs I'm thinking of that I'd like to show you after breakfast."

"Hooray. I hope they are crocheted components for a painting."

"They are. Now that we are creating together, my mind seems to be filled with ideas."

"Good. Grab your breakfast and let's head out to watch the cold day in warm comfort."

The two women sat on their patio, looking out across Lake Sammamish. Both had their laptops open and were checking emails.

ME was lifting a spoonful of yogurt to her mouth but stopped and said, "This is weird."

"What?"

"I've received an email from Heather Alderson that she is going to Europe for two weeks with her benefactor, Hadar Hamal. They will go to several auctions and she hopes to bring home some fine pieces for the gallery."

Lena shook her head, her curly red hair touched with white bouncing. "That makes little sense. We talked with her ten days ago and she scheduled an appointment to come here tomorrow."

"I'm frankly shocked. In all the time I've known Heather, there hasn't been a single time she has made an appointment and not kept it. The email doesn't allude to our appointment at all. I've also never known her to travel to Europe for art. She's always had only Pacific Northwest artisan work in her gallery. That's the whole point of her gallery name and her goals for the area."

"More than that," Lena pointed to the computer, "She says one of her employees will take over the business temporarily."

ME shook her head. "I really dislike Tamal, and I'm shocked Heather would turn the business over to her for even a day. I was going to talk with her tomorrow about my feelings related to Tamal. She is a beautiful woman and certainly talented, but there is something totally off, creepy even, about her."

Lena nodded. "Yeah. I think she is what we'd call a snot back home. She thinks she is marvelous, but she's snot."

ME laughed. "How very middle school of you."

Lena shook her head. "You know I'm right. She also sort of reminds me of your painting of your chameleon power animal, Owen. Not that Owen isn't marvelous. It's more that her beauty and grace hide something more sinister than she seems on the surface; something even more vile than her arrogant way of being."

ME shuddered. "I think you are spot on. I'm going to call Heather. Surely she has her cell phone with her."

"She probably does. Besides, I don't think she'd just forget her appointment with us."

ME dialed Heather's phone number. When it went straight to voice mail, she left a message asking Heather to call her at her earliest convenience. "That's weird. I've never had to leave a voice mail for Heather, at least not one that went straight to voicemail."

"Well, let's get on about our day and try again in a few hours. She might have turned the phone off while traveling."

"If she's traveling, which I don't believe for a minute, she'll return my call. She and Hadar are grand friends, and he has been a real boon for her life, but they've never traveled together. None of it makes any sense."

Roger picked up Basanti right on time. Once she was in the car she said, "I'm worried about Tamal."

"Me too, but I can't change her direction in life. I wanted you to know I've told her I would not contest any divorce proceedings. I'll be going to my lawyer after we finish with your lawyers and bankers. I'm deeding our house over to her and taking my name off the joint accounts."

Basanti patted his hand. "You are a good man, Roger. I hope you will not forget you are my son, although I didn't give you life."

He smiled. "Amma, I could never abandon you. My parents are both deceased. You are the most important person in my life now that Simon is gone and Tamal is leaving me."

"She may find her love for you again, Roger."

"I don't think so, Amma. I think her love is restricted to her own adoration of herself and art."

"What if she sells your beautiful home?"

"That will be fine."

"Where will you live?"

Roger glanced at his mother-in-law then said, "I need to share something with you Amma, but it may make you more sad than you already are."

"I can handle my sorrow. Is it about Simon?"

"Yes, several years ago, shortly after I met and married Tamal, Simon and I shared where in our homes our personal documents were. He was concerned that something might happen to him and no one would know what to do. I had the same misgivings, so I agreed, and we shared information. I opened his safe yesterday evening and found his will."

Suddenly Roger was overwhelmed with grief. He brushed tears away and said, "Saying it out loud is harder than I thought it would be. I can't believe how many tears there are, Amma."

"More tears than all the stars in the Universe, Beta. I've been sharing my tears too."

He smiled at her endearment she used occasionally as a dear son for himself and Simon. "Simon left me his home and his entire estate."

Basanti crossed her hands to her chest. "I'm so relieved. What a grand man he was."

"Yes, he was. He also told me he expected me to be sure Tamal is safe and taken care of, but to not lavish money on her needlessly. Otherwise, he trusted me to be generous and help as many people as I could with his estate. I've moved into his house, Amma. Pavlov is happier there, and I feel comforted in my best friend's home."

She sat quietly for several minutes. When they arrived at the bank and Roger parked the car, Basanti turned to Roger. "Before we go in, I too, need to tell you some important things."

Roger turned to his mother-in-law and nodded.

She smiled and touched his cheek. "My will today will be very similar to Simon's. I've deeded my house to Tamal upon my death. After my death, my home is her home. I've left her a small trust fund to help with the upkeep and taxes on the home. If she decides to sell my house, she of course may keep that money, but the trust fund will be void. I've made you the executor of my estate to use the money to help other people. I've emailed my lawyer about the details already just in case something terrible should happen to me."

"Did you expect something terrible to happen to you?"

"Not really, but I'm uneasy. First my dear Paresh died driving his adored car. It should have been on a junk heap years ago. It looked like a tired, ancient bathtub turned upside down with wheels rumbling underneath. Even so, it was shocking the way he died."

Roger chuckled. "I remember that Volvo. He loved it second only to you and your children."

"Yes. The police couldn't make up their minds whether it was an accident. I assumed it was the old car giving up in the end, but now I wonder about his death."

"Because Simon died?"

"Yes. We know for sure Simon was murdered. I wonder if Paresh was murdered too."

"Do you suspect Tamal? I can't see her being able to do such a thing."

Basanti touched his hand. "My son, never underestimate the power of a woman. Not only can we squeeze enormous babies out of our bodies and be up cleaning and cooking within hours, we can do whatever it takes to get what we need in life. Some women go further, striving for what they want in life, not just what they need."

"I'll remember Amma, but I'm not sure I could stand the heartbreak if Tamal is the one who killed Simon."

"We are both in the same boat there, Roger. Let's go in and change my bank accounts so they are private only to me and you."

"Do you think your current accounts are not private now?"

"I know they are not. The bank agrees that someone has been poking around electronically, looking at my accounts."

"You think it is Tamal?"

She nodded, then took a deep breath. "I keep trying to figure out how I've been so terribly wrong about my beautiful daughter. At dinner last night she said, 'You know Amma, Taman and I really talked together in your womb. I'm glad I got to come out first. Taman and I argued about who would go first. I wanted me to be the one you saw first. I wanted you to love me before you even saw Taman.' Her words made me nauseated. I had to work hard to not shudder."

Roger felt a chill creep up his spine and into his throat. He swallowed hard, hoping he wouldn't choke. He whispered, "I'm so sorry, Amma."

"Me too."

CHAPTER TWENTY

Roger stopped at a home improvement store in West Seattle on his way home. He wanted to get new door locks, a new garage door opener, an electronic doggie door and electronic alarm system as well. After talking with Basanti earlier in the day, he decided for his safety and that of Simon's home; he wanted to be the only one with keys or garage door opener pad. He felt sad knowing what he was really doing was making sure Tamal couldn't come into Simon's, now his, home without his permission.

He never again wanted to take the risk that Pavlov wouldn't be able to get outside when he needed to. Simon had never installed a doggie door because he was afraid of raccoons, rats or other critters coming into the house. Roger had done the research and knew exactly which doggie door was the safest for the humans, the dog and the home. It took a few minutes to install the doggie door. When he finished, he fastened the special collar on Pavlov. With a few treats, the dog quickly got the idea and was running in and out of the house with ease.

Roger said, "What a smart doggie you are, Pavlov."

Roger's phone rang, and he saw it was Stan. "Hey, Stan. What's up?"

Stan asked, "Are you home?"

"I'm at Simon's house. Want to come over?"

"Yes. I need to share something with you and need to talk to someone who loved Simon as much as I did."

"Great. Come on over. Pavlov and I have lots to show you."

When the doorbell rang, Pavlov raced to the living room window and started barking with glee, turning around and around in fast circles. Another friend was here.

Roger opened the door and told Stan, "Come on in and see what we're doing."

He showed him the doggie door, and Pavlov willingly showed how to use it. Roger said, "Try to open that door."

Stan pushed with his hand and then his head with no luck. "Hey, that's great. I might want to get one for our dogs. We don't have a patio sliding door, though."

"They make them for regular doors too."

"I'll talk with Renee about it. I can do the heavy lifting, but she's the engineer in the family. I don't get why you are doing this though, with Simon gone."

Roger pointed to the refrigerator. "Let's grab a couple of beers and go back to Simon's study. I'll explain it all back there."

Stan opened the refrigerator, pulled two bottles of beer from the shelf, and followed Roger and Pavlov back to the study. Pavlov curled up on his mat under the television and chewed on a bully stick. The two men sat down in the recliners and Roger handed Stan Simon's will.

"Is it okay for me to read this?"

"Yes. I've already talked with Simon's lawyer. He will file the probate for the will as soon as we have the official death certificate. Since I'm the executor of the estate and taking care of Pavlov, I'm moving on with Simon's lawyer's permission. There are a lot of things to take care of legally, and the lawyer will take care of that stuff. I'm taking care of what I can."

Stan nodded. "Control your controllables, is what Simon always said." He opened his beer.

"Yep. He was right, too. It's helping me a lot, having actual hands-on things I can do."

"What about your work?"

"I've got three projects going. They all three have excellent team leaders. I've alerted them I'm taking a few days off because of a death in the family. They'll do fine without me for a bit. I'm available by phone if any team leader needs me."

"I haven't heard the term team-leader from you before. Why not foreman?"

"Well, foreman didn't sound right when we have several women on the teams, and one is a team leader."

"That's cool. What about Tamal? How are things on that front?"

"Not great. She's at her mother's house for now. Read the will. There's a lot to talk about."

ME called Heather again. And again, it went straight to voice mail. Lena said, "Let's email Hadar. We don't have a phone number for him, but he gave us his email address. He will know for sure if Heather is with him."

ME laughed. "Yes, he will. I don't know why I didn't think of that earlier."

"Or me," Lena said and chuckled.

ME emailed Hadar then told Lena, "I heard someone died on Little Si over the weekend."

"Was it a hiking accident?"

"No. Murder."

"Holy shit. That's creepy."

Before ME could answer, her email dinged. "It's from Hadar." She read the email, then turned to Lena. "He says he and Heather had no trips planned. He does not know where she is."

"What should we do?"

"I don't know. She has no family around here."

"Do you know where she lives?"

"Yes," ME answered. "She owns the building where the gallery is. It is a three-story building. She had the whole second floor of her building remodeled for climate-controlled storage of art pieces. The third floor she had redesigned as a fabulous apartment. It's nearly three thousand square feet."

Lena sat thinking and after a few minutes said, "I don't think we should call the gallery. IF someone hacked her email and sent it to us, then going around to the gallery might put her in danger. Besides, we'd have to deal with Tamal, which neither of us is interested in doing."

"Then what do we do?"

"We could email Stan or better yet, Darren Jordan, the detective we met last year when that bat-shit crazy piano tuner Persephone was kidnapping the jazz piano players. He came here to talk enough times that he has become a friend and already knows about our artwork and the gallery."

"That's a great idea. I'll send him an email with what we know. If there's anything going on, he might know about it and be able to help Heather."

Lena said, "If she is in trouble and not actually traveling."

"I don't think she is traveling."

"What do you think?"

"I think something has happened to her."

Lena shuddered a little. "Damn. I hope not. Send Darren the email right now. Be sure to tell him about Tamal and that we're available if he needs to talk with us. Let him know you think something has happened to Heather."

"Will do. I'm hoping she is fine, and someone just hacked her email."

"Getting hacked being the best outcome feels really weird."

Stan looked at Roger. "This must be hard for you to take on top of Tamal and her anger."

Roger nodded. "Thanks, Stan. I was worried folks would think I was taking over too soon. I ignored anyone else's critical ideas and did what's best for Pavlov and me. We both feel better here than anywhere else. I'm going to make Simon's house my home."

"Renee and I feel shattered by Simon's death. Did you tell the rest of the Old Man Coffee fellas?"

"Yep. Lucky duck Harvey is in Cozumel with his wife. She set up a surprise second honeymoon trip for him this week. He's really torn up about Simon but said, laying on the sand, in the sun, watching his wife in her pink, polka dot bikini makes it all a lot better."

Stan laughed. "I bet it does. I'm glad he didn't know about this before the trip began."

"Me too. Jack is really upset and having a hard time. He and Simon went to high school together. He and his husband, Arthur, are coming over later this evening to have pizza and beer with me. Want to come over?"

"I would, but we already have plans for this evening. I wanted you to read something though."

"What?"

"You know about the Core Shamanism stuff I've started lately, right?"

"Sure. You think it is helping with the bipolar issues?"

"Maybe a little. It helps keeps me more centered so I can see what I can and cannot control. That's a big deal for me. It helps with the worry and anxiety too."

"Good. Did you want me to read something about Core Shamanism?"

Stan shook his head. "No. I wanted you to read a journey I took last night. Journey is what we call it because when we are in a deep meditative, shamanic state we can go to other realities and talk with our power animals. Mine is a young male elk who is a total goofball and grins all the time."

Roger chuckled. "I'd be glad to read your journey."

Stan handed him his journal, then said, "I hope it might help with Simon's murder. Since the detective on the case is Darren, he'll understand. He knows about Core Shamanism. I scanned a copy and sent it to your email so you can send it to Darren if you think it would help."

Roger opened Stan's journal and was soon crying again. When he finished reading, he nodded. "Darren needs to see this. I'll send it to him in a few minutes."

Both men stood up, and Stan hugged Roger. "I'm here for you if you need me."

"Always."

CHAPTER TWENTY-ONE

After talking with Lena and ME, Hadar felt a chill race down his spine. He muttered to himself. "I think something evil is afoot." He picked up his phone and dialed a number in Edmonds, Washington.

A soft, lilting voice answered, "This is Odetta."

"Good afternoon, Odetta. This is Hadar."

"How nice to hear from you, Mr. Hamal."

"Please, Hadar. Are you settled in your new home?"

"Yes, I am. It is beautiful looking out across the sound and just a few blocks from the gallery. I'm excited to meet Ms. Aldersen. We have a dinner appointment later this evening."

"Dear girl, I've a great favor to ask of you."

"Certainly. I owe you many favors, Hadar."

"Do not go to the dinner meeting. In fact, I'd feel much better if you'd go to the Four Seasons Hotel for the next few days. I've a penthouse suite there and I've alerted the staff of your coming there today."

Odetta was puzzled, and a little shaken. "What is wrong, Hadar?"

"I may be overreacting, but I feel I'm not. You may be in danger. I've sent a driver who will take you to the hotel. His name is Sander Torrin. I'm sending you a photo of him. Do not open your door unless you recognize him. I'm on my way to Seattle and will be there in a few hours. Go to the suite, lock the door, and let no one in other than those I tell you about. You will hear from Danny Jukes, a bodyguard and special ops trained person I trust with my own life. Danny will meet you at The Four Seasons."

"You're scaring me, Hadar."

"Good. I'm frightened too and want absolutely nothing vile to happen to you. Will you do as I ask?"

"Yes, of course."

"Thank you, Odetta. Sander will be at your doorstep in thirty minutes or less. Can you be ready by then?"

"Certainly."

"Try not to worry, but please be vigilant. Do not order room service just in case you are followed. Call 911 if anyone tries to break in, even though Danny will be with you. I'm sending you the alarm codes for the suite. There is plenty of lovely food and refreshments in the suite. I recommend no alcohol for now. I want you to be alert at a moment's notice."

"I'll be very careful, Hadar. I trust you will explain everything when you arrive."

Next, Hadar called Danny Jukes. Danny answered on the first ring and asked, "How can I be of service, sir."

"I've a car picking up a young woman who is in danger. Do you remember Sander Torrin?"

"Yes, sir. He's a good man."

"Yes, he is. The young woman is Odetta Thomas. She was to meet with Heather Aldersen for dinner. Heather had agreed to give Odetta a start in the art industry. I believe Heather has come to harm."

"I'm sorry to hear that, sir. I really like Heather."

"And she likes you too, dear girl. I want you at the entrance of the Four Seasons Hotel to meet Odetta. Please stay with her and guard her until I arrive."

"Yes, sir."

"I'm sending you a photo of Odetta. She is a brilliant artist from Haiti and I'm sure you two will get along famously. She is a jewel I do not want harmed."

"I'll take care of her, Hadar. Please relax and enjoy your trip here to Seattle."

"I'll relax when I see both of you women safe and sound."

"We'll look forward to it."

Once on board his private plane, Hadar started a video call to ME and said, "Is Lena there with you?"

"Yes, she is. What's up, Hadar?"

"Heather and I had planned this to be a surprise tomorrow evening. Things have changed and you need to be careful."

Lena asked, "What do you mean?"

"I worry you two might be in danger and I wanted to relate the surprise now so you would understand."

"Sure," ME said. "We've gotten in the habit of keeping all the doors and windows locked and the alarm system on. Do you think we need further security?"

"Perhaps not. I would suggest you not go near the gallery or call Tamal."

Lena said, "We agree and in fact have alerted the police about the issues. What is the surprise?"

He smiled. "It's not what, it is who. Heather had already decided she needed more help in the gallery but was uncomfortable with Tamal. A young woman I've been mentoring in Haiti is in Seattle now. We were going to introduce you to her tomorrow evening at dinner."

"Is she safe?" ME asked.

"I've made arrangements for her safety. Maybe Tamal is unaware of her joining the team, but it may also be she is aware. Whatever has happened with Heather, I feel strongly is by Tamal's hands."

"Do we need to help keep Odetta safe?"

"No, I have that in hand, but I want you two to take extra care of your own safety. You may not be in Tamal's field of vision yet, but I feel it is important to be alert."

ME nodded. "I understand. We'll be careful."

"Good. I'll let you know when I'm with Odetta and safe. We'll go from there. I'm sure two artists such as yourselves will appreciate her keen eye and her art."

Lena said, "We look forward to meeting her and seeing you again."

They ended the conversation. Hadar leaned back in his seat and allowed himself peaceful rest. His mind always worked better when he could sleep a few hours before any important confrontations.

Odetta would have enjoyed the ride in the luxury car had she not been afraid. Her life in Haiti had not always been easy, but seldom was she afraid other than during hurricanes. The big city was unfamiliar to her, its mere size made her uneasy. She was grateful Hadar had provided her a home in Edmonds facing the water. Everything was cleaner and more modern than she was used to, but the water helped her to feel more at ease.

Edmonds was a small enough town she could easily walk to work from her home. She'd walked by the gallery but had obeyed Hadar and not entered the beautiful art establishment. She dined in a few of the local restaurants and felt she was beginning to feel settled in her new environment.

When the driver, Sander Torrin, pulled up at the entrance to The Four Seasons hotel, she was nearly overwhelmed. She knew there were many taller buildings in Seattle, but to be in front of the tall and elegant building was nearly overwhelming. Sander came around to her door and opened it. He held out a hand to help her out, then turned to a tall, beautiful, black woman with short curly black hair cut in a short pixie style. Her eyes were black as obsidian and nearly as shiny.

"Hi, Danny," he said. "Nice to see you again."

"You too, Sander." She turned to Odetta, held out a hand and said, "I'm Danny Jukes. I'm here to stay by your side and be sure you are safe."

Odetta smiled. "Thank you for being here. However, you are too beautiful to be a bodyguard."

Sander snorted. "She beats my ass every time we work out together."

Danny smiled. "Not every time, but most of the time. Come on Odetta, and let's get you inside."

Odetta turned to Sander and said, "Thank you for the ride. It was really fun."

He grinned. "Having fun is what I live for."

Danny rolled her eyes and muttered, "Men."

Odetta laughed and turned to follow Danny into the amazing hotel.

CHAPTER TWENTY-TWO

Sally Quinn entered the Pacific Arts Gallery in Edmonds, Washington, a few minutes after it opened. She waited as Tamal Chowdhury talked with a customer on the phone. "I'm sorry this presents an inconvenience for you, Mr. Snow. Our gallery is heading in new directions. I'll arrange for your pieces to be returned to you by special courier."

Tamal waited a few moments while the man on the other end of the call shouted, cursed, and belittled both her and the gallery. When he was finally quiet, she said, "I quite understand your dilemma, Mr. Snow. I'll relay your concerns to Ms. Aldersen upon her return." She ended the call before he could say another word.

She looked up at the police officer sitting in front of her. She smiled and said, "I'm appalled you had to hear such a vile conversation. I hope it did not distress you too much."

"No. I've heard much worse," Sally answered, thinking, *but I haven't seen as many ice queens as cold as the woman in front of me.*

"Good. Now what was it you wished to speak with me about? Ms Aldersen is in Europe right now."

Sally opened her small notebook and said, "It was actually you I wished to speak to, Ms Chowdhury."

Tamal cocked her head slightly and smiled. "Whatever could you possibly need to speak with me about?"

"Your brother's murder."

Tamal gasped but quickly pasted a sorrowful face and became the epitome of a grieving sister. She pulled a linen handkerchief from the cuff of her deep navy and ivory silk tunic. She dabbed at the corner of her eye without quite touching her skin. "Dear Simon's death shattered our family."

Sally nodded, looking at the stunningly beautiful woman. Her dark, wavy, sleek hair gleamed and fell nearly to her waist. As the woman moved, her hair also moved, seemingly with a will of its own. Her dark eyes glistened and were nearly as black as her hair. Her dark skin gleamed, with obviously tenderly cared for elegance. "I'm sure losing your brother in such a violent way is difficult to bear. If it is okay with you, I'll record our conversation. It keeps me from mistaking what you've said or intended. Will that be okay?"

"Oh, certainly. I'm an open book."

Sally started the digital recorder, then asked. "Do you have any idea who would do such a thing to your brother?"

"Why, no, of course not. I thought perhaps some animal, say a cougar, had killed my brother."

"No, ma'am. A human being definitely killed him."

"I'm shocked," Tamal said, and sniffled a little for emphasis.

Sally struggled to not smile and said, "I understand, Ms. Chowdhury."

Tamal reached across the desk with a beautifully manicured hand and said, "Please, dear, call me Tamal. It is my given name."

"Certainly. Tamal is a beautiful name."

"Thank you. In our family, we honor our Indian heritage as much as is possible. My name is a treasured Indian name meaning dark tree."

Sally felt a bit of a chill on the back of her neck but smiled in response.

Tamal asked, "What does your name mean, dear?"

"It is the diminutive of the name Sarah, which means princess."

Tamal, of course, already knew the answer. She smiled a tight smile, but her eyes darkened. "Yes, every little girl wants to be a princess. Personally, I never understood the fascination. I'd much rather be in control of my own life than living as a princess with everyone cow-towing to me, but not really adoring me."

Sally struggled to not raise her eyebrows at the word *adoring*. Instead, she said, "I agree. I never understood why any girl would want to be a princess. They wind up being used by men for political, financial, or power reasons, or all three. I've got different goals for my life."

"Good for you, Sally. I so admire when young women of limited means work to climb the ladder."

"Oh, it's not money I'm after."

"Then, dear girl, what are you after?"

"Killers."

Tamal paled a little, tucked the hankie in her sleeve and leaned back in her chair. Sally noted the response in her notebook. Then she said, "Now Tamal, back to your brother's murder."

Tamal flipped her hair back over her shoulder. It moved a little as it settled against her neck and back. "First, I didn't kill him. Murder is a messy business and I loathe mess. Second, I think I'd rather you address me as Ms. Chowdhury after all. Third, I don't know who killed my dear brother. Fourth, I've work to attend to. I'm the only one here today and can't spend my time chatting with policewomen. If your *detective* needs to speak with me again, I'll happily do that as long as *he* arranges the discussion with my lawyer."

Sally smiled, wishing for the first time that Darren was a woman. She answered, "I understand, Tamal. I'll share your thoughts with Detective Jordan." She picked up the recorder but didn't turn it off. She slipped it into her breast pocket, picked up her handbag and started to walk away.

Tamal shouted, "You ignorant peasant. I never want to speak with you or be in your presence again. I'm an important woman and you are nothing but dirt beneath my feet."

"I understand, Tamal. Thank you for your time."

Sally turned away smiling while Tamal Chowdhury shouted and cursed her as she left the art gallery. She pulled the recorder from her pocket, murmured into the microphone, "Interview over."

Once she was in her patrol car Sally said, "Yippee, detective! I think you'll enjoy what Tamal had to say." She started up the car and headed back to headquarters.

ME and Lena composed an email to send to Detective Jordan. After editing the message a few times, ME said, "I think this expresses our doubts, concerns and even fears."

"I agree. I hope Heather is okay, but I've got a deep feeling she is no longer on this plane of existence."

ME paled but said, "I'm emailing this right now." She clicked on the send icon and then said, "I want to journey."

Lena nodded. "I agree. If we validate our suspicions, we may want to talk directly with Detective Jordan."

"Let's journey and then decide what to do."

"What's the intention?"

"For me, straight and to the point: *is Heather alive and well?*"

"Good. You journey on that intention and I'll journey on *where is Heather?*"

ME agreed. "I think that covers the pertinent anxieties we have."

The two women pulled out their yoga mats, lay down, and turned on the drumming app to begin their journeys.

Darren listened to the recording of Tamal Chowdhury's interview. He shook his head and looked up at Sally. "What was your impression of her?"

Sally licked her lips, then scowled, not sure how to answer. She expressed her impression but was very clear about the evil she'd encountered. "Have you read *The Lord of the Rings?*"

"Sure. I don't think there are more than a dozen humans on the planet who haven't read the trilogy."

She chuckled. "Oh, there are a lot of knuckleheads out there who haven't read Tolkien's work. However, do you remember Shelob?"

He shuddered visibly, nodded and said, "I loathe spiders. I nearly vomited during that scene in the movie version."

"Well, imagine if Shelob was sitting in front of you, just waiting to pounce. Tamal reminded me of that spider. BUT. I think she is even more dangerous than Shelob."

"Why?"

"She is stunningly beautiful and almost as tall as you. When she looked at me, I felt nothing but malevolent intent. It was disturbing to hear her clear, beautiful voice yet feel the way I felt. Sitting before me was the most beautiful woman I've met, but I would not have been surprised to see nasty black spiders flowing from her mouth intending to devour me. Her hair is glorious. Stunning in fact. She shuddered again. "Her hair seemed to move of its own accord as if it were an entity separate yet a part of Tamal."

Darren closed his eyes and was quiet for several seconds. When he opened his eyes he said, "I want you with me every moment I'm in her presence."

"Okay, but if real shit goes down, I'm running."

He chuckled. "Then you'd better be faster than me."

When Lena and ME sat up after journeying, they each took a drink of water, then sat writing in their journals the events of their journeys. When they finished writing, they looked at each other.

ME said, "I don't like this one bit."

Lena nodded and squeezed ME's hand. "I'm so sorry. Shall we read each other's journeys?"

"Yes, and then I'll write another email for Darren."

Both women cried as they read their journeys.

Lena said, "I'll go make some tea. I think if Darren has the time, it would be best for him to read the journeys directly from our journals."

"I agree," ME said, then her phone rang. She looked up at Lena. "It's Darren."

"Good. The sooner we share with him, the better for Heather."

"It won't bring her back though."

"No, it won't."

ME answered the call and Darren said, "If you ladies have time, I'd like to stop by and chat."

"Yes, please. We've just journeyed and really need you to read what we learned."

"Good. I'll bring my new partner, Sally. She has something to share you might want to hear."

"We've got tea and gingersnaps at the ready."

Darren smiled, recalling his conversations with the women on a previous investigation. The women always had hot tea and gingersnaps when they were stressed. "We'll be there in twenty to thirty minutes."

CHAPTER TWENTY-THREE

Tamal turned the door sign to closed, turned out the lights in the gallery, then went upstairs to the third floor. She walked through the elegant apartment with white cotton gloves on her hands, touching every surface. This was where she belonged. She knew she would have to wait until someone decided Heather Aldersen wasn't coming back. *I might want to hurry that along.* When Heather's new will was discovered, Tamal would finally live in the luxury she felt she deserved.

The white, gray and pink marble of the entryway seemed to beckon her forward. Heather had decorated the apartment with contrasting colors and textures. On one small wall in the entryway was an antique hall tree with gleaming brass fixtures. Above her head was a stainless steel and copper chandelier with tiny sparkling lights. Throughout the apartment the juxtaposition of modern gleaming stainless steel and lights side-by-side with ancient pieces of furniture and art created a sense of feminine mystique and luxury.

She checked the main bedroom and bath to be sure there was no lingering scent of Lily of the Valley. Poor Heather slipped in the tub and inhaled the water filled with the sweet-scented poison. There was no blood to clean up, for which Tamal was exceedingly grateful. She'd considered leaving the body in the tub for the police to find. She simply couldn't bear the thought of a rotting body in the tub where she herself would spend many luxurious hours soaking in the deep, antique tub. Luckily Heather had installed an elevator for carrying heavy items, including luggage.

Tamal had packed Heather's body into an enormous suitcase lined with thick plastic. It wasn't easy to do, but with a push here and a shove there, Heather was packed and ready to go. Tamal had taken a taxi to the airport. At the airport she used Heather's ticket with Heather's name and ID, including passport, on Icelandic Air from Seattle, Washington to Paris, France. At the check-in counter, she paid the extra money for the very heavy case. She'd been a little nervous since Heather was a few inches shorter than her and her photo IDs showed her hair was dark but shorter. Having her hair pulled up and back helped and as she'd thought, letting her knees buckle a little, the desk clerk and TSA person didn't check close enough to notice the difference of height. Of course, her flowing sari made the semi-squat of her knees invisible and the scarf covering her head hid most of her hair.

Once in Paris, Tamal simply picked up her small suitcase, cut the tags off the large suitcase and walked away from the terminal. She left the enormous suitcase, with no identifying tags, spinning on the luggage carousel.

She spent a lovely night in a high-priced hotel before flying to London with her own ID and passport to spend another night of luxury, then back home to Seattle. Her stay in The Mandarin Oriental at Hyde Park was everything she fantasied she deserved in her life. The food was elegant and exquisite, the service sumptuous and lavish, the suite a paragon of divine beauty and luxurious comfort. She'd have loved to stay longer but didn't dare leave the gallery unattended for long. Someone would surely raise a fuss if the gallery didn't open at the appointed time. She was not ready for fuss. At least not yet.

A few days later, she waited in the deep woods of Washington State for the coup de grâce of the last day of the year. Simon was on Little Si, a mere few feet away from her. She shook her head in disgust. The insipid man, her older brother, watched the sunrise. She did not understand the fascination with the sun, moon, stars, or even the Universe. She took them for granted as part of the environment in which she lived. They were there, but not worth noting, other than as they served her. Certainly, they were nothing to be awestruck about.

Today was the first day she'd allowed herself to enter the apartment she hoped would soon be hers. She opened a bottle of champagne and drank a glassful. Then she poured the rest down the drain, washed, and dried the glass. She pulled off the white cotton gloves and carried the empty bottle downstairs to a dumpster behind the building a few doors down.

Back inside, she opened the gallery again and began planning how she would transform the little Pacific Northwest Gallery into a much sought-after place for real art rather than the insipid local yokels who thought they were artists. There would be no more charity auctions. As soon as the place was officially hers, she'd get rid of all the mundane pieces, especially the fiber art. She snorted, "As if anyone would think fiber could be art. Old granny threads aren't anyone's idea of art."

Detective Jordan pulled on to Interstate 90. He glanced at the police officer and said, "So, Sally, I want to ask a question, but I want you to take it without feeling I'm judging you. I just want an open and honest answer. Can we do that?"

"Of course. You can even refer to me a policewoman and I won't get my knickers in a twist."

He laughed. "Okay. Here goes. Are you religious?"

"Not a bit. I'm not sure there is a god of any sort. I am sure however there is evil in the world. We deal with it every day."

"Good. Have you ever heard of Core Shamanism?"

"No, but I know a bit about historic Shamanic practices. I majored in anthropology in college before I started taking legal and criminal law classes."

"What was your major when you graduated?"

"I had a dual degree in anthropology and criminal law at Stanford University."

"I had no idea. Did you get your Juris Doctorate?"

"Yep, and my master's in anthropology. I passed the bar and I'm legal to practice law in California, Oregon and Washington."

He glanced at her and shook his head. "Why the hell are you not practicing law?"

"I volunteer a couple of weekends a month with Legal Aide, but I want to be a detective. I keep up with my law licenses and do a lot of research on the legal ramifications of our cases, but I want to be a detective."

"Okay. Well, that was unexpected information. I'll work hard to not feel intimidated."

She laughed. "No need to feel intimidated. If I hadn't wanted to be a detective since I was a kid reading Nancy Drew novels, I'd have been a perpetual student. I love learning new things. Why did you ask me about religion?"

"The two women we are going to talk with, practice personal Core Shamanism. It isn't a religion at all, but a spiritual path of enlightenment for them."

"I'm open to learning more about it. Is what they have to tell us connected to Core Shamanism?"

"In a way, but as information not the shamanism itself."

"Hang on," Sally said. "I want to research this a little." She pulled out her small laptop, connected to the internet and started reading. Darren smiled, watching his intent sidekick going through page after page of information. In a few minutes she said, "Well, I'll be damned. That's pretty incredible stuff there, detective."

He grinned. "Yes, it is, and later I'll explain how much it has helped me in solving cases. For today, I want you to be open to what they have to say."

"Will it come from their power animals?"

"Yep."

"Cool. I'd heard of Michael Harner, but it didn't trip any triggers for me."

"Well, after today it might."

"I'm game for anything that helps us solve cases."

"I'm relieved. My last partner was so solidly Christian he couldn't accept that any information could come from anywhere other than the Bible. I call it esoteric information."

"Well, I've learned a lot from reading holy texts. I've also learned that no matter who the god is or what the religious concepts are, humans behave the same way all over the world. Some texts feel like justification for doing harm to others. I'm not okay with that approach."

"Neither am I."

He took the exit off Interstate 90 to East Lake Sammamish Parkway then said, "These two women are incredible artists. You won't believe their place."

"Are they a lesbian couple?"

"No. They are an asexual couple. There's another thing you should look up."

She grinned. "Already on it, boss."

CHAPTER TWENTY-FOUR

Darren and Sally got out of the car at ME and Lena's home. Sally said, "This is a beautiful place."

"Yes, it is. ME refurbished the whole place nearly single-handedly."

"Well, it is lovely. Hopefully, someday Paul and I can afford a house that is this beautiful."

The front door opened, and Lena said, "Come on in, you two. Tea's ready."

Darren waved and said, "We're on our way." He turned to Sally, "I have faith in you and Paul. Someday the right house will come along, and you'll know it is meant for you."

"Thanks, boss."

He chuckled, and she blushed a little. She knew she didn't have to call him *boss*, but it just felt right.

Once they were seated at the patio table, with the propane heater going, Darren said, "My new partner here has been looking up information about Core Shamanism."

"Good for you, Sally," ME said.

Sally blushed a little and said, "I've got a degree in anthropology and learned some about shamans but had never heard of Core Shamanism before."

"Well, for myself and Lena, it is a spiritual pathway that helps us with problems in our lives. In fact, in my journey Owen, my Power Animal talked mostly about a tall, dark woman, but then at the end mentioned, there would be a princess who wants to meet me and talk about Core Shamanism."

Sally laughed. "I'm not a princess, but that is the meaning of my name. Plus, I'm very interested in the Core Shamanism."

"Great! After we finish talking about my journey, I'll give you some information and local resources."

"I'd appreciate that."

"Good," ME said, then turned to Darren. "First, detective, I want you to read a series of emails to set the stage. I printed them out for you. After you two read them, we'll ask you to read our journal entries from today. I've scanned and printed those out too if you want to take them with you."

Darren and Sally read the email chains between Heather Aldersen, ME and Lena, and between the two women and Hadar Hamal. Then they both read the journal entries from ME and Lena's journeys.

Darren looked at Sally, then at the other two women. He said, "Okay, here is a journey Stan took last night." He handed them a sheet of paper and continued, "His power animal, Nelson seems like a total goofball but very empathetic and really nice and kind."

ME said, "He sounds a lot like Stan."

Darren nodded. "I agree. You ladies read Stan's journey, then we'll talk."

When the three women finished reading, Darren turned to Sally. She had a bemused look on her face. He smiled and asked, "So what do you think, Sally?"

She tilted her head thoughtfully and said, "In all my life and studies, I've never read anything like these three journeys. Yet all three of them clearly have much of the same information." She looked at Lena and ME. "Did you two talk about your journeys before you wrote them out in your journals?"

Lena laughed and shook her head. "I can understand why you would ask, but no, we never speak at all until we have written our journeys. And we haven't talked with Stan lately. It would be cheating for us. Core Shamanism and our Power Animals are too important to cheat."

Darren pulled out his smart phone and said, "You ladies discuss the issues. I'm going to check out a hunch."

Sally said, "I have to say I've never read anything like this. In all three journeys, your power animals related Simon's death with similar descriptions of the killer. The killer is tall, female, and very quick and aggressive. However, ME and Lena, both your power animals support the supposed email from Heather that she is in Europe. Mr. Hamal and you two ladies don't believe she is in Europe."

ME nodded, "I really think there is something wrong with Heather. What do you two think about her being at a lost and found place in my journey and riding around and around in a suitcase in Lena's journey, both in Paris?"

Darren looked up and said, "I may have an answer, ME. It's gruesome though."

Sally said, "Gruesome is a part of our job description."

"Yes, but it isn't part of ME or Lena's job description or life experience."

Lena snorted a chuckle. "I think my life has been filled with gruesome."

He nodded and smiled understanding her thoughts. "Fair enough, and of course, you have had more than your fair share of the dark side of life. I think I may have found Heather but will need to get back to the office and verify the details. Then I'll have to go through diplomatic channels to be sure."

ME shuddered. "You think Heather is in Paris but is dead and stuffed into a suitcase, don't you?"

"Yes, I do. I checked with Interpol when I got your email about your concerns related to Heather being gone and leaving Tamal in charge of the gallery. Heather checked into a flight from Seattle to Paris over a week ago now. All of her luggage except for one large case was picked up, but they didn't know it was her case until they opened the case."

Lena paled, and Darren rubbed his hand over his face. "According to the Paris police, the fingerprints of the woman in the suitcase match Heather Aldersen's prints I sent to them earlier today. Their medical examiner says cause of death was drowning and poisoning."

ME cried, but through her tears she asked, "How could she be killed twice?"

"The water in her lungs contained toxins present in Lily of the Valley plants. She also had the same toxins in her stomach. The smell was sweet and the medical examiner is fairly sure she was dying before she drowned. Whether she ingested the toxins voluntarily or not, we can't tell. We know she didn't put herself in the suitcase and go through airport security by herself."

ME jumped up and ran inside to the kitchen sink and vomited. Lena quickly went to help her. Both women were crying, shocked that their friend and benefactor was murdered.

Darren turned to Sally and whispered, "Let's just quietly wait here. They deserve to have a bit of time to settle and process. Heather wasn't just the woman who helped them with their art. She was also their friend. For now, what are your thoughts about the case?"

"I have a gut feeling that the murderer of Simon is Tamal Chowdhury. I think she probably killed Heather Aldersen too."

"Do you think she had the strength to do either of the murders?"

"The woman I talked with earlier today might move mountains with a glance and a flick of her fingers, then smile at her accomplishment. I had to work to not be intimidated by her."

"I haven't met her yet—it's high time I did. We'll go there next."

"Good. I think anyone who is around her, related to her, or a threat to her goals is in grave danger."

"I agree," Darren said and nodded. "Now we need to get the evidence to support our conclusions. I want to listen to your interview with her again on the way to Edmonds. Then let's head back to West Seattle and talk with Roger again. I think he and his mother-in-law are both in danger."

"Why would she kill him now? He's given her the house and agreed to not stand in the way of the divorce she wants."

"I'm not sure anyone was ever in her way. With Simon, I think she was just fed up with his playing the role of the patriarch a little too strong. According to Roger and Basanti, Simon was always saying things to her about how and what she should be doing. Simon said a lot of things to her that made her bristle."

"I hated that game."

"What game?"

"Simon says."

Darren felt a chill and nodded. "I think it is why he died. Too many times of Simon telling her what she should do."

"Simon Says as a game always made me want to punch someone's lights out. The boys thought they always got to be Simon and rule over the girls. Made me glad my brother's name is Mark."

Darren smiled, but when he looked at Sally's stern face, he was glad he hadn't pissed her off.

CHAPTER TWENTY-FIVE

On their way to Edmonds, Darren and Sally listened again to her interview with Tamal. Sally said, "Let's stop by Mrs. Chowdhury's house and be sure she is okay."

"Good idea. We need to protect anyone who is around Tamal. Let's see if she'd consider going someplace for a few days."

"Do we have enough evidence to bring Tamal in for questioning?"

He looked at her. "You're the lawyer. Would you be able to keep her out of prison based on the evidence we have now?"

"Absolutely and I've never tried a criminal defense case in my life. My lawyer skills have been volunteer legal aid experiences only."

"So, if a lawyer without lots of criminal defense skills can get her off, then we do not have enough evidence. I want to try to get enough evidence in today and tomorrow to tie her up with a bow."

Sally laughed. "Make sure it is an ugly bow. Her hoity-toity attitude really rubbed me the wrong way. She assumed I was impoverished."

"Are you?"

"Now that's a really personal question detective, but no, I'm not impoverished. I'm not rich, but I have a generous monthly stipend from my grandparents' estate. It's the only way we could have the life we have. Someday, when Paul has graduated with his doctorate in nursing, things will be easier, and we'll have a nice home. He works a few shifts a month which helps a lot, plus he takes care of Gabe whenever he can. For now, we will watch the pennies. Police officer's pay, at least at my level, isn't enough to live in Seattle."

Darren slapped the steering wheel, and Sally jumped.

He said, "I'm sorry, but we didn't get you the information on Core

Shamanism ME was going to give you."

"I'm sure she and I can be in touch later. I don't want to bother her right now. She is reeling enough with Heather's death."

"Go ahead and call her, or at least text her a message. She won't mind at all."

She smiled. "Okay, boss, I will."

"Don't call me boss."

"Can't help it, unless you come up with a better idea."

"Just call me Darren."

"I'll try, but it will be hard. I kind of like calling you boss."

"Yeah, well, I hate it, so knock it off."

"Yes, boss...I mean Darren."

"Good. Text ME."

"I already did." Her phone dinged with an incoming message. She grinned. "She sent me a reading list and information on local training events."

"Good. Now let's concentrate on putting Tamal away for a long, long, time."

"She'll look terrible in orange."

Sally smiled a little. It would be a shame to waste all that orange cloth on a woman like Tamal, but some things just couldn't be helped.

Roger finished installing the new garage door opener and the security system. Next on his list was the front door lock. Pavlov followed him around the house, watching everything he did. At one point, the dog came up to him and laid his head on Roger's feet. He grinned and sat down with the dog. "I bet you don't understand what's going on, do you fella?"

Pavlov laid his head on Roger's lap and sighed. He patted the dog's head then said, "I'll tell you what. Let me finish the front door lock and set up the security system. After that, we'll go for a walk." The dog jumped up and raced to the study. He came back with his leash in his mouth. Roger laughed. "Give me ten minutes and then we'll go."

Hadar Hamal arrived at the SeaTac airport mid-afternoon. His driver, Sander Torrin, was waiting beside his car. Hadar said, "Thank you, Sander, for being here promptly."

"My pleasure, sir. Are we going to the Four Seasons?"

"Not yet. Let's check in with Danny and Odetta, but I want to go to Edmonds before settling in at the Four Seasons."

"Yes, sir. I checked to be sure the video link is up and working in the rear compartment."

"Perfect." Once Hadar was settled in the back of the limousine, he started the video call to Danny.

Her smiling face greeted him. "Hello, sir. How was your trip?"

"Restful and uneventful."

"The best kind."

"Indeed. Is Odetta around?"

"Yes, sir, she is. Would you like to speak with her privately or shall I be present too?"

He smiled, appreciating her willingness to not listen in but also knowing Odetta might need her support. "Let's have it be the three of us."

When Odetta was sitting beside Danny, she said, "Thank you, Mr. Hamal, for making this so painless. Danny has been very kind and is fun to be around."

"Good. That's exactly how I want it to be. I hope you had a restful night."

"Absolutely. Everything has been perfect, and I feel safe with Danny here."

"You are safe with Danny. I'd trust her with my own life. Have there been any calls from Heather or Tamal?"

"Tamal called, but I let it go to voicemail."

"Excellent. Talking to her will only increase your danger. If you'd inadvertently slipped and let her know where you were, I'm sure she'd try to get to you. Now, ladies, I wanted to alert you I'm here, but I'm going to the gallery in Edmonds before coming to see you two."

Both women nodded. Odetta smiled and said, "I'm eager to see inside the gallery."

"I know you are. But for now, keeping you safe is more important."

Darren and Sally sat with Basanti Chowdhury in her kitchen. She made her favorite Darjeeling tea and small, soft, lemon-blueberry cookies laced with cardamom and anise. Sally took a sip of the tea and said, "I've never had tea like this. It is really nice."

Basanti smiled. "It is a favorite for our family. It's Darjeeling with a bit of cardamom, cloves and honey."

Darren nodded. "The tea is very good, but these cookies could be sold in any upscale restaurant."

"You're too kind," Basanti answered. "I've been experimenting on small tasty treats hoping to sell them."

He looked up and asked, "Are you going to open a bakery?"

"No, I want to do all the work here at home and then deliver the goods to establishments in the area."

"If you'll wrap a few of these cookies to go, I'll share them with my husband. He's head chef, downtown at Apple Dapple Restaurant."

"You think he would want to serve them?"

"I'm certain he would. They are tiny, lovely, and taste better than any lemon cookie I've ever had. The spices seem to enhance both the lemon and blueberry. I think Martin will love them."

"Maybe I should make a new batch for him."

He grinned. "No. These are perfect. Can I give him your phone number?"

"Of course."

He touched her hand. "How are you doing?"

She shook her head and tightened her lips to avoid crying. When she was sure she could remain composed, she said, "The baking helps, but I miss my son terribly. I don't know what to expect or when I'll be able to bury him."

"Do you know what he wanted for his body?"

"He bought a plan from a company here in Seattle who will let his remains naturally degrade. After the process is complete, there will be some soil to donate and a small amount for me and my garden."

Sally said, "I read about that. It sounds like a perfect solution."

"Yes, that's what Simon said. I understand his intentions, but I wish he were here with me."

Darren nodded. "I can't imagine how hard it is for you. What about Tamal? I heard she is living with you."

"Yes, she is, but I don't think she will live here for long."

"What makes you say that?"

"She says she'll be taking over the gallery and may even get to live in the apartment above the gallery."

"I didn't know there was an apartment there."

Basanti nodded. "Oh, yes. It is a very elegant place. I went to dinner there with Tamal, Roger and Simon at a special event at the gallery. It is beautiful, but too elegant for my tastes."

Darren looked at Sally and nodded. She stood up, walked a little away from the kitchen, pulled out her phone, and requested a search warrant for the gallery and the entire building. When she returned to the table she nodded and then asked Basanti, "Do you feel safe here?"

"Oh, yes. This is my home and I love every inch."

Darren smiled. "Please be careful and if you ever have any doubts about your safety, please call me—anytime—day or night."

"I will. Let me wrap up the cookies for your husband. I hope he'll like them."

"I have a feeling he'll be your first customer."

CHAPTER TWENTY-SIX

Hadar sat in his limousine across the street and a few car lengths away. He watched the door of The Pacific Arts Gallery. Through the glass window front, he could see Tamal sitting at Heather's desk, speaking on the phone. He tapped Sander on the shoulder. "I'd like you to accompany me, Sander. You have your weapon handy if needed?"

"Yes, sir. Do you think we'll need it?"

"I'm uncertain, but I do not trust Tamal Chowdhury."

He walked across the street and down the sidewalk to the gallery. He briskly opened the door and walked with a purposeful stride to the desk. Tamal's eyes looked up, startled. She licked her lips and simply hung up the phone mid-sentence. She quickly pasted her best and most fake social smile on her face. "Mr. Hamal. What an unexpected pleasure."

He did not smile, but simply nodded.

Tamal walked from behind the desk to stand in front of him. She said, "I'm sorry, but Heather isn't here at the moment. You surprised me because I thought you were with her in Europe."

Before he could say anything, the door of the gallery opened. A tall, handsome man with a petite police officer entered the gallery. Hadar stepped back away from Tamal as he turned and smiled at the two who had just entered.

Darren pulled out his identification, including his detective shield as he introduced himself. "I'm detective Darren Jordan. This is officer Sally Quinn. I'm sorry to interrupt, but we had a few questions for Ms. Chowdhury."

Hadar smiled and said, "As do I." He took a step or two toward Darren with his hand outstretched. "I'm Hadar Hamal and this is my driver, Sander Torrin."

Darren nodded and shook the man's hand. "It's a pleasure to meet you. I've heard about you and even met you briefly about a year ago."

"Yes, I thought I recognized you from the charity auction last year."

"That's it. You bought that incredible painting of a friend of mine."

"Ah, ME is a true talent. Her chameleon painting of her Power Animal captivated my heart and soul from the first moment I saw it."

Sally said, "You look a bit like him, too."

"That I do. It's part of why I bought the painting."

Tamal couldn't stand it a moment longer. "Excuse me, detective. I made it clear to your little sidekick there, that I'd be delighted to talk with you as soon as you arrange a formal time with my lawyer."

A slight smirk touched Hadar's face as he stepped back a bit and looked at Tamal. "You surprise me, Tamal. I would have thought you might be a bit more concerned about Heather's disappearance."

"She hasn't disappeared. She is in Europe."

Darren asked, "Do you know where in Europe?"

Sally was busy taking notes but had turned on her recorder too. Tamal noticed and turned to Sally. "Please put away your notebook and turn off the recorder."

Sally looked her in the eye and said, "When Detective Jordan requests I do so, I certainly will."

Tamal's lips tightened but before she could say another word, Hadar asked, "I'd be very interested in listening to this conversation but first I want to know *why* you think Heather is in Europe and *why* you've told all her customers, I am with her."

"Yes," Darren said. "I'm interested in having the same answers."

She pursed her lips then said, "All right. If you must know, Heather asked that I tell everyone she was in Europe so she could take a nice quiet trip for herself. She hasn't had a vacation in years."

Hadar put his hands behind his back, smiled briefly and licked his lips. Sally had the distinct impression he was preparing, like a chameleon, to dart out his tongue and eat Tamal in one sticky tongued swipe.

His voice was deep and a little rumbling as he said, "No vacations for years, other than the vacation she took early last summer to hike in the Utah mountains for a week with friends. Oh, and then there was her trip in the fall to Vancouver, British Columbia and the Northwest Canadian islands for two weeks. She was researching native arts of the Northwest and wanted to expand her offerings here in the gallery."

Undaunted, Tamal said, "Well, since I wasn't made aware of those trips, I assumed when she said she hadn't had a vacation in years she was telling me the truth."

Darren bit his lip to keep from laughing out loud and asked, "When did you start working here?"

"I started mid-October."

He nodded, then turned to Hadar Hamal. "I know you are a great friend and benefactor of Heather Aldersen. When was the last time you spoke with her?"

"About a week before Christmas."

"Did she say anything about a trip to Europe?"

"No, but she might not have told me about it."

"Did she tell you about her previous vacations?"

Hadar smiled. "Yes, she did. She generally did let me know what was going on here."

"Did she close the gallery during her vacations?"

"Yes, always. She felt it was the only way to be sure everything here was safe."

Sally asked, "How often did she travel?"

"Oh, once or twice a year. Usually once in early summer or late spring and another in early fall. Those times are slower times for the gallery."

Darren turned back to Tamal and asked, "When did you last see Heather?"

"When I drove her to the airport for her vacation trip with Mr. Hamal."

He nodded and then turned back to Hadar. "Would it surprise

you to know Heather is in Europe?"

"Indeed, it would. I've tried to reach her by phone and personal email."

Sally looked up when Tamal gasped. Hadar smiled his slow, predatory smile, again with a slight poke of his tongue licking his lips. "Did you not know she has a private personal email?"

"Of course, I didn't know. I'm a trusted employee, not a friend. I'm surprised though she would share private information with you."

He nodded. "I'm sure you didn't know that Heather and I are very close friends. It will decidedly be my goal in life to find her and bring her safely home."

Sally swallowed but kept quiet.

Darren cleared his throat. While watching Tamal closely he said, "We put out a missing person alert a few days ago when none of her friends or close acquaintances could reach her. We also heard complaints from some of her artists when you, Ms. Chowdhury, told them the gallery would no longer be supporting their work."

A soft growl emanated from deep inside Hadar Hamal. He asked, "Where in Europe do you think she is Ms. Chowdhury?"

She shrugged her shoulders a bit. "I do not know. She did not give me an itinerary of her trip."

"When do you expect her back?" Sally asked.

"I fail to see why that is any of your business."

Darren stepped closer to Tamal. "We expect her body to be back in the United States and Seattle in a few days. The details of when are not worked out yet, but we know where she is now. She is in a morgue in Paris, France."

Hadar gasped and stumbled a little. Sander quickly reached to help his employer to keep from falling. Hadar shook his head as tears streaked down his face. "Are you sure it is Heather's body?"

"Yes, I'm sure. I have a search warrant for the entire building, Ms. Chowdhury."

She shook her head. "That isn't possible. I don't have keys for anything other than the gallery itself. You're more than welcome to search the gallery."

Hadar said, "I have keys to every lock in this building and the combination of the company safe and her personal safe. Heather gave them to me from the first as a security measure should anything happen to her."

Tamal lifted her manicured right hand to her throat. She did not know there was any safe other than the company one. The presence of the personal safe might complicate things for her. It was difficult to tell what her emotions were, but for the first time, in the whole of her life, fear tickled her belly. Cold, dark fear crept in.

CHAPTER TWENTY-SEVEN

Harry Bishop was the overseer at the Sallal Grange in North Bend, Washington. Sometimes the weeks were busy at the Grange, other times not. He'd come by and check on things a time or two a week, even if not much was happening. When the Grange had special events throughout the week, he'd spend most of his days and evenings at the Grange.

All the Christmas and New Year's doings were finished, and things had been a little slow. The upcoming weekend was a different story. A bluegrass band, All Together Now, from Duvall was set to play both Friday and Saturday evening. He was eager to hear them again, especially their singer, Laura.

Harry drove to the back of the Grange building to park his truck in his usual spot. He was surprised to find a black Subaru SUV parked in his favorite spot. He tried to open the door of the vehicle, but it was locked. He looked in the car windows and saw the car keys lying on the dashboard.

"Well, I'll be damned. Whoever owns this is one lucky son of a bitch. Stealing cars is child's play, especially when you leave the keys out in the open."

He shook his head and pulled his phone out of his pocket. He called the Snoqualmie Police Department, who did the policing for North Bend, and said, "Hey, this is Harry Bishop, caretaker over at the Sallal Grange in North Bend. This isn't an emergency as such, but there's a strange car parked behind the Grange. The car's locked up tighter than a drum, but the keys are lying on the dashboard. I don't know who you've got on patrol duty today, but I'd appreciate someone coming by and looking."

"Give me the tag number and I'll make sure whether it's been reported stolen."

Harry gave the operator the tag number then she said, "Give me your phone number and I'll get back to you in a bit."

He grinned and asked, "How long's a bit?"

She laughed. "Look it up, Harry. Now give me your number."

He did and then said, "I'll be here awhile so no big rush. I don't like having folks park here for no darn good reason."

"I understand, Harry. I call back soon no matter how long awhile it is."

He chuckled and shook his head. He liked when joking was a back-and-forth thing. It brightened his day to laugh a little, even with small humorous encounters. He ended the call, took out his keys and went into the Grange. He was busy sweeping the floors when his phone rang. He pressed the little green phone icon and smiled. No one who was born after about 2000 would even know there had ever been phones that looked like the icon.

He said, "Hello. This is Harry."

"Hey, Mr. Bishop. This is Chief Phipps in Snoqualmie."

"Hi Chief. I'm surprised to hear you be the one calling me back."

"Well, turns out that SUV is on a BOLO for that fella that was murdered on Little Si a few days ago."

"You're kidding."

"Nope. I've alerted the Seattle Police Department, who is handling the case. They'll be sending a truck to haul the car away and a forensics team. Can you hang around for about twenty minutes until I can get an officer over there to guard the car?"

"Sure. I'm just sweeping and cleaning, getting ready for the bluegrass band."

"I'm looking forward to hearing them myself. I hear they are great."

"They are. Don't rush on sending someone here. I'll be here most of the day."

"Thanks for calling it in, Harry. Hopefully, it will help find the killer. I don't know about you, but I hate like hell having folks murdered in our area."

"Me too. I just hope it wasn't someone from around here."

"You and me both. Thanks again, Harry."

"Yep."

Harry decided he'd wait outside and watch the SUV just in case someone tried to mess with the evidence. Now that he'd found the car, and it was important evidence, he felt it was his civic duty to stand guard.

Roger walked with Pavlov around the neighborhood. In front of Stan's house, he was surprised when Stan opened the front door, waved, and said, "Hold up, Roger."

He and Pavlov stopped. Stan said, "I'd invite you in, but my dogs are all in a dither already seeing Pavlov."

"Hey, no problem. I didn't expect to see you."

"Let's walk and talk a bit," Stan said. "The dogs will settle down quicker if they don't see us."

When they were far enough away from Stan's house that the dogs were no longer interested in them, Stan said, "There was an alert on my phone from KIRO 7. They found Simon's car."

Roger stopped and asked, "Where?"

"Apparently, parked all this time behind The Grange in North Bend. Here, look at the video from the KIRO 7 helicopter." He pulled out his phone and opened the video. The two men stood watching the scene of a big tow truck pulling the SUV of their friend onto the bed of the truck. Police vehicles, officers from Snoqualmie and Seattle were standing looking at the car.

Roger said, "I'm glad they found Simon's car. I hope they learn something from the find."

"Yeah, me too. Darren is on the case, but he's not one of the policemen in the video."

"My guess is he is busy tracking down other leads. He can't do much there behind the Grange."

"You're right. Besides, there were forensic folks there taking photos. My guess is that other than the photos, they won't find much until they get the car back to Seattle."

Roger sighed. "I'm glad they found his car, but damn, it feels more real somehow."

"I know. I feel that way too. I told Renee a part of me was hoping it wasn't Simon on Little Si, despite all the evidence. Finding his car without him in it, feels like pounding nails into his coffin."

Roger hugged Stan and Pavlov whined. Stan smiled and kneeled down to pet the dog. Pavlov put his head on Stan's shoulder. When Stan started to cry, the dog sighed and rubbed his head against the man's neck. Roger couldn't help himself. He kneeled with the dog and Stan. After a few minutes, Stan chuckled. "I don't know about you, but this feels weird."

Roger laughed, brushed his tears from his face, and stood up. "Me too. Stand up, buddy, and pretend to be a man."

"Pretend is all there is." Stan grinned and wiped his face with his sleeve. He shook his head then said, "I wish Harvey and Jack were here."

"When I get home, I'll call and see if they want Old Man Coffee in the morning."

"I don't think Harvey will be home yet."

"Well, damn. I'll call anyway. As soon as he is back where he belongs, we'll get together and have a good old-fashioned wake for our dear friend."

Stan nodded. "I'll head back home. Just thought you'd like to know about the car."

"Thanks. I appreciate it a lot. Take care and hug Nina and Renee for me."

"I will. And you, Pavlov, take care of my buddy there."

The dog yipped. Roger waved as he and Pavlov walked away and headed back home.

Stan smiled. *My luck and my life are tied up in love. I love all the fellas in Old Man Coffee almost as much as my wife, and daughter, and family. Love isn't just a four-letter word, Joan and Bob. Sometimes it's a six-letter word called Sorrow.*

He knew living was a risk to his heart, but it beat the hell out of the alternative.

CHAPTER TWENTY-EIGHT

Hadar said, "I want to go upstairs to the apartment, detective, if that's alright with you."

"Certainly, but I'll go with you." Darren answered. He turned to Tamal. "There's no need for you to accompany us since Mr. Hamal knows the building well."

"I certainly do. I spent many days with Heather, planning and designing the interior of this structure. Later, when it was completed, I came to visit a few times a year. I know this place like I know my own home."

Tamal paled and asked, "What shall I do?"

Darren said, "For now, since we do not know what will happen next, and since the owner is deceased, I want the keys to the gallery please. Then you can go home."

"But I'm supposed to run the gallery while Heather is away."

"Every inch of this building is now a possible crime scene. I'll happily throw you in jail if you violate the scene. I'll take the keys now." He held out his hand. Tamal hesitated, then finally went to the desk, opened the top drawer, and pulled out the keys to the facility.

When she handed them to Darren, Hamal reached out and asked, "May I see those, Detective?"

Darren handed them to Hadar, who compared them to the ones on the ring of keys he had. He shook his head and looked up at Tamal.

Sally drew in a quick breath at the dark intensity on his face. Once again, Hadar Hamal seemed to be a predator. He cracked his lips open slightly as his glare intensified. The tip of his tongue touched his upper lip. He took a step toward Tamal. The air seemed to quiver as his voice became brutal ice.

"Ms. Chowdhury—you—are a liar. Every key, to every door in this facility is in the set of keys you've been using."

She said nothing but lifted her chin and looked away. Darren nodded to Sally, who tucked her small notebook into her pocket. She reached behind her back and pulled handcuffs from her belt. She watched, alert as she approached the tall, elegant woman. As she reached for her hands, Tamal quickly turned to swipe Sally's hands away. Sally had expected such an attack. Before either man could come to her aid, she had Tamal on the floor with both arms twisted and pulled up behind the taller woman's back. Sally quickly put the cuffs on Tamal.

Detective Darren Jordan lifted his chin and said, "Tamal Chowdhury, I'm arresting you for interfering with an active investigation, lying to police during said active investigation and assaulting a police officer."

"She is the bitch who assaulted me."

"Yes, in self-defense. I made a similar mistake with Sally one time in the gym. I never expect to win against her. That's a lesson you might take to heart. You have the right to remain silent. Anything you say can and will be used against you in a court of law. You have the right to talk to a lawyer for advice before we ask you any questions. You have the right to have a lawyer with you during questioning. If you cannot afford a lawyer, one will be appointed for you before any questioning if you wish. If you decide to answer questions now without a lawyer present, you have the right to stop answering at any time. You have a right to be silent. Do you understand your rights?"

"I understand you are a fucking heathen, not worthy to be in the same room with me."

"That's as may be. Do you understand your rights?"

"Yes. I'm not an idiot."

Sally grinned thinking *assumes facts not in evidence,* but she said, "I'm going to help you stand up. If you try to take me down again, you'll be face down on the floor. Again. Do you understand?"

Tamal nodded but said nothing.

Darren turned to Hadar. "I'll help Sally confine Ms. Chowdhury in the patrol car, call for backup and the forensics team. I'll be back with you in a few minutes."

Hadar nodded. "I'll lock the door and put up the closed sign. I'll watch for your return. Then we can both go together to Heather's apartment."

Darren nodded. "Okay Sally, let's help Ms. Chowdhury into the car."

As they walked to the police vehicle, Tamal screeched and screamed and shouted obscenities. People turned to stare at the beautiful woman in handcuffs. Many pulled out their smart phones and videoed the scene before them. Once they had Tamal in the backseat, Sally said, "I'll do the calling, sir. You go back with Mr. Hamal. I'll ring you when the rest of the crew arrives."

"Thanks, Sally. Do not open that door or get in the car with her. I do not trust her as far as I can spit. With this brisk breeze today, that's not very far."

She grinned. "Yes, sir."

"Darren."

"Yes, Darren—sir."

He chuckled, shook his head, and walked back to the gallery.

Stan called Roger and said, "Holy shit, Roger, turn on the television. You won't believe what is happening. I'll be right over."

"I'll leave the front door unlocked."

Roger went to the study and turned on the huge television. He switched to the local KIRO 7 station. He watched in amazement as his wife screamed and fought against the tiny policewoman, Sally Quinn. She and Detective Darren Jordan put Tamal Chowdhury in the backseat of the police car.

The newscaster said, "We aren't sure what is going on in Edmonds this afternoon, but I wouldn't want to tussle with that tiny policewoman. She seems in total control. Let's watch the video again. We have multiple videos being sent to us. Chopper 7 is on the way to the area. We've had a busy and exciting day so far, folks."

Stan came into the study and said, "I'm so sorry, Roger."

"I guess I am too, but I do not know what's going on."

"You want to call her mom?"

"No! I'm hoping Amma hasn't seen this yet. She rarely watches television during the day. I don't know exactly what I should do."

His phone rang, and he saw it was Officer Quinn calling. "Hello, Officer Quinn. What's going on?"

"Call me Sally. You may see the videos of your wife, Tamal, on television."

"Yes. Is she under arrest?"

"She is, but there may be more charges later. I thought perhaps, before everyone gets wind of what's going on, go to her mother's home. If you can help her get away from the area before all hell breaks loose, that might help her a lot. Every news person in the area will want to talk with Mrs. Chowdhury."

"Great idea, Sally, and thanks for thinking of it. I wasn't sure what I should do. I'll head there right now."

He ended the call and said to Stan, "I'm going to talk my mother-in-law into coming to stay with me for a few days until things settle down a bit."

"Yes, I agree, that's best for her. Go on. I'll head back home."

Roger nodded. "I'll set all my new alarms, lock up, and go to Edmonds. With the doggie door, Pavlov will be fine until I get back with Basanti."

Roger pulled into his mother-in-law's driveway as his phone rang. It was Basanti calling. Roger pressed the answer icon and said, "Amma, I'm here. I just pulled in the driveway."

"Do you know what is happening?"

"Yes, in part at least. We'll talk inside."

He ended the call, and before he got to the front door, she was standing in the open doorway. He hoped both he and Basanti were up to the tasks and days ahead of them. *It's going to be a shit show. Taking care of Amma, Pavlov and me is all I can do. For now.*

At the door, he took his mother-in-law, Basanti, into his arms. She wept on his chest. He said, "Amma, I'm so sorry. Let's get a few things packed and get you out of here. You shouldn't have to deal with all the looky-loos and reporters."

"Okay, but I want to know what's going on."

"I don't know very much. I'll tell you what I know, and we can talk about it on the way to Simon's house. Let's get you a bag packed for a few days. We'll work everything out as it comes along, but I need you to be safe."

She patted his cheek. "You are a fine son. Come with me and tell me what you know as I pack."

CHAPTER TWENTY-NINE

Hadar Hamal and Detective Darren Jordan walked up the steps to the storage level of the Pacific Arts Gallery. Hadar said, "The area beyond those glass doors is a climate-controlled area. The rest of this floor is for storage of boxes, tubes, and extra tables and chairs for events. Heather also kept paper, toner, and other office supplies up here. One flight up is Heather's apartment."

Once they were on the landing to Heather's apartment, Darren said, "Hang on," and handed Hamal nitrile gloves and shoe covers. "Try not to touch anything unless it is necessary. The forensics team will be here soon and coordinate with the local law enforcement folks. For now, I want to just look and get a feeling for what might have happened here."

"You think Heather was murdered here?"

Darren nodded. "I won't tell you the details, at least not yet. You know her apartment well and can share your impressions with me."

Hadar nodded. "I'm relieved to be of some service." He unlocked the door and stepped into the hallway. He stood still, lifted his head a little as he looked around the entryway and open spaces of the living area.

Darren asked, "Any sense of anything?"

"Yes. I smell something incredibly sweet. I'm sure it is a flower but can't call it up yet. I will. Otherwise, it feels totally devoid of life."

"I feel that too, but my sense of smell isn't as good as yours. I don't smell anything."

Hadar smiled, "I've always had acute senses. It's both a blessing and a curse, as you can imagine."

"If you'll slowly take me through the apartment, that would be a great help. Tell me anything you sense. Is it okay if I record your impressions?"

"Certainly. In fact, I think it is an excellent idea. First impressions can become clouded as time goes by."

Darren turned on the recorder and followed Hadar into the open living area. There were several seating areas, a floor to ceiling fireplace and a dining room that could easily seat twenty people.

"This is the formal living area. Heather has a small, cozy apartment I'll show you as well. This room is more for looks and entertaining than comfort. This room and the kitchen comprise about eighteen hundred square feet. Heather's apartment is about twelve hundred square feet."

"I can see this as an elegant venue for any top end event. It is a lovely room."

Hadar nodded. "Yes, it is. Along the length of the glass wall is an outside balcony. When the weather is mild, Heather could open the glass wall, adding even more room for guests. She had impeccable taste in everything." He swallowed a little, then sighed. He realized he had used past tense regarding his dear friend. "Let's go into the kitchen." He turned away from the open living area and walked through the doorway to the kitchen.

"Wow," Darren said, "I wouldn't dare show Martin this kitchen."

"Is Martin your significant other?"

"Very significant. We've been married for a few years now. He is head chef at the Apple Dapple Restaurant in downtown Seattle."

"Lovely restaurant with some exquisite dishes as I recall."

"I'll tell him you said so. It will of course go to his head, but he'll love hearing what you've said."

"Heather enjoyed exploring food and learning new techniques. She wanted a professional yet beautiful kitchen so that entertaining for the gallery wouldn't be a burden."

"Did the guests come up here?"

"Yes, but not all of them, only special benefactors of the arts in the area."

Darren cocked his head. "I'm surprised she would have them come through the storage area."

Hadar smiled. "Let me show you the elevator system." He led the detective back into the living area and said, "There by the door we entered you see a lovely antique mirror. That's the guest elevator."

Darren nodded. He walked over to the mirror. He stood in front of the seven- or eight-foot-tall mirror with gold leaf framing. "The mirror is recessed. I could see it being a door. Does it stop at all three floors?"

"Only with a key. On nights that Heather entertained large groups, the second floor was locked out of the elevator system. She also locked her personal spaces, so that guests were free to roam in the open public areas of the apartment."

"Sounds like a perfect way to use the space. Can we check out the elevator?"

"Certainly," Hadar answered. He lifted his hand and touched the mirror at the right upper corner. The mirror slid into the wall, revealing an elevator door. Hadar shook his head.

"What's wrong?"

"The smell is stronger here. Do you smell it?"

"No, I don't."

Hadar nodded and pressed a button to open the elevator. As soon as Darren stepped in, he said, "Now I smell it. You're right, it is very sweet and floral."

Hadar stood beside him. "It is Lily of the Valley. It is so strong here, there is no mistaking the scent."

"Lily of the Valley?"

"A small, beautiful flower that blooms in early Spring. It's also known as May Bells and Mary's Tears. It is deadly if ingested."

Darren shuddered a bit and felt the hair on his neck rise. "My mother taught me about Lily of the Valley and a few others. She told me the sweetest flowers may bring your true love or your death. She cautioned me to always look beyond beauty."

"Yes, that is similar to folk lore I've heard. I'd heard the flower lured nightingales to each other, but also protected gardens and homes from evil. It's deadly not only to humans but to animals as well."

Darren sighed. "The toxicology report from the Paris medical examiner revealed that Heather was poisoned. Lily of the Valley is the culprit."

"Such a beautiful flower and alluring scent destroyed an incredible woman, and one of my dearest friends."

Darren touched Hadar's shoulder. "I'm so very sorry. When you are ready, will you show me the rest of the apartment?"

"Of course. I'll lead the way." He left the mirror open, knowing the police would need to have access to the elevator. "All this big open space with lots of seating areas is the public space of the apartment. The rest of the apartment is actually Heather's personal space."

He walked across the large living and entertaining area to a wall with floor to ceiling bookcases. They were filled with small pieces of art, artifacts, and first edition books. At the end of the case, on the fourth shelf, was a book labeled *The Secret Garden*. Hadar, using the tip of his finger only, pulled the book down. The wall clicked, and the bookshelf slid to the left, revealing a short hallway with a door at the end.

Hadar led the way to the door.

CHAPTER THIRTY

At the end of the hallway, Hadar unlocked the door. "Here we are at Heather's personal apartment."

There was a stone fireplace, also floor to ceiling, but not as big and imposing as the one in the guest living room. A mixture of antiques and modern designs pulled together with soft gray and rose colors creating a warm environment. The floor was covered with soft gray carpet with a few throw rugs of various designs. There were no obvious electronics in the room, not even a television.

Darren said, "This is lovely too, but cozier and more feminine."

"Yes, exactly. Let's go over here to the balcony." He slid the balcony door open and stepped outside. He pointed to the wall on his right. "That wall divides this balcony from the public balcony. It has a terrific view of the sound."

"Yes, it does. Yet another reason I don't want Martin to see this place. He'd want to live here."

Hadar laughed. "Those words, or similar ones, have been verbalized by many people. Come, let's look in her bedroom and bath. I think the bathroom is probably where she was murdered."

"I'm sure it probably is," Darren agreed. "You mentioned she had a private safe and a business safe. Are they both in this apartment?"

"No, the business one is on the second floor. Her private safe is behind the toilet in her bathroom."

Darren laughed. "I've never heard of such a place for a safe."

"She was a quirky woman, but a practical one too. She spent a lot of time planning and thinking about her personal space. She wanted it to be luxurious like the rest of the apartment, but a safe haven too. When the bathroom was being built, she asked the plumber if he could create a clean and dry place behind the toilet for her to have a personal safe. He talked her into having the secret space above the toilet, away from the pipes. It works. Let's go into her bathroom and look there first."

Darren followed Hadar to the bathroom. Above the toilet was a beautiful painting of a woman bathing. Hadar said, "This is a reproduction of a famous painting, *Femme a sa Toilette* by Edgar Degas. Try to lift it from the wall."

Darren reached up and found he couldn't move the painting in any direction.

"Now you have the key ring in your hand. There is a fob that looks like an automobile fob. Press the green button with your right thumb."

Darren did so and nothing happened. "So, how does this work?"

Hadar said, "Only two thumb prints will move the painting to reveal the safe. Mine and Heather's." He pressed the green button with his thumb and the painting raised to reveal a safe. There was only one button on the safe. Hadar pressed his thumb to the button, and the safe opened.

Darren smiled. "So even if whoever killed Heather knew about this safe, unless you are the villain in this story, they could never get into the safe."

Hadar shrugged. "I'm not the villain of this story, but I still would not assume it would be impossible to get into the safe. The first step would be knowing it was here. You saw Ms. Chowdhury's face when I mentioned a personal safe."

"Yes. She was shocked. My guess is on her way to the Seattle jail, she fretted and worried about where the safe is."

"I agree. Further," Hadar said, "I believe she thought the only safe was the one downstairs." He reached into the safe and tapped on a thin brown leather case. "In there is Heather's Will." He then left the contents of the safe where they were and closed the safe. In doing so, the painting closed automatically. He turned to the detective. "I closed the safe because if my suspicions are true, there will be a will downstairs in the business safe, but it will not be the same as this will."

"Why do you believe that?"

"Because Tamal thought she was getting all of this. I know the contents of Heather's will."

"Which are?"

"For me to find another woman to replace her and give all this to that woman with the proviso that the gallery always supports Pacific Northwest artists only."

A slow smile crossed Darren's face. "Tamal is not that woman."

"Most certainly, she is not."

Darren saw the stern expression on Hadar Hamal. He nodded but said nothing. The man standing beside him was not a man to trifle with. His phone alerted him to a text message from Sally. *We're here with Forensics team.* He looked at Hadar and said, "Let's go let the forensics team in. Do you mind working with us for an hour or two?"

"Not at all. I want to find who murdered Heather, although I have suspicions."

"A tall, dark, stunningly beautiful woman."

Hadar nodded. "Exactly, and without an ounce of human kindness, or perhaps, even without a soul."

By the time the forensic team had cataloged all the areas of the building, including both safes, it was early evening.

Hadar said, "If you are up for it, Detective, I'd like to meet your husband."

Darren grinned. "I texted him what you said about his culinary expertise. He told me to be sure and be extra nice to you."

"Good. I've made a last minute, reservation for an early dinner. I'm ravenous."

"Terrific. It will need to be a quick dinner, for me. I want to interview Tamal before her lawyer kicks up a fuss."

"I do not envy you that task. You'll ride with me to the restaurant and then I'll be happy to drop you at the police station whenever you're ready. I'm not looking for a feast but a good meal and to meet your husband. Afterwards, I too have work to do."

"Thanks, that will be perfect," Darren said. "I've never ridden in a limousine."

Hadar smiled. "I started to say it's just a car, but of course, it is not. It's a lovely way to travel. Come, Sander is waiting at the curb for us."

"Let me tell Sally where I'm going and that I'll meet her at the station. Then I'll be ready to leave."

Once inside the limousine, Hadar pulled out his phone and sent a message to Danny Jukes. *I'm having a quick dinner with Detective Jordan and then I'll bring dinner with me for you and Odetta. Things are moving quickly. I'll need your services for several days. Is that workable for you?*

She responded: *Absolutely. I'm enjoying Odetta's company. You've picked a jewel, Mr. Hamal.*

Sally called her husband, Paul, and said, "I grabbed a sandwich on the way back to the station. I'll be late coming home tonight."

"Thanks for the heads up. Your mom just left. Gabriel and I will have a yummy pizza delivered."

"When the cat's away, the mice will play."

He laughed. "This mouse is ready to play. I don't have to work tomorrow. I'd volunteered for an extra shift at the hospital, but they ended up not needing me. Do what you need to at the station. We'll be here when you come home."

"Thank you. I love you."

"I love you too, Sally Quinn."

She smiled as she ended the call and went back to work. *I'm a lucky woman.*

She drove to the police station and started working on the white boards and evidence they'd gathered. She transcribed the interviews with Hadar Hamal as well. Ms. Chowdhury was raising a fuss, but for the moment a little more peaceful, talking with her lawyer.

Sally thought, *she needs a good one!*

Darren, Martin and Hadar enjoyed a lovely meal together. Hadar said, "The meal is just as delightful as I remembered. Please, let me know if there is anything I can do to help you, Chef Daniels."

"Dining with you and showing appreciation for my cooking is all you need to do."

"Well, the meal was as lovely as I remembered from my previous time. What did you think of Basanti Chowdhury's lemon cookies?"

"I loved them. They are delicate and filled with bursts of flavor. I'll be calling her to discuss putting them on the menu."

Hadar smiled. "They are a treat and just right to follow up a rich meal. Now, Detective, shall I drop you at the police station?"

Martin said, "No need. I've finished for the evening here. I started bright and early this morning. Besides, the drive will be the only time we have together today. Thankfully, I don't work until after the lunch crowd tomorrow."

"We'll keep in touch, I'm sure, Detective. I'll be staying here in town at The Four Seasons until the case is resolved and I can bring my new protege on board at the gallery. Please take this card and get in touch if you need me. That is my personal number and personal email. Very few people have that information."

"Here's my card, Mr. Hamal. I'll keep your information confidential. When I know anything I can share with you, I'll be in touch."

Hadar stood with the two men, bowed his head slightly and walked out of the restaurant.

Martin said, "I don't know what to think of him. He is very nice and seems kind, but he is also intimidating."

Darren nodded. "There's a wildness under his skin."

Martin shuddered as he took Darren's hand. "I hadn't thought of it that way, but yes, wildness simmers inside him. I'm glad he likes us."

Darren chuckled. "Me too."

CHAPTER THIRTY-ONE

Roger and Basanti sat side-by-side in Simon's study. She reached for Roger's hand and squeezed. "I hope you know, none of what has happened is your fault."

"Yes, Amma. I do. However, I wish I had understood how strongly Tamal felt about Simon."

"So, you believe she is the one who killed him?"

He nodded. "I do, and so does my friend Stan and his Power Animal. It breaks my heart, but I can't see anyone else doing this to Simon. Tamal was the only person I ever heard say a cross word about him."

"I heard Simon mention his friend, Stan, and Core Shamanism. The Power Animals remind me of the sacredness of all animals in Hinduism."

"I've tried to learn more about your religion but found myself mired in confusion."

She smiled and patted his hand. "Unless you were raised Hindu, it can be confusing. All those gods and goddesses! There are hundreds and it's easy to lose track of them. As time goes on, I too find myself feeling much the same as you. I've learned to stick with those elemental beings and ideas that work well in my life. As a child growing up as Hindu, it all just progressed along. I took our religion as being magical and personal, especially the elephants. Ganesh, a god with the head of an elephant who rides on a mouse, is one of our most important gods. I count on Ganesh's wisdom every day."

"I've heard of Ganesh and wondered about an elephant as a god," Roger said. "In the religions I know of, mostly human likenesses of gods exist."

She nodded and said, "Parts of every god or goddess may seem human, but they are separate from us in form. As a child I grew up learning each part of Ganesh has a symbolic function. As humans, we too can use the god's symbols in our own lives."

Roger smiled. "That's amazing, Amma. Tell me about his symbols."

"Well, his head symbolizes how we all have the ability to acquire wisdom and knowledge. His beautiful, big ears give us the gift of patience to listen carefully. His eyes, like human eyes, are small. This is so he can focus clearly to behold the future and recognize truth. His long trunk sniffs out good and evil. His big belly reminds us we have the grace to digest both the best and worst in life. The tiny mouse upon which Ganesh rides, represents the ability to move quickly and decisively. From these skills, we learn that once we know what must be done, we should get on about it."

He laughed. "That's how Simon was. He would think about a problem and then shake his head. He would say, 'Control the controllables and let everything else go.' And he would."

Basanti smiled. "Yes, that sounds like my dear son. He too loved Ganesh." She pointed to the elephant statue of Ganesh on the shelf under the television. "See, Simon kept Ganesh close to him always. I taught my son that all obstacles, no matter how big they seem, can be rooted out by worshipping Ganesh."

"That's where I don't understand things. How can we worship Ganesh?"

She chuckled and patted Roger's hand again. "By paying attention to all his symbols. Gain knowledge that may help you be wise. Listen carefully to what is said around you. When you smell evil, avoid it. Look to the future, for there is where your life must go. Learn to swallow the good with the bad. It is important to digest both the good and bad; take it as it comes, if you will. When action is required, act."

He nodded. "Your words make sense, Amma."

"Good. As an adult, Hinduism, but especially Ganesh, helps me stay grounded in the Universe and the natural order of all things. Elephants are ever near me. A specific elephant comes to talk with me in my dreams. He is a young elephant named Max."

"I've never heard you speak of an elephant before, Amma."

"For me, Max is a very close, sacred, personal friend. Perhaps he is like your friend Stan's power animal."

Roger nodded then asked, "Amma, did your Max talk with you about Simon and Tamal?"

She sighed and shook her head. "At first, all he would tell me was I might try to talk with Simon about his bossy nature. I tried. However, Simon was more his father's son than his mother's son in that regard. He was always gentle, kind, and loving with me. However, he believed in the hierarchy of the male head of household. Both he and his father were brilliant men. Their incredible minds, saw how things could be. Over time, their thoughts became how things should be. Their minds created danger for them. At least that is my fear and belief."

"How so?"

"The more they learned, the more they understood how life works in the modern world. Sadly, they lost sight of how their words had become weapons."

Roger shook his head. "I never felt threatened by Simon's word or by Paresh's words."

"Of course not. They did not lash men with their words, only women."

Roger felt tears coming but swallowed them back. "That's how I began to feel with Tamal. Then I found myself becoming more and more demanding, more and more insistent on her doing things as I wanted them done."

"Yes, and that is how it began with Paresh and Simon."

"How could you put up with it, Amma?"

"I simply smiled and said, 'we'll see.' I went on and lived my life my way regardless of what they had to say. But I always lived my life with love in my heart where my true self becomes the real me. Tamal rebelled against their words instead of living from her true self. Living a false life is hard, tiresome work."

He nodded. "I remember you saying 'we'll see' to Simon and Paresh both. I also remember Tamal railing about your meekness when you gave the men your answer and smiled."

"If I had ever wanted Paresh, Tamal, Simon, or you dead, I could have easily done so and left no trace. When I love, it is with hidden strength. I keep love as the focus of my life in that strength."

"How so?"

"I am the root of the family. When a mighty wind blows, why doesn't every tree around us fall over and die?"

"I never thought about it, Amma."

She patted his hand and said, "Of course not. Most people do not consider where the real power lies. Power is with the one who can hold it all together and can keep the tree standing in the face of a mighty wind."

"But trees do fall."

"Eventually, just as all living beings eventually die. If the root is old and weary, or the ground becomes too soft, or disease takes over, or someone cuts down the tree, then the tree will fall. That's as it should be, even with humans. My roots are strong, but not strong enough to keep someone from chopping down the tree or a branch of the tree."

"I understand, Amma. Tell me, has your elephant Max said anything about Paresh or Simon's death?"

"Not directly. However, he did say Paresh was driving too fast, but the brake line had been tampered with. He also said, Simon should have known better than to trust Tamal. And Max is right. Tamal has never been trustworthy as a child or an adult."

"Do you trust her, Amma?"

"No. I love her, but it is not safe to trust her. I see she is suffering. I see that her inner self is not in balance with the Universe. I see she doesn't understand love. But maybe it is more that she thinks the love offered to her is isn't worthy of her being. Love is the only truth we can abide in day after day. We share love physically but also emotionally, psychologically, spiritually, and socially. When we are balanced from our inner being, we share it all equally and create even more love. The more love we share, the more love grows and the stronger we become."

Roger nodded and was silent for a few minutes. Finally, he said, "Thanks for sharing your thoughts with me, Amma. I'll work to be more balanced from within my nature. I feel I've let myself be pulled out of my true nature. For my own survival, and perhaps for Tamal's, I must not participate further in betraying my inner truth. Tamal and I will divorce, but I'm going to work on my inner truth for my future."

"Good man, but don't forget, external, physical strength can still kill you. An axe can still fell a mighty tree."

He nodded and was quiet for a few minutes. Then he asked, "Do you think Tamal is strong enough physically to have killed Simon?"

Basanti chuckled and shook her head. "Ah, Beta, you truly are a man in many ways. You haven't noticed, have you?"

"Noticed what?"

"She has been working out and building up her muscles. She's also been learning and honing her skills in martial arts."

His mouth dropped open. "You're right. I did not notice. How do you know that?"

"A friend of mine in Edmonds owns a gym and martial arts studio. Tamal spends at least two hours a day there. When she can, she is there even longer. She lifts weights, runs on the treadmill and rides at least ten miles every day on the electronic bicycles there. Then she practices and trains with a martial arts teacher, too."

Roger shook his head. "I had no idea. Obviously, my observation skills need work too."

"Remember Ganesh's eyes." Then Basanti asked, "Did she bring everything with her to her apartment?"

"Not everything. There are still some files in the file cabinet at home and more clothes than she could wear in a year. Why?"

"I took her to outpatient surgery while you were on your trip a few months ago."

"Really?"

Basanti nodded. "She told me you knew she would have minor surgery. When I returned to pick her up later that day, she said, she was a little sore but not to worry."

"Do you know what surgery she had?"

"No, but when I asked, she said, 'Don't worry, Amma. No matter what else happens in my life, I'll never have a baby.' I was confused because it seemed to come out of the blue. Later on, I thought per-

haps she had some surgery to keep her from becoming pregnant."
Roger leaned forward with his hands over his face and wept.

CHAPTER THIRTY-TWO

Kirsten Holt was a senior associate lawyer at Warren, Givens, and Holt Attorneys at Law. Her father, Howard Holt, was a senior partner and president of the company. Kirsten had every intention of following in his footsteps.

She watched the woman sitting across the table from her, reading the contract the lawyer had given her. She didn't like Tamal. Liking her client wasn't necessary but forming a bond of trust was. The bond was especially important for violent crimes.

Getting to the facts and facing the realities of the client's involvement was paramount to her success. Whether her client was guilty, or innocent was immaterial to Kirsten. Getting the best outcome for her client was all that mattered to her.

Tamal looked at the tall, beautiful woman with flowing, gleaming red hair. She seemed too beautiful, too perfect to fight in the gutters of the legal system. Besides, Tamal always expected to be the most beautiful woman in any room. The woman sitting across from her might be a good lawyer, but she might also compete with Tamal's beauty. This worried her a bit. She ignored her own insecurities, for now.

She asked, "How many major cases have you been the lead attorney for?"

"Many. Do you need to know exact numbers, or would you prefer to shop around and find a discount lawyer?"

"Money isn't the issue. Getting me out of here and the police off my back is all that matters. You don't really look like an attorney."

"It would be a mistake for you to let my amazing red hair, startling green eyes, luminescent skin, and perfect body fool you. They are just the icing on the cake. My brain is a million times better than my body."

Tamal smirked. "Well, if you say so. You are beautiful and I'm willing to say your beauty is not merely skin deep. Your beauty tells me nothing about your brain."

Kirsten didn't bat an eye. "Then you are in for a pleasant surprise. I have kept some clients out of prison and in every case, they have gotten less prison time than the prosecution expected."

"So, you haven't kept all your clients out of prison."

"That would be impossible. However, I'll work my prodigious brain to the maximum to keep you out of prison. The outcome isn't fully under my control. Whether you go to prison, depends on the evidence and the jury. What is in my control, is how long you might be in prison. The length of incarceration depends entirely on my skill as an attorney."

"I want out of here immediately."

"Then you need to whip out your magic wand and make it so. That's the only recourse at this moment. It is beyond my power to get you out of here immediately." Kirsten started packing up her briefcase and slid her chair back a little from the table.

Tamal reached her hand-cuffed hands across the table. "Wait. Please. I need your help now."

"Yes, you do. If you wish to have me as your attorney, sign the contract in your hands. You will pay on time, without fuss, complaints, or excuses. I allow no late payment grace. One missed or late payment and I'm off the case. Immediately. You'll also have to agree to let me defend your case as I think best. You have to trust that I know I can create the best outcome for you."

Tamal sighed and shook her head. "I've read the agreement. It isn't necessary to verbalize what I can understand for myself. What guarantees can you give me?"

"The only guarantee I can give you is that while I'm your lawyer, I will work hard for your best interests. I will not guarantee the jury will find you not guilty or that you won't have some prison time. My job and all my energy will go to getting you the very best outcome available by evidence and circumstances."

"I want out of here now."

"Again, not possible. I haven't looked at the evidence or the charges. I won't ask questions or spend any effort on your behalf until you've signed the contract and paid the twenty-thousand-dollar deposit. The deposit is nonrefundable. If I need more money to defend you, I'll let you know and will expect that money in my hands within twenty-four hours."

Kirsten set her briefcase back on the table and scooted her chair forward a little. She folded her hands in her lap and waited for Tamal to respond. Tamal read the contract two more times.

Kirsten looked at her watch. "I've a dinner engagement in three hours. Would you like me to return tomorrow, or would you prefer to sign the agreement and give me your information for how you will pay?"

Tamal looked up from the documents and looked directly into the lawyer's eyes. She said nothing for several seconds and then asked, "Do you have a pen?"

Kirsten reached into her briefcase, pulled out a sleek burgundy pen and handed Tamal the Montblanc pen. She watched as Tamal's eyes widened a little at the classic, very expensive pen. Tamal touched her tongue to her lips, then signed the documents. She held the pen, not wanting to let go of it, but knew she must. Just as she was about to hand the pen back to her attorney, the attorney handed her more papers to sign. It relieved Tamal to be allowed to hold the pen a bit longer.

Kirsten watched her new client holding and using the pen. She knew Tamal had never held one of the iconic pens. She smiled a little and understood her new client coveted the best this world offered. This knowledge would help keep her client in line. She said, "Now, you need to fill out this form with the details of the money we will withdraw as soon as I'm back in my office."

Tamal wrote the details with the elegant pen. She used one of her offshore banking accounts for the payment to the attorney. She had no intention of revealing everything about her full financial status, but this would be her ticket to getting out of jail.

When the documents were signed, Kirsten reached across the table and took the pen from Tamal. Tamal felt the loss of the elegant pen but determined someday she would own such a pen.

Kirsten was aware of the slight dimming of her client's eyes as she took the pen and placed it on the table beside her briefcase. She pulled out a blank yellow legal pad and smiled. When she looked up, she saw Tamal's greed written all over her face.

Greed was a powerful, unforgiving beast. What Tamal would never understand, was that since she wasn't satisfied with the life she had, having everything she desired would not satisfy her either. Kirsten knew she could use Tamal's greed to keep her in line. She suspected greed was the basis of her client's life, and therefore her life would never meet her perceived needs.

The lawyer understood what Tamal did not. The universe of greed is infinite.

CHAPTER THIRTY-THREE

Kirsten took a digital recorder out of her briefcase and turned it on. "Now, I'd like to ask you a few routine questions."

"Are you going to record everything I say?"

"Absolutely. You should also be prepared to be recorded at all times by the police. You may not even be aware of being recorded."

Tamal nodded, surprised that the attorney would record everything. She didn't know that the police might also record everything she said. It meant she would have to be careful with every word she spoke. She was not accustomed to censure herself.

Kirsten asked, "What is your full legal name?"

"Tamal Basanti Chowdhury."

"Were you born in the United States?"

"Yes."

"My name is Kirsten Diane Holt. I am a criminal attorney at law here in Seattle, Washington. I'm licensed to practice law in the state of Washington. I am a member in good standing with the Washington Bar Association. Do you understand my role in your case?"

"Yes."

"Do you wish to be my client?"

"Yes."

"Do you understand, that after this evening, I will make no efforts on your behalf until the twenty-thousand-dollar retainer fee is paid in full. That fee is due within twenty-four hours."

"I understand. You have the information in your hands to make it so."

"Good. Now, please tell me in your own words what happened today."

Tamal smiled then asked, "Today only?"

Kirsten did not smile. "Yes, today only."

"Good." Tamal gave a detailed and honest telling of all the events of her day except for the few minutes she was in Heather's apartment drinking the exquisite champagne. She ended her accounting of her activities with, "I have no idea why the police thought throwing me to the floor, handcuffing me, and hauling me unceremoniously to the police station, was appropriate behavior."

"Did they say you were under arrest?"

"Yes."

"Did they say *why* you were under arrest?"

"Yes, they accused me of lying to them and assaulting a police officer."

"What did you lie about?"

"I did not lie. I had a ring of keys to The Pacific Arts Gallery where I'm employed. I did not know what all the keys unlocked, but assumed they belonged to doors or places I had not been oriented to."

Kirsten smiled a tight, slow smile and shook her head slightly. "Now do you know why the police thought you lied?"

"It turns out, the keys I didn't recognize were for places other than the main gallery."

"Do you know where and what those places are?"

"Of course not. If I had known, I would have told them."

"Do you plan to use that reasoning for the rest of the trial?"

"It's the truth. Heather Aldersen, my employer, showed me the keys and which places they opened."

"And you were never curious about where else they might lead?"

"It wasn't my job to be curious."

"Did Ms. Aldersen ever say you were not to use the other keys?"

"Not at all. She said she trusted me to do my work well and make it possible for her to not be tied up every moment of every day."

The lawyer nodded. "Did you assault a police officer?"

"Not really."

"That was a yes or no question, Ms. Chowdhury. You gave me an ambiguous answer."

"Well, when that little waif of a policewoman came at me with handcuffs, I just reacted. I had no intention of harming her, but simply reacted. I know of no one who would take kindly to having handcuffs on their wrists in the middle of a conversation."

"Do you know any other reason the police were questioning you in the first place?"

At this point, Tamal raised her cuffed hands and touched the corner of her eye with the tissue in her hand.

Kirsten was tempted to smile at the show Tamal was putting on, but remained the stoic, professional lawyer she was.

Tamal said, "My dear brother, Simon, was murdered on Little Si a few days ago. I think they were there to talk with me about his brutal death."

"I'm surprised your employer didn't make allowances and let you be off work so soon after your brother's murder."

"Ms. Aldersen is traveling in Europe. I thought she was with Hadar Hamal."

"The billionaire?"

"Yes. I'd always thought he was a kind and generous man, but he lashed out at me and called me a liar."

"About what?"

"About the keys and where Ms. Aldersen was."

"Why did he question either fact?"

"He has a full set of keys to the gallery."

"Did you know that before today?"

Tamal blushed and tried to talk in a calm voice, but the volume of her voice raised as she spoke. "No. I did not. I was totally blindsided."

Kirsten nodded. "Did you learn anything else in the interview?"

"I learned Heather was in Europe, Paris to be precise."

"And when will she be coming back to the states?"

"I don't know. A few days is what the detective said."

"What else did you learn?"

"Poor, darling Heather is dead and stuffed into a suitcase."

Kirsten looked up and glimpsed Tamal's small smile and eyes alight with glee. She paused the recorder and said, "You need to control your facial features, Ms. Chowdhury."

"Please call me Tamal."

"No, not in this lifetime. I'm your lawyer and I'll do a damned good job of it. But. I will never be your friend."

Tamal's visage darkened, but she didn't push the issue.

The lawyer continued. "To underestimate the police detective who arrested you would be the biggest mistake of your life, Ms. Chowdhury. He has an excellent success rate in solving major crimes, including murder. Now I'm going to stop our interview for now. Detective Jordan is due here soon. I need a break and a quick bite to eat before he arrives to interview you. It is your choice whether you spend most of the rest of your life in prison, have a shorter sentence, or maybe even get your case dismissed. No one who will interview you, including me, is your friend. No one will make any allowances for you. Do you understand?"

Tamal felt queasy and nodded.

"If you ever want to see the light of day again, Ms. Chowdhury, you'd best be ready to quit expecting everyone in sight to pull the forelock to you. Not a single person will. Your beauty will get you nowhere. The justice system is really, truly, mostly blind. The only things that really matter are the evidence, the statements, the questions, and the answers. But most important to your future is you being honest with me, and me building a good case."

"Can you get me out of here tonight?"

"Maybe, but do not count on it. One thing I can tell you is, I'll never ask you direct questions about what illegal things you have done. The less you tell me on those accounts, the better your chances will be. But even a slight slip of your tongue, or facial expressions, can change the path of your life."

"When will they take these cuffs off me?"

"Not anytime soon. The better your behavior is and the more humble you can be, the better your chances are."

"Humble? Why should I be humble?"

"IF you wish to be some bully woman's bitch, just keep going the haughty way you've been going. If you wish to have some sliver of possibility of leaving jail or worse yet, prison, you've got to change your behavior and attitude. Immediately."

Tamal nodded. *How can I be humble? How can this be happening to me? I don't deserve this horrid situation.*

Kirsten Holt picked up her briefcase and walked out of the interview room. *It's hard to believe Ms. Chowdhury can seem to be so smart and yet stupid at the same time.* Of course, it wasn't the first time Kirsten had seen exactly the same thing in criminals.

Sadly, for Tamal, this was just the beginning.

CHAPTER THIRTY-FOUR

Darren read over the transcripts of the day's interviews with Tamal Chowdhury. He shook his head. "We can charge her all we want to on the lying and obstruction, and probably even make it stick. We do not have enough to charge her with the murder of her brother or Heather Aldersen."

Sally Quinn said, "I agree. The forensic team is working on both Simon Chowdhury's car and The Pacific Arts Gallery. Maybe they'll give us more solid clues than the ski mask."

"Fingers crossed they find DNA on the mask. We know it is her mask but tying it to Simon's death is the key. Let's go through what we have before we interview her."

"We have her fingerprints for the charges we have already made. Hopefully, her fingerprints can be matched to something incriminating either in Simon's car or at the gallery."

He nodded. "We want to be careful to be sure the evidence is incriminating and not wishful thinking. It's important to keep in mind that she may not have killed anyone."

Sally snorted. "Do you believe that?"

"Not for one moment, but we cannot rush to judgement either."

There was a knock on his door. One of the forensic techs walked in with a champagne bottle in an evidence bag. She said, "We found this bottle in a dumpster in the alley behind the gallery. It was a few doors down, but we looked in all the dumpsters for anything that might have fingerprints or be related to the case."

Darren shook his head. "Why would you pick up a champagne bottle?"

"There were wine bottles in a few of the dumpsters. The wines were good wines, but this one stood out for three reasons."

"Okay, I'll bite. What are the three reasons?"

The tech smiled and said, "This bottle was Krug Brut Vintage 1985. It goes for a thousand dollars a bottle or more."

Sally asked, "For real?"

"Oh, yes. I was lucky enough once to have a small sip, and it was delish. I wouldn't spend that much money on it, but it was great."

Darren prompted, "What are the second and third reasons?"

"The second reason is the gallery has a stock of this champagne. There are several boxes unopened, but there is one with eleven bottles in the box. This is also the only box upstairs in the apartment and not on the second-floor storage area. It was in the pantry in Ms. Alderson's private apartment. There is evidence the box was recently opened. The third and best reason? Your perp's fingerprints are on this bottle."

Darren grinned. "Thank you. Great work."

"You're welcome. Want me to leave this with you?"

"Absolutely. You made my day."

The tech placed the bottle in the evidence bag on Darren's desk and said, "We aim to please."

"Any other juicy evidence?"

"There's a lot to process. I already gave you the evidence bag with the ski mask. We found a few spots that might reveal DNA such as around the eyeholes and nose hole, but we haven't gotten the DNA results back. There are also hairs that look like hers, but we need her DNA to compare to any results we might get."

"I understand. Without her DNA we won't know for sure it connects her to the ski mask, and perhaps she might have been in Simon's car at one time and lost the mask."

"We'll keep working. I have a feeling there won't be a lot of hard evidence, but I'm sure there will be more evidence than we have now. We need her DNA."

After the tech left, Darren said, "Go see if Tamal's lawyer is present and ready for us to ask a few questions. Then come back here. For the interview, I want you to watch until I pull my left earlobe. Then come into the exam room with the evidence bags we have. I want both the champagne bottle and the ski mask to be a bit of a surprise to Tamal and her lawyer. Don't say a word, just sit down and put the bags in front of me."

"Got it, boss."

He shook his head but said nothing.

Sally grinned and left the room.

Darren went over the evidence they had, which included the black ski mask with Tamal's name on the tag and a few strands of long, black wavy hair. It would be interesting to see what she had to say about the ski mask. The forensic team had found it wedged between the driver's seat belt receptacle and the edge of the seat.

Sally came back into his office and said, "The lawyer is ready but wishes to speak with you first. She is waiting in the hallway."

"Great. I'll go talk with her. You take these two evidence bags to the viewing room and shut the door. Try to avoid letting the lawyer see what you have."

"I'll take them and put them in my desk drawer. I won't leave the area until you and she are in the interview room."

"That'll work."

He stood up and followed Sally out of his office. She went to her desk and placed the evidence bags in a drawer of her desk. Darren walked out to the hallway and said, "Ms. Holt. It's good to see you again."

She smiled, and they shook hands. "I'm hoping to beat you this time."

He chuckled. "Good luck with that. It's my aim to bring the bad guys or gals in and toss away the keys."

"And it's my aim to prove Ms. Chowdhury isn't the bad gal."

He nodded. "Well, let's get to it then. After you."

He watched her walk away, slowly, making sure her hips were swinging in the provocative way of sensual women. He shook his head. *Wasted on me, but you have an alluring body. For a woman.*

When they arrived at the interview room, he unlocked the door and held it open for her to enter first. Although he wasn't attracted to women, he made sure when dealing with them to be gentlemanly and yet not suggestive. He firmly kept his eyes up, looking across the room as she glanced to see if he was watching her body. He'd learned from watching videos that many women wanted to be sure men were watching. He did not mind disappointing them.

He stood behind his chair at the table and waited for Ms. Holt to be seated beside her client. Once she was seated, he leaned across the table and removed the handcuffs from Tamal's hands. She rubbed her wrists but said nothing. He sat down across from her and laid the cuffs on the table beside him.

He pulled a disposable ballpoint gel pen from his pocket. He laid the pen and a blank, yellow legal pad on the table. "Ms. Chowdhury, during this session I will ask you a lot of questions. I will record everything we say during this session. Do you have questions before we begin?"

"Where's your little waif?"

"Sally? I don't think of her as a waif, but she'll be along soon. Can I get you anything to drink or eat?"

"I'm not hungry and have no intention of going to the restroom in this squalid place."

"I understand. I'll start the recorder now." He turned on the recorder and related who was in the room, then said, "I'll now read you your Miranda rights."

She rolled her eyes. "Please do not bore me with that drivel again."

He said, "Regardless, I will read you your rights." After he read the Miranda Rights to her, he said, "Do you understand your rights?"

"Yes, yes, yes! Just get on with it."

He pulled on his left earlobe and asked, "Can you state for the record your name, address, and occupation, please?"

She did so, and as she finished, the door opened, and Sally walked in with the two evidence bags. Tamal grinned, "There she is! The darling little girl who wants to grow up to be a police officer."

Sally smiled a little and nodded. "Nice to see you too, Ms. Chowdhury."

Darren said, "For the record, Officer Sally Quinn has entered the interview room with two evidence bags."

As Sally sat down beside Darren, she put the two bags on the table in front of the detective. Kirsten Holt asked, "Is this evidence from the gallery?"

"In part," Darren answered. "We'll get to them in a few minutes."

Sally watched Tamal's face and could see her eyes tighten a little. More importantly, her face paled when she looked at the bag with the ski mask found in Simon Chowdhury's car.

Darren asked, "Do you have anything you'd like to say, Ms. Chowdhury?"

She raised her head, looked him in the eye and said, "No. Not a fucking thing."

CHAPTER THIRTY-FIVE

Darren watched Tamal's face. She couldn't control the tightening around her eyes or her pupils constricting when she saw the evidence in front of her. He nodded and asked, "Which bothers you more, Ms. Chowdhury, the champagne bottle or the ski mask?"

"Neither bother me at all."

"Do you recognize them?"

She shrugged but didn't answer.

"For the record, Tamal Chowdhury has shrugged her shoulders. I can't tell if that is a yes or no, Ms. Chowdhury."

"They are common items. I've seen plenty of champagne bottles and ski masks."

"Do you own a ski mask?"

"I own several. Skiing is the only sport I enjoy. However, protecting my face from the brutal cold and wind is important to me. I always wear a mask when skiing."

Darren nodded. "I know many people do. I could never abide the confined feeling of a ski mask."

Tamal smirked. "It shows on your skin."

"Perhaps, but I'm not a stunningly beautiful woman."

Tamal smiled, licked her lips and asked, "Who do you think is more beautiful? Me or my lawyer?"

"First, we aren't here to judge your beauty. Second, I've learned to always tell every woman she is beautiful no matter how she looks. I get more honest answers if she believes I think she is beautiful."

Kirsten bit her bottom lip to not laugh out loud, but Tamal blushed and said, "You are a silly man, detective."

He smiled briefly. "Probably so." Then he asked, "Is this your ski mask?" He pushed the evidence bag to her.

"I've no idea."

"Do you label the inside of your ski masks with your name?"

She nodded. "I hate having anyone wear my ski mask. My husband often just grabbed a mask and pulled it on. I had to train him to look and be sure he wasn't putting on my mask."

"If he wore your ski mask, what would you do?"

"I'd yank it off his head and toss it into the fireplace."

"But surely you wouldn't mind having your husband's hair on your ski mask?"

She couldn't stop the look of disgust and even shuddered a little. "I never, ever share my clothing with anyone, even my husband."

Darren nodded and took a few notes, letting a full minute pass before he looked up and said, "Your name is on the label inside this ski mask."

"Then it's mine."

"Do you know where we found it?"

"In my home?"

"No, we haven't gone to your home yet."

"Then I've no idea where you found it, detective."

Kirsten asked, "If you think the ski mask is important, Detective Jordan, please skip the theatrics and tell us where you found it."

"Certainly," he said and smiled at Kirsten. Then he let his smile fade as he looked at Tamal. "We found it wedged between the driver's seat and the driver's seatbelt clasp in your brother Simon's car."

Where once she blushed, now she paled. She kept her mouth tightly closed.

Darren continued, "We got real lucky with Simon's car. They found it parked behind the Sallal Grange in North Bend, with the keys tossed on the dashboard."

Kirsten asked, "Is there a point detective?"

"Yes, there is, Ms. Holt. His car was missing for over forty-eight hours after his death."

"What does that have to do with Ms. Chowdhury?"

"Her fingerprints, and her ski mask, were found in the car. Her fingerprints were also on the keys as well as the inside and outside of the car. There were boot prints beside the door that seem to be a woman's boot. With the recent snow melt, the mud gave us a great impression of the sole of the boot."

Tamal shrugged. "I've been in my brother's car a lot of times and have even driven the car a time or two."

"We thought of that, but with your ski mask wedged where it was, we started to wonder."

He didn't say anything else but waited while he watched Tamal. When she could no longer stand it, she asked, "Okay, I'll bite." Kirsten reached out and touched Tamal's hand. She jerked her hand away from the lawyer. Tamal asked, "What did you wonder about, detective?"

"What size of shoe you wear and whether you had similar boots to the boot print."

"It doesn't matter what boots I might or might not have. I wasn't in North Bend and certainly wouldn't go anywhere near such a silly thing as a Grange. Those places are for people who have menial lives."

Sally gripped her hands together in her lap but said nothing. Her thoughts, however, were less quiet. *What a bitch!*

"Well," Darren said. "Don't worry about it. We have a search warrant for your home in West Seattle, and the apartment you were living in at Redmond. We are also in the process of getting a search warrant for your mother's home, where you stayed the last few days."

Tamal said nothing, for which Kirsten was grateful. The lawyer said, "Have you started the search?"

"Not yet, but it is next on our list to do tomorrow. We would have searched her home today had we not searched all day at the gallery."

She nodded and made a few notes before asking, "Are you charging my client with some crime related to Simon's car?"

"Not yet."

"I need to see the search warrant and the cause you used for the warrant before you start the search."

Darren nodded. "That will be fine. Now on to the champagne bottle. Have you had some of this champagne recently?"

"Yes, Heather and I had a toast before she left for Europe."

He made a note. "Well, your fingerprints are on this bottle."

"They might be. We both poured glasses of the champagne while we talked about her future plans."

Darren nodded. "Heather's fingerprints are not on the bottle."

Sally watched Tamal closely but saw no response.

Darren continued, "According to public records, the dumpster where we found the bottle, was emptied on Friday, the morning after Simon's death. So this bottle couldn't have been the one you shared with Heather before she left for Europe, a week before his death."

Tamal sat still as a stone but said nothing. Her lawyer leaned over to her and whispered, "Lying will not help you."

Tamal nodded but said nothing. Her only thought was, *I shouldn't have had that moment of weakness.*

"Tell me, Ms. Chowdhury, your activities on the day of your brother's death."

"Just the usual sort of day, other than it was New Year's Eve."

"Did you have special plans for the evening?"

"No, I did not. I don't celebrate silly changes on the calendar. One day is much like the next day to me."

"What days do you celebrate?"

"Oh, occasionally Christmas or Thanksgiving, but even those are boring and trite."

He nodded. "What about your birthday?"

She glared at him. "I hate celebrating my birthday, although my mother always insists we celebrate."

"Why do you hate celebrating your birthday?"

"First, I hate anyone to think I'm getting older, although I suppose we all must, or we die young. Second, I hate the feeling of blame, of guilt, from my mother."

He shook his head slightly and said, "Why would you feel blame or guilt on your birthday?"

She sat still as a stone for several seconds, then blew out a deep breath she'd been holding. "My twin brother died during our birth. I came out first and mother said she adored looking at her beautiful daughter. My twin and I argued about who would come out first. I made sure I did."

Darren felt the hair on the back of his neck rising. Sally felt a cold heaviness seep into the pit of her stomach. Kirsten Holt ducked her head to hide her face while she gripped her hands tightly in her lap.

Darren softly asked, "How did you make sure you came out first, Tamal?"

"I pushed Taman out of the way. Once I was in the birth canal, he couldn't be first. Amma, my mother, blames me for his death."

"Why?"

"His umbilical cord was wrapped around his neck and my ankle. When I came out, it caused his umbilical cord to tighten around his neck. So, in a very real sense, I caused my brother's death. Not Simon's death, but Taman's death."

The detective watched her carefully, and for the first time he thought he saw some real human emotion. "Surely no one blames you, an infant in the process of birthing, for your twin brother's death."

"They say they don't, but I know they do. I know Amma wishes I'd come out second. I couldn't let that happen. I wanted my face to be the first one she saw and adored."

The room was quiet. Darren couldn't speak, and Sally was feeling lightheaded. She said, "Excuse me, please. I need some fresh air."

Sally stood up and left the room. Tamal smiled, "She may be a better martial arts fighter than I am, but deep down she is weak."

Darren said, "End of interview," turned off the recorder, picked up the evidence bags, stood up and followed Sally into the hallway.

She brushed away a tear. "I'm sorry, Darren."

He shook his head. "No worries, Sally. Let's go to my office. I need a drink."

She nodded. "Me too."

CHAPTER THIRTY-SIX

"Odetta, you look lovely," Hadar said. "I worried you'd feel too confined the past few days."

She smiled. "No sir, not at all. Danny is the best company I could have had for the past 48 hours."

"I'm pleased. Let's sit down and chat while you two eat. I've already had my dinner but brought dinner to you."

Danny said, "I'll plate our dinners, then we can chat. How about a glass of wine?"

"A nice Riesling would be perfect."

She smiled, opened the chilled wine and set it with three wine glasses on the table. Hadar said, "Allow me to pour the wine while you plate your dinners."

In a few minutes, they were sitting together in the dinning area of Hadar's elegant suite at The Four Seasons. Odetta said, "This pork loin stuffed with apples and walnuts is divine. I taste some exotic spice, but I can't figure it out. I will though."

Hadar laughed. "I know the chef. My guess is if you ask nicely, he'll tell you exactly what it is."

"That would be great. I love to cook and experiment with new foods."

Danny said, "I'm a steak girl most of the time, but this is superb. I like the sweet potato chips with it."

"It's one of my favorites," Hadar agreed. "I like how he uses fresh pink pepper and rosemary on the chips. Keeps them from being too sweet, but pairs nicely with the pork and apples."

"Well," Odetta said, "It is a lovely dinner. I've never had sweet potato chips. I really want to experiment with those."

Hadar smiled. "I'm glad and I look forward to eating some of your culinary delights. Now ladies, we have some business to attend to."

Danny shook her head. "We watched all the hoorah at the gallery. Was that Tamal Chowdhury being taken away in handcuffs?"

"Yes, and it complicates things on an emotional level for me. I've never liked the woman, but because of her skills with art, Heather wanted to give her a chance. When it was obvious that she wasn't what we wanted at the gallery, I brought Odetta to Edmonds."

Danny asked, "Why would not liking her, complicate your emotions?"

"I feel I should have stood my ground about her in the first place, or acted sooner. Perhaps if I'd done either of those two things, all would be well."

Odetta asked, "Was I going to replace Tamal?"

"Yes, but now that cannot be."

Odetta nodded and lowered her head. She worked hard to not cry, but struggled to swallow the food in her mouth.

Hadar wished he'd spoken differently. He touched her hand and said, "Let me tell you ladies the full story. You, Odetta, have big things ahead of you. So cheer up and don't choke on the fine meal in front of you."

She nodded, chewed a bit more and let the food go down before she took a sip of wine.

Hadar asked her, "Do you trust me, Odetta, to have your best interests at heart?"

She smiled and nodded. "Yes, I do. It's just I was looking forward to working with Heather and The Pacific Arts Gallery."

"You have bigger fish to fry now, dear girl. Please finish this lovely dinner, then we'll talk over coffee. Besides, your desserts are lovely lemon blueberry cookies that I think are treasured little gifts."

She smiled and said, "I'm hungry and this food is terrific. I'll do what my Momma always said."

"What's that?" Danny asked.

"God made you to be the beautiful, talented woman you are. Let no one tell you different. Chin up and take the bull by the horns!"

Hadar nodded. "Your mother was a stunning, insightful woman. She was also a force to be reckoned with, as you will also be."

"With your help."

"Yes, with my help you will be even more amazing than you are now. Let's change the subject for the moment. How do you feel being in America rather than Jamaica?"

"Well, I truly miss the island life. Things seem to move so quickly here, it's a little hard to adjust."

"I feel that way every time I'm in the states. Living on an island, I naturally live with the rhythm of the sea."

She grinned. "Yes, that's it exactly. But there are other things for which I'm very grateful."

Danny watched Odetta, and when Odetta caught Danny's eye, she smiled. "Do you know, Hadar, men who love men and women who love women can actually show their affection publicly here without fear of death?"

He smiled and nodded. "I know that."

She took another sip of her wine. "I saw two women sitting at a very nice restaurant holding hands. It warmed my heart to see them. When their dessert was brought to them, one woman, got on her knees and gave the other woman a ring!"

He smiled. "They were probably becoming engaged."

She nodded. "Probably. But the most amazing part of the episode was everyone in the restaurant applauded and shouted lovely blessings on the two women."

Danny swallowed and worked to hold back tears. She asked, "What would have happened in Jamaica if those women had done such a thing."

Odetta shook her head. "They would have been beaten and probably killed. If they weren't killed, they would have been sent to prison for at least ten years."

Danny reached across the table and said, "I'm so very sorry."

"Thank you, Danny. The relief I felt with the two women in love has made it impossible for me to return to Jamaica."

"Ever?" Danny asked.

"Ever." She looked at Hadar. "I can't go back there, Hadar. Hiding who I am and putting up with men's hands all over me—I can't go back."

He patted her hand. "You never have to go back."

"Thank you."

"It is my honor. If you two have finished eating, let's go to more comfortable seating and work out what we will do from here."

Odetta let out a sigh, but Hadar just smiled at her. *What a jewel she is and how lucky I was to find her.*

CHAPTER THIRTY-SEVEN

Hadar sat with Odetta and Danny in the sitting area of his suite. "For now," he said, "I'm asking you two ladies to remain here in the suite. I'll be staying in my bedroom here but will be in and out. I do not think you are in further danger, but I want to be sure."

"You thought I was in danger?" Odetta asked.

He nodded. "I may have over-reacted at first. I know now, indeed I'm certain, if the police had not been quick in their reactions, you might well be dead."

Odetta gasped, and Danny reached out and held her hand. "You mean murdered, don't you?"

"Yes, that is exactly what I mean."

She shook her head. "I can't imagine anyone would want to murder me. Even more difficult is to imagine why."

"I think greed is at the heart of it all. Greed is difficult for me to speak of. I'm a man of nearly unlimited wealth. I enjoy my delights of living in luxury, yet I think I can honestly say, I never sought the delights themselves, but more I really loved playing with money. As a child, I always won at Monopoly, but my father said I'd never be wealthy because I gave so much of my money to players who were losing."

"But you are wealthy," Odetta said.

"Yes, I am, but it is a mystery to me how I became so wealthy. I think it was mostly a matter of luck and not desiring more than I can afford. However, because I am wealthy, I seek people with talent but limited opportunities."

"Like me."

"Yes, dear one, like you."

Danny said, "I've never heard how you found Odetta."

"She was the curator in a small gallery on Sam Sharpe Square in Montego Bay, The Parrotfish Artists' Gallery."

"I loved working there but also wanted bigger things in my life," Odetta said. "If Hadar had not walked into our gallery on a day I was working, I would still be there, working and hoping."

He smiled. "When Odetta started talking about various artists and their work, I was enchanted. For the first time in a long time, I knew for sure, just as I did with Heather Aldersen, here was a woman with a genuine love for art and artists."

Odetta laughed. "When he asked which painting was my favorite, I panicked a little."

"Why?"

"I loved them all."

Hadar chuckled and shook his head. "It was a struggle for her and I could see the struggle on her face. She finally said, 'this one I will miss less if you buy it. I will still miss it, but I won't grieve too much.' Then I knew she would be perfect at The Pacific Arts Gallery."

Odetta smiled and shook her head. "He made me tell him which one would cause me the most pain. I told him and he bought it."

"Yes, I did. Now it hangs in your home in Edmonds."

"And it brings me joy."

"What a terrific story," Danny said. "I know there are many issues around all of this, Hamal, but what can you share with us? Why did you think Odetta was in danger?"

He sighed and shook his head. "Heather Aldersen was an incredible woman who was making a difference in the art scene in the Pacific Northwest."

Odetta touched his hand. "You speak of her as if she is gone."

"Yes, she is gone. She was murdered and her body is now in Paris, France, but will soon be back in the United States and here in Seattle."

Both Danny and Odetta gasped at the news, then Odetta asked, "Is that why you told me to not go to the dinner appointment?"

He shook his head. "No. I believed the woman whose place we had planned for you to take, is a murderer. I now believe she murdered Heather. I also believed and still believe she would have murdered you too."

Tears rolled down Odetta's face. "Why? She doesn't even know me."

"Greed. Greed is the why of everything that has been going on."

"Did she know I was going to take her place?"

"I do not think so, but the dinner date was on Heather's calendar and I feared Tamal would show up in her place. I'm sure she'd have given you an excuse for Heather's absence, but I also feel strongly she would have murdered you and done so quickly."

"None of this makes any sense, Hadar," Odetta said. "I was no threat to her."

"She might not have perceived reality in the same way you would. She wanted it all—the gallery, the apartment, Heather's position in the world."

Danny said, "How very sad it sounds."

He nodded. "Yes, it is. Tamal drugged Heather, then drowned her. Next she put Heather's body into an enormous suitcase and took it to Paris, France. She used Heather's ID and passport. Once in Paris, she left the body and suitcase at the airport. I'm not privy to any more information about it all. But, if she would go to those extremes with Heather, it would be child's play for her to eliminate you as well."

Danny said, "Surely someone would have noticed Odetta's death?"

"Why would they? Odetta had been here a week before all this happened. No one really knew her here other than me. Even Heather hadn't met her yet. She was accepting my recommendation that Odetta should replace Tamal."

Odetta nodded. "She could have disposed of me anywhere and without ID on my body, I would be another black woman, name unknown, murdered for no apparent reason. Dead black women are not mourned by the legal systems of the world."

Danny shook her head. "It well and truly pisses me off, but you are probably right, Odetta. Black women and black men are killed daily. The justice system works very slowly for them, if at all."

Hadar took both women's hands in his own. "You are both correct in your assessments. For now, though, I can keep you safe, here in my suite. I have faith in Detective Jordan and Officer Quinn. I'm certain in a few days, we can reopen the gallery and you, Odetta, will be the curator and owner of the gallery."

"Owner? Why would I be the owner?"

"Heather's will is explicit. In the event of her death, her gallery, the apartment upstairs, the entire building belongs to whoever I chose to be the next curator."

"She owned the gallery?"

"Yes, and the entire building. The top floor is an amazing apartment that will legally be yours in a few days."

"Her family wouldn't want to have the gallery?"

"She has no close family ties—no siblings, her parents are deceased, as are her grandparents. The gallery was her life, and now it will be yours."

"I don't know what to say other than I am not worthy."

Danny chuckled. "Of course, you are. If Hadar says you are, then you are."

Hadar turned to Danny. "Thank you for the vote of confidence. I'm also asking you if you will be with Odetta at the gallery, at least until we find someone else to take her place as assistant curator."

"Sure, but I don't want to do it full time. I like freelancing when you don't need me."

"I understand. Now, ladies, I don't know about you, but I'm exhausted. I need a hot shower and go to bed. Unless you have other questions."

Odetta said, "I'll probably have a million questions, but right now I need to wrap my mind and heart around all that has happened."

He smiled. "Good. I'll see you both in the morning."

As he walked away Danny stood up, held out a hand, and said, "Come on, Etta, let's get to bed ourselves."

Odetta smiled, took Danny's hand, and stood up. "My Muma always called me Etta."

"I hope it is okay I called you Etta."

"More than okay."

As they walked to their bedrooms, Danny thought, *she is beautiful and talented. I could fall for her in a New York minute.* At Odetta's bedroom door, Danny kissed her cheek and said, "Sleep well, Etta."

Odetta smiled, opened the door, and went inside. She went to the private bathroom, brushed her teeth, undressed, and pulled on her pajamas. She smiled as she climbed in the bed and laid her head on the down pillow. She sighed then thought, *I really like Danny. I think she is gay, but I'm not sure. I could love being in her arms. Here in America, I could be in a woman's arms without fear of torture, rape, or imprisonment.*

She closed her eyes and dreamed of Danny, her protector and friend.

CHAPTER THIRTY-EIGHT

Sally drove the police cruiser with Detective Darren Jordan in the passenger seat. He was going over the warrant for the home of Tamal Chowdhury and Roger Cookson. He wasn't worried about the search but felt sad for Roger and his mother-in-law.

He sighed. "I think Roger Cookson is a good man who is dealing with a lot of grief and trauma."

"You've met him before, right?"

"Yes, and he has been very helpful. He and his mother-in-law will meet us at his house along with Kirsten Holt."

"I thought Roger was going to live in Simon's home."

"He is, but he still has joint ownership of the home he and Tamal lived in."

She shook her head. "I can't imagine how hard it is for him, or frankly any family, when one member of the family goes off the rails. Tamal's mother's grief must be immense."

"I'm sure you are right. I wonder how much do we *really* know about the people closest to us. I don't think Martin could or would do such a thing, but how would I know? Do I really know him the way I think I do?"

Sally glanced at him and said, "I know you're the head honcho, but surely you know there are secrets in every relationship."

"I'd never thought of it before. What secrets do you have in your relationship with your husband?"

She laughed. "Once again, boss, a really personal question."

"I know, but seriously do you have secrets you don't share with Paul?"

"Okay, I'll share one little secret, but if you rat me out, they'll never find your body."

Darren laughed and said, "Okay. Give it to me."

"I really hate that sometimes he chews his food with his mouth open."

"Have you ever said anything about it?"

"No, but, one time his mother said, 'Paul, for the love of all that is holy, shut your damned mouth when you chew!' Then she looked at me and asked, 'How can you stand him chewing with his mouth open?'"

"What did you say?"

"I shrugged my shoulders and said, 'He's great in bed.' The conversation stopped cold for a few seconds until she laughed out loud. Paul blushed and his father said, 'Way to go, son' and grinned like a monkey. I still never say anything about it, but he sometimes catches himself and closes his mouth to chew."

Darren laughed. "I'm impressed, Officer Quinn. But no big serious hidden secrets?"

"Not a chance. Life is hard enough as it is. Without a man like Paul in my life, I'd be miserable. He works hard as an ICU nurse with ten and twelve-hour shifts, all while he is going to school for his DNP. Yet, he always helps me around the house and with our son. When I have horrible hours, like on this case, he makes special efforts to be sure I take care of myself. When he has double shifts, I make sure he doesn't have to come home to a mess or have to help cook a meal. I also take time off for special family time and don't feel a moment's guilt."

"I appreciate that you simply took time off for your son's birthday. A lot of folks wouldn't do that, especially in the middle of a big murder investigation."

"There is no ladder, in any career, worth not spending special time with family."

"Sounds great, Sally."

"It is, but it isn't always easy. I sometimes wish I was a stay-at-home mom, but I know I'd go crazy, and the money would be really tight. Then the next day, I'm working on a case and wish I'd not had a child, but I adore Gabriel. He is a delightful boy. When I get home and he races into my arms, I love my life. When Paul tells me I'm an amazing police officer, wife, and mom, I know I'm doing the right things in the right order. Big secrets would spoil the whole thing."

He nodded and looked out the window. "I think I'll talk with Martin about secrets."

"Do you have big secrets you keep from him?"

"No, I don't. In fact, I don't think I have any little secrets."

"Good," Sally said. "Just be kind with him in case he has any secrets."

Darren chuckled and said, "You're good for me, Sally."

"And you're good for me, boss."

He shook his head and laughed as she pulled the car into the driveway of Roger and Tamal's home. The Forensic Team was already there waiting for him and the search warrant. "Let's get busy and see what we can find."

The Forensic Team started the search in the closet of Tamal Chowdhury. Roger asked Darren, "Do you have a few moments to talk with me?"

"Sure, what's up?"

"I'd like the conversation to be private."

Kirsten Holt heard them and said, "During the search I expect to be apprised of anything and everything related to the search."

Before Darren could answer her, Roger said, "This is personal and nothing to do with Simon's death or Tamal's arrest."

"Then now isn't the time, Mr. Cookson," she replied.

Darren shook his head. "If it's all the same to you, Roger, it will be easier for both myself and you if we delay any private communication."

Roger looked from Darren to the attorney. He gritted his teeth and decided to share what was on his mind. "First, Ms. Holt, you are nothing to me and I could care less about anything you have to say unless it directly relates to me. Second, I was going to inform Detective Jordan that I had followed through and filed for divorce, and signed the deed to this house over to my wife."

"So, you are saying this is no longer your home?"

"That's exactly what I'm saying. I've already taken all my belongings to my new home."

"I need to know what those belongings entail, Mr. Cookson."

"You'll need to get a search warrant, Ms. Holt."

Darren bit his lip but couldn't stop the smile on his face. Kirsten Holt said, "You had no right to remove anything from this home."

"Of course, I did," Roger said. "I already checked with my attorney. My personal property is none of your business unless you have a credible reason for searching my personal property. Now, if you'll excuse me, my mother-in-law doesn't need to keep standing here in the cold while the search continues. She has been through more than enough the past several days."

He nodded to Darren, turned briskly, and walked to his mother-in-law. He took her hand and said, "Amma, let's go. There's nothing for us here."

Kirsten grabbed his arm and said, "I thought Basanti was Tamal's mother's name."

Basanti looked at the woman and said, "I am Basanti Chowdhury. Amma is a term of endearment for beloved mothers. It is not a term you should even think of using in speaking with me. In fact, my given name is also not one you should use. I am Mrs. Chowdhury."

Kirsten swallowed and said, "Yes, ma'am. I'm sorry if I offended you."

"Is there a question you wish to ask me?"

"No, ma'am not at this time."

"Good. I'm fatigued with all the turmoil." She turned to Roger and said, "Beta, please take me to my son's home."

Roger walked with Basanti to his car and helped her in. Once they were driving away from what had been Roger's home, Kirsten asked, "Why did she call him Beta?"

Darren smiled softly. "It is a term of endearment for a beloved son."

"Roger isn't her son."

"He is her son in her heart and now her only living son."

Kirsten stood silently looking at the detective. She saw earnest truth in his face and said, "Forgive my rudeness, please."

He nodded and turned to continue helping with the search. When he was out of the lawyer's sight, he texted to Roger. *Are you okay?*

Roger responded. *Yes, and I appreciate your courtesy in asking. I wanted you to know that I took personal papers and my personal property. I'd prefer to show them to you without the lawyer present.*

Darren texted back; *May I drop by later?*

That will be fine. It is also okay if Sally is with you, but not the bitch lawyer.

Darren chuckled and put his phone back in his pocket.

One tech came up to him and said, "I think this boot is a match for the boot print at the Grange."

Darren pulled up a photo of the boot print and showed it to the tech. He said, "The pattern is exactly the same."

The tech agreed. "We'll know for sure when we compare the print to this boot. There is still mud in the grooves on the boot. We may be able to match the dirt in the boot to the dirt behind the Grange."

"Good work," Darren said. "Do you need us here anymore?"

"No, sir. We've just about finished."

"Any other surprises or finds?"

"Just that there are no personal papers anywhere in the home. Otherwise, all we found are Ms. Chowdhury's clothing, belongings, and this pair of boots. Oh, and a diary in the bedside table you might find interesting."

"Can you get the diary to me as soon as they process it?"

"First thing this afternoon."

CHAPTER THIRTY-NINE

Officer Sally Quinn and Detective Jordan drove to Simon Chowdhury's home and parked across the street. She started to get out of the car, but Darren put a hand on her arm. He said, "Let's sit here a few minutes and see how things pan out with our lawyer friend."

Sally looked at him and asked, "Are you expecting trouble from Ms. Holt?"

"Not necessarily, but it sure as hell wouldn't surprise me."

"Do you know her?"

"Yes, on cases I've worked where she was the defense attorney and by reputation. I think she and Tamal Chowdhury are cut from the same bolt of cloth. They are bold, determined and beautiful women. The only actual difference is I don't believe Kirsten Holt is an evil or even a bad person."

Sally nodded. "I think Tamal is pure evil."

"Well, she certainly is singularly focused on herself."

Sally looked up and pointed to a car coming their way. "Well, here comes the she-wolf in lawyer's clothing, all set to pounce."

He grinned. "I thought she might try something." He lowered his window as Kirsten walked to the cruiser. "Are you lost, Ms. Holt?"

"No, I'm not. You know I'm not lost. What are you doing here?"

"Sitting and talking over the day's events and what's next with Officer Quinn."

"In front of Simon Chowdhury's house? Seems a little too convenient to me."

He shrugged his shoulders but said nothing.

"You're here to talk with Roger Cookson privately."

He just looked at her with what he hoped was a blank expression.

"I'm entitled to any communication you have with Mr. Cookson."

"Really? Is he your client?"

"No. He is the husband of my client."

"And because of that, you have a right to *all* communication I might have with him?"

She pursed her lips and admitted, "No, only as it pertains to this case."

He nodded. "Well, I will certainly let you know if anything I talk with Mr. Cookson pertains to this case."

"What other reason could you have to speak with him?"

"He's a friend of mine."

She stomped her foot and shouted, "Since when?"

"None of your business," Darren answered in a very quiet and calm voice. "My life and my friends are my personal business, Ms. Holt. Now if you'll excuse me…"

"I will not excuse you."

"You simply don't have that power, Ms. Holt, and you do not intimidate me." He opened his car door and stood up close to her. "I'll be going to visit my friend now, Ms. Holt." He turned to walk away, and she grabbed his arm and pulled him back.

"You aren't going anywhere detective."

He looked at her hand on his arm and said, "You are making a mistake, counselor. Either let go of my arm, and leave me alone, or I will arrest you for assaulting an officer of the law."

Sally got out of the car and reached behind her back for her handcuffs.

Kirsten looked at the officer and then back to the detective. "You wouldn't dare."

"Maybe. Maybe not. We could play out this little scene and see what happens. It might be fun, at least for me. I'm sure you'd enjoy sitting in a cell waiting for your father to come to your aid." He grinned and continued, "Just think of the headlines!"

Her hand dropped from his arm, and he walked away. Sally quickly followed Darren as she tucked the handcuffs back in her belt.

Kirsten shouted, "You'll regret this."

Darren didn't respond but kept walking toward Roger's new home, the home that used to be the home of Simon Chowdhury, the murder victim. Darren felt more certain than ever that Simon's sister Tamal was the murderer. He didn't turn around when Kirsten Holt sped away in her fancy Beemer. He grinned and said, "So sad she doesn't know how to peel out."

Sally chuckled. "Not even a little bitty spot of rubber on the road. Total rookie."

They sat at the kitchen table in Roger's home. Pavlov lay with his head on Basanti's feet.

Roger said, "I'm sorry if I caused you any trouble."

"Not at all. She is Tamal's lawyer and is an adversary."

Basanti touched his arm. "Will she be a problem for you?"

"No, and even if she is, I can handle it. Please don't worry about me. You have enough on your plate as it is."

She nodded. "If it's all the same to you, I'd prefer to go sit in my room and read for a bit. Roger bought me an oversized recliner so Pavlov and I could sit together. I've had all the drama I need for some time to come."

Darren stood up and held her chair for her. She patted his hand and said, "You are a good man, detective."

He said, "Thank you, Mrs. Chowdhury."

"Please call me Basanti."

"Only if you'll call me Darren."

She nodded and said, "Thank you, Darren." She left the kitchen with Pavlov following her. The dog loved Basanti nearly as much as he loved Simon.

He looked at Sally and said, "See how easy that is?"

She laughed and said, "Yes, boss—Darren." She turned to

Roger and asked, "Would you like me to leave?"

"No, this isn't private other than being a personal wound."

Darren sat back down. "Tell me what is going on, Roger."

"Well, Basanti informed me, while I was out of town a few months ago, my wife had outpatient surgery."

"You didn't know she was going to have surgery?"

Roger shook his head. "No. If I had known she needed surgery, I would never have gone on the trip. It was just a business conference for home builders. It wasn't important enough to let her go through surgery alone."

"Why didn't she tell you?" Sally asked.

"She had a tubal ligation. She even forged my signature on the forms. It looked like my signature too. I found the copies of all the forms and bills earlier this morning in our office at home."

Darren said, "I'm so sorry. I take it you wanted children."

"Yes, I did. Basanti told me about the surgery yesterday afternoon on our way from Edmonds to here. This morning, I decided to look for evidence of what she did before you and Ms. Holt arrived. After I found the documents and talked with Basanti, she suggested I tell you just in case."

"Just in case what?" Sally asked.

"Just in case Tamal forged documents related to Simon's death or Heather Aldersen's death. When Basanti went to the bank to change her accounts, she found Tamal had added herself as a signatory on all Basanti's accounts using Basanti's signature. We both think she has been forging signatures for a long, long time."

"Holy smokes," Darren said. "She could have ripped Basanti off completely."

"She tried, but one of the bank Vice Presidents who had known Basanti for a long time, called her and asked about the large withdrawal a few days ago to an off-shore account. When I took her to the bank, to look into the matter, she found that over thirty thousand from her savings account had been withdrawn."

Sally asked, "Can't Mrs. Chowdhury file a claim or get legal help?"

"Yes, and the bank suggested she do exactly that. Instead, she opted to empty the accounts and create new accounts using her maiden name, Bakshi, for her banking accounts. She also signed papers requiring in-person account changes unless she is deceased. I'm her beneficiary and executor now."

"Why isn't she pressing charges?"

"She feels her daughter has enough burdens right now. She also wants to let her use the money for her defense fund."

Sally shook her head. "She is a better woman than I am."

"She is a truly good woman. She is filled with grief over her son's death and now feels responsible because she believes her daughter killed him."

Darren shook his head and clinched his teeth. "I feel such overwhelming sorrow in this case. I'm so sorry, Roger, that she couldn't be honest with you about not wanting children."

"She was honest with me. I just thought she would finally come around to having a child."

"Would you have stayed with her if you'd known she wanted the surgery?"

"No, I would not. I want to build a family. I thought she was the woman to make it happen. Like you, I'm filled with sorrow. My best friend is dead. My wife is the most likely suspect for his murder. I feel ashamed to have not seen her for what she truly is. Yet, I feel blessed to have Basanti and Pavlov still in my life. It's just one big mess."

After a few moments Darren asked, "Roger, is it okay if I take those papers in as evidence? If it would be easier for you, I can get a warrant for the documents."

"No need. I've got copies of the forged signature of Basanti's bank cards as well as my forged signatures. Amma has agreed to let you have them." He stood up and went to the kitchen counter and picked up a large manila envelope. On the back of the envelope were two pieces of tape with Basanti Chowdhury's and Roger Cookson's signatures taped across the flap of the envelope.

"If you need anything more related to these documents or the forgeries, please let us know. Basanti will be staying with me until all this has settled down. We'll both testify in court or give depositions as needed."

Darren took the envelope and stood up. He wrapped his arms around Roger and said, "I'm so very sorry, Roger."

Roger wept in Darren's arms as Sally sat quietly. She was glad that her small secrets hadn't caused pain of this magnitude. *When I get home, I want to talk with Paul about secrets. Even little ones are too much. I have a suspicion that small secrets can grow and become vile.*

CHAPTER FORTY

Odetta and Danny were bored. After Hadar left to go to the gallery and see how things were there, Danny said, "What do you want to do today?"

Odetta smiled and sat on the sofa beside Danny. "Get out of this luxurious jail."

Danny laughed. "Want to watch a movie?"

"I'm all Netflixed out! I couldn't watch another movie right now."

"Tell me about your homeland then."

"Jamaica is a beautiful place, but it is also a difficult place to live sometimes."

"Because of the gay issues?"

"A little because of those issues. Many people create gay relationships and do fine. They have to do it secretly and quietly, though. They are always at risk. For me, the biggest issue was the rampant drug industries, gangs, and violence."

"We have that too, in America."

Odetta nodded. "I love my homeland, but now that Muma has passed on, I've nothing to bind me to the island. Once I took the risk Hadar offered, I was ready to leave and not look back."

"Well, for those of us who are not heterosexual, even in America it can still be difficult. Add being African American and it can be a real tough go. Also, I know for sure, working hard and taking care of your resources doesn't always mean your life will be successful."

Odetta laughed. "Sounds as if you are trying to talk me out of America as my new homeland."

"No, but I am saying this isn't some sort of glorious utopian land."

"Ah. Well, I gave up on Utopia a long time ago. I lived where everything around me looked like paradise, but often beneath the beauty was nothing more than vile, roiling rot. At the same time, Jamaica is beautiful and wonderful, and I love my birth country. Most of the people I knew were kind, loving and generous. As a lesbian woman, it meant I had to have nothing I wanted in my life unless I could lie to myself, and the world around me."

"What do you wish to build, Etta?"

Odetta laid her head on Danny's shoulder. "A life filled with love, art, compassion and fun. What about you?"

"The same. Do you have a partner?"

"No. I did have a wonderful partner for a short period. But, her father insisted she get married, which she did. Three days after her marriage, her husband beat her to death. They gave him no jail time because she admitted she was lesbian."

"Were you in danger?"

"Yes, but by then I'd met Hadar. He took me to his island home for a few weeks before he convinced Heather to take me on in the Pacific Arts Gallery."

"So, you have a visa to be in the United States?"

Odetta chuckled. "Yes, I do, plus a green card. Hadar can make miracles happen when they are needed. What about you? Do you have a partner?"

"No and haven't for a long time."

"Why?" Odetta looked at Danny and watched her face as she told her story.

"I was married to a lovely woman. She was a member of the Duwamish Tribe here in the Seattle area. We wanted to raise a family, so she became pregnant with sperm donated from another Duwamish member. When she was about five months along in the pregnancy, she was raped and beaten. Both she and our son died that night."

Odetta's tears streamed down her face, listening to Danny's story. "I'm so very sorry, Danny. Did they find who killed her?"

"No, but there was a note left about how she'd betrayed her ancestors being married to an African American woman and not a Duwamish man."

Odetta pulled Danny into her arms and whispered, "You are worthy of love, affection and grace, Danny. Please tell me her name so I can remember her in my prayers."

"She was Angeline, named after Chief Seattle's daughter. Our son was to be named, Curtis after one of Angeline's friends in the historic days of Seattle."

The two women sat, holding each other. Odetta knew the emotions of the past few days might bring new joy, but also could bring new fear. She hoped that joy would always overcome fear.

Hadar talked with Detective Jordan, "When do you think we can re-open the gallery?"

"We finished up with the gallery early this morning. The gallery and building are ready to be back in business. I think it would be safe for Odetta to move into the apartment, or back to the house she was living in."

"She is getting stir crazy. She isn't a woman who does well trapped indoors all day and all night."

Darren smiled. "She seems to be a remarkable woman. I'm glad you are here though. I need you to look at something with me."

"Certainly. Anything I can do to help, I'll be happy to do."

"I want you to look at the will you pointed out in Heather's hidden safe and compare it to one we found in the safe in the storage area."

"Are they different?"

"Decidedly so. The one from her hidden safe is just as you say. The one in the business safe leaves everything to Tamal Chowdhury. We have handwriting experts looking at the wills and some other documents we think she forged. To my eyes they are identical."

"And of course," Hadar said, "The will in the business safe was dated a day or two before Heather's death."

"Yes, it was." Detective Jordan handed Hadar scanned pages of both wills.

Hadar read the wills but had difficulty controlling both his anger and his grief. When he finished reading, he shook his head and asked, "Was the latest will forwarded to the courthouse?"

"Yes, it was posted legally at the courthouse. However, it was posted two days after Heather's body arrived in Paris, France."

"By whom?"

"Tamal Chowdhury."

"Then Tamal has made a serious mistake."

Darren agreed. "More than one serious mistake, I fear. I'll share with you some of those mistakes if you feel you need them, but I ask you not to discuss them for the time being."

Hadar nodded. "I would prefer to not know anything not directly connected to the gallery. When those things are known publicly, will be soon enough for me."

Darren nodded. "Thank you, Mr. Hamal. Now let me give you back the keys to the gallery building." He opened the desk drawer and took out the keys. As he handed them to the billionaire he said, "I'm certain there are going to be legal hoops to jump through but I don't think Tamal will win any of them."

Hadar stood. "Thank you, detective. I appreciate your candor. I'm going to proceed as if the will I know to be legal, will be judged so by the courts. I want to get Odetta settled in the gallery."

"You will also want to check with the current artists who's works are there. Tamal was busy getting rid of local artist's work to bring in what she thought of as real art."

"She has a very limited view of the world, including the world of art. Odetta is a much smarter woman in that regard. It has been an eye-opening experience again, detective. I look forward to more pleasant times with you and your remarkable husband."

"Thank you," Darren said and shook hands with the enigmatic man he could only think of as being related to ME's chameleon. He grinned and shook his head. ME's chameleon was her Power Animal and a painting. Hadar Hamal was all human and a powerful man.

Sally walked in a few minutes after the billionaire left the office. She held up an evidence bag. Darren grinned and asked, "Is it good news, Sally?"

"Oh, yes, and worthy of any gruesome novel. Here's Tamal's diary."

He nodded his head. "Give me strength and a shot of whiskey."

"You will need both, boss."

He ignored her use of the word 'boss' and asked, "Does Ms. Holt have this new evidence?"

"Yep, she sent a courier to pick up her copy."

"Well, we'll see what she can spin out of this."

"Nothing pretty, I can guarantee," Sally said.

CHAPTER FORTY-ONE

Hadar entered his suite at the Four Seasons Hotel to find the two women sitting quietly chatting together on the sofa. He smiled, thinking, *I feel a bit of romance in the air. These two women in front of me deserve every bit of love they can share.* He said, "Hello, ladies."

Odetta smiled, "You look happy, Hadar. Does that mean you have good news?"

"Indeed, it does. You can move into the Gallery immediately."

She stood up and took his hand. "Can we talk about the gallery before we make any moves?"

He nodded but asked, "Do you not wish to be the owner and curator of The Pacific Arts Gallery."

She grinned. "Yes, I want to be the owner and curator. However, I'm missing my house by the beach, looking out on the sound. Is it possible for me to live there and own the building?"

"Of course, it is. You already, or soon will be the owner of the entire building. I also gave you the deed to the house on the beach. You may live wherever you wish."

"Good, then Danny and I have another idea, but you maybe should sit down for this idea."

He chuckled. "I'll take a seat, but I told Sander to ring for us in about thirty minutes."

"This won't take long and we're both already packed."

He sat down and Danny said, "We've been thinking about Tamal's mother."

He sighed and shook his head. "Among all the horrible, unjustified events, Tamal's mother's sorrow is one of the worst parts of all of this."

Danny said, "We agree. She seems to be a really lovely woman and needs all the love and support we can give her. We were wondering if she might want to live in the apartment above the gallery?"

"Hmmm. I hadn't thought of her living there. Give me good reasons why it should be so."

"Well," Odetta said, "I can't see her wanting to live with Roger, or in Roger and Tamal's old home. I also can't see her wanting to live in the home she raised her children in."

"Why ever not? It has been her home for many, many years."

Danny said, "You said she was talking about wanting to create a pastry and delicacies business for restaurants and other venues."

"Yes, but I don't see how living in the apartment above the gallery will help."

"The big industrial kitchen would be perfect for her. The small, private apartment is one I think she might like. It is very feminine and comfortable. Additionally, she could help with the hostess duties at the gallery and build her business."

He smiled. "You are assuming this is what she will want to do."

Odetta nodded. "Yes, we are, but if she wants to, will that be all right with you?"

He laughed and shook his head. "It isn't my property or place to decide."

"Oh. Right. I forgot I own it all," Odetta said and grinned. "It will be a while before I'm used to being the owner of such a fortune."

"First, it isn't really a huge fortune, although it has substantial monetary value. Without careful tending and stewardship, it could all collapse."

She nodded. "I get that part and hope I can learn quickly the ins and outs of it all."

"I'll help you get the ball rolling in that regard. Also, if Basanti agrees to your plan for her life—which I remind you she hasn't heard of the plan or voiced such a longing for her life—she can also be a big help for you. She has kept track of every penny her family has earned and done a fine job of it. She isn't wealthy, but she is certainly financially very well off."

Odetta smiled. "That is how I think I'll approach her. I'll need help and support with the gallery. I have a feeling we would enjoy working together. Plus, she'll have that lovely kitchen with every modern convenience she could want or need. I'm hoping that will be hard for her to resist."

He nodded. "That might just work, and I think it is a stellar idea. You've been missing your own mother, and she is a fine backup mother for anyone."

The doorbell chimed and Hadar said, "That will be Sander. Let's take you ladies home and then to the gallery."

Danny said, "I'll follow you to your house, Odetta. I want to see this home you can't live without."

When they arrived in Edmonds, Washington, Sander drove Hadar Hamal and Odetta to her home on Cary Road. Danny followed and parked behind Sander's limousine. She smiled and thought, *no wonder Etta wishes to live here. Her home of white clapboard siding with turquoise trim suits her. The ocean is right in front of the house too.*

Odetta waved to Danny. "Come see my home. You'll love it."

Hadar smiled and whispered to Sander, "I think this will be *their* home soon."

Sander nodded. "They look like they belong together, sir."

"We won't be long, Sander."

"Take your time. I'll enjoy the view."

Hadar smiled, nodded, and followed the two women into the home of Odetta Thomas.

Odetta sat with Danny and Hadar in the sunroom off the

kitchen. It was glass fronted, floor to ceiling, looking out on the sound. The water was crystalline blue today, with glints of golden sunshine on the gentle waves. They could see the closer islands and far across the water, the Olympic Mountains covered with snow.

Danny said, "I haven't seen this view so perfectly before. You are a lucky woman, Etta."

"Yes, I am, thanks to Hadar."

He smiled. "I have great confidence in you, Odetta. I expect you to carry on the traditions of excellence that Heather Aldersen started. I just wish you'd met her."

"Me too, Hadar. I'm happy to have this home and look forward to working at the gallery. It feels like too much."

"It will only be too much if you don't follow through on your dreams."

She touched his hand. "It's nearly overwhelming though."

"Let's do it the elephant way."

She grinned and nodded. "Yes, one bite at a time."

He nodded and pulled out the two key rings filled with the keys for the gallery. "Let's set the fobs for your fingerprints, Danny's fingerprints and my fingerprints."

Danny asked, "Are you sure, Hadar?"

"Yes, I'm sure. You will work with Odetta for a few weeks, or at least until Tamal Chowdhury is sure to remain in the custody of the legal system." He shrugged his shoulders. "Then it will be up to you and Odetta to decide what will be your life and relationship in the future."

"But, if both Danny and I have keys, what about you? Don't you need a set of keys?"

"Yes, I do. There is a spare set in the safe in Heather's apartment. That will be my set until I can have another duplicate set made."

Odetta smiled at the man who had become a father figure for her life. "I'll do my very best."

"Of course, you will. I have faith in you. Now, let's get the keys and fobs synced, then head to the gallery. It's been closed for too many days."

Once they put away Odetta and Danny's few belongings from their time at the Four Seasons and set up the key fobs for the women, they walked back outside to Hadar's limousine. He said to Sander. "If you don't mind going with us, to the gallery, I'd appreciate it. I want your assessment of the safety measures in place as well as Danny's assessments. I want Odetta to always feel secure in the gallery."

Sander smiled, "I'd be happy to assist."

CHAPTER FORTY-TWO

Sally and Darren sat at their respective desks. Each was reading a copy of Tamal Chowdhury's diary. Most of it was the mundane musings of a self-centered woman and her recording of her daily life.

Sally found it hard to read. Tamal was so self-absorbed even in her diary, the words created a deep feeling of unease for the police officer.

Darren's thoughts were similar, but with the added feeling of delight that he was not attracted to such women. For both police officers, the last few years of the diary entries, the tone and tenor of the writings changed.

Sally muttered, "Incredible. I never really understood egocentric, narcissistic behavior before. This is amazing and chilling too." She continued to read, highlighting passages she thought might be relevant to the case in yellow. Several such entries could result in further charges. In pink, she highlighted passages that she thought might help to understand Tamal's behaviors and choices.

After three hours of reading and highlighting, she stopped to do research on sociopaths versus psychopaths. She shook her head, *it's as if every article defines Tamal Chowdhury. I wonder how many people she has actually killed and how many thousands of dollars she has stashed away.*

Thirty minutes later, Sally took her notes with the highlighted passages to Detective Jordan. He looked up and said, "I've just finished reading her diary. What are your thoughts?"

She handed him her copy of the diary and said, "I've highlighted several passages as you'll see."

Darren looked at her highlights and asked, "Why two different colors?"

"Yellow highlights might be directly pertinent to the case, or possible additional charges. For example, she detailed how she waited for Simon, how she killed him, buried him and hid the car. I also highlighted her killing Heather, taking her to Paris, then spending a luxurious evening in London before coming home. That creeped me out to the max. It was hard to read all the things she did to Heather to get her body into the suitcase. I'm glad I never had to see her body in the suitcase."

"I agree with you on that. It will be terrible enough to see her body here at the morgue."

Sally nodded. "The pink highlights might—and I emphasize might—help us understand her motivations and behaviors. For example, her desire to be sure her mother saw her first when she and her twin brother were being born. And, it wasn't just to be first, it was to be most adored."

Darren shook his head. "It's hard to imagine such profound egocentric expectations. I like your approach, Sally. Good work."

"Thanks. I also printed off some information about various personality disorders, too. I thought it might be helpful in understanding her."

"Maybe, but I doubt I'll ever understand her completely. I knew she suggested she might have been part of the reason her twin bother died. But in the diary, it seems she thinks or feels she purposefully killed him."

"Yeah, and that made me want to puke. Surely, an infant couldn't form such direct ideas and intent."

Darren sighed. "I sure as hell hope you are right. I also circled the places where she wrote about thefts of precious things just because she thought she deserved them or wanted to give them as gifts. Even then, the gifts were only to glorify herself. In one paragraph she said, 'Whatever I want is mine. Surely the rest of the world sees that.' And then this passage," he thumbed through a few pages. "Yeah, here it is. 'Amma will adore me, perhaps more than Simon, when I give her this diamond bracelet. Five carats is a little much, but as a gift for Amma, from me, perfect.' Totally creeped me out."

"Yeah, and that really pissed me off, too. The words 'uppity bitch' comes to mind. I'll check with the burglary and theft folks and see if they recognize any of the items she described."

"Good, but also check and see if we have taken any of those items as evidence. If we haven't, let's see how many of them we can find. We can add theft charges on top of the murder charges."

"What about the things she stole but gave as gifts?"

"Well, legally they are still stolen, but getting them back may be difficult."

"The emerald and diamond earrings stood out to me. We saw Basanti wear earrings, just like her journal described the first time we interviewed her. Since then she has worn plain silver studs."

Darren nodded. "I noticed them too. I hate like hell to pile more distress on Mrs. Chowdhury."

"Me too. But I think she may suspect the fancy things Tamal gave her were stolen."

"Let's see what we can learn about which items were reported stolen and go from there."

Kirsten Holt sat across from Tamal Chowdhury, whose handcuffs were locked to a steel bar on the table.

Tamal asked, "When are you getting me out of here?"

"No time soon, I'm afraid."

"Why not?"

"You were at the bail hearing, Ms. Chowdhury. The charges against you are significant and bail was denied."

Tamal shrugged. "Then get the charges dropped."

"I can't do that. You've incriminated yourself, six ways from Sunday. On top of your self-incrimination, the police have been very careful and have violated none of your rights."

Tamal seemed to ignore the words from her lawyer. "Look at these awful clothes they make me wear. Orange is not a color I would ever wear, but most especially not baggy, utilitarian clothing."

"In prison you do not have a right to fancy clothing or even plain clothing of your choice. Every woman in this jail wears the same clothing."

"I'm not every woman!" Tamal fumed and tapped her fingers on the table. "I've never said I committed any crime. How can you sit there and say I've incriminated myself?"

"You seriously don't know?"

Tamal glared at her lawyer but said nothing.

Kirsten shook her head and pulled a stack of papers out of her briefcase. "First, here's your ticket from Paris to London, and the next day from London to Seattle. Do you deny being there?"

"No, of course not."

"Where's your ticket from Seattle to Paris?"

"Not my problem to find out."

"Okay, fair enough," Kirsten said. "Here's the receipt for your dinner and luxury hotel stay in London."

"So what?"

"The wages you made at the gallery, did not support this lifestyle."

Tamal smiled. "I saved up for the trip."

"Do you know what the rest of this stack of paper is, Ms. Chowdhury?"

"No, why would I?"

Kirsten tapped on the pages. "This stack of paper is a copy of your personal diary given to me on discovery."

"Did you enjoy reading my private thoughts?"

"Not especially. Worse yet was reading the details of the deaths of your brother and Ms. Aldersen."

"Brothers, you mean," Tamal said.

Kirsten Holt felt a cold chill race from the top of her head to her toes. Nausea threatened to overwhelm her.

Tamal laughed. "You silly woman. Of course, I didn't kill anyone. How could I, as an infant, have killed my twin brother? It's ridiculous."

"I might agree with you had I not read the details in your handwritten diary."

"I make up stories all the time. I love writing about things I only wish I had the skill, courage, and wherewithal to do."

"So you are going to tell me and the court this entire diary is fiction?"

Tamal shrugged. "Sure. Why not?"

Kirsten watched her client's face and realized Tamal was actually enjoying herself. She shook her head.

Tamal asked, "Are you having fun yet, lawyer girl."

"No, I'm not."

Tamal smiled. "You can't tell anyone, anything I say, is that right?"

"Yes."

"Then ask me any question you want, and I'll tell you the truth."

"Are you capable of telling the truth?"

Tamal shrugged. "If I choose to do so."

"This diary covers only the past few years. Are there other diaries the police haven't yet found?"

"Certainly, but where they are is no one's business."

Kirsten nodded then asked, "Did you kill your brother Simon?"

"Yes."

"Did you kill Heather Aldersen?"

"Yes."

"Who else have you killed?"

"More people than you can imagine. I just missed an opportunity by one little day to kill that silly little Jamaican girl. I saw her walk by the gallery and look in the windows. Hadar Hamal thought he could foist her on me."

"Why do you kill anyone?"

"Because I need them out of the way of my goals for my life."

Kirsten folded her hands on the table and leaned forward. "What are your goals in life, Tamal?"

Tamal smiled. "So finally, you use my given name. Does this mean we are going to be friends?"

Kirsten sat still and quiet. She regretted using Tamal's given name.

Tamal leaned forward, as far as her restraints would allow, and caressed Kirsten's hands. The lawyer didn't move or look down at her hands. She kept her eyes on the woman across the table from her. Tamal licked her lips then said, "My goal in life is to be adored by everyone who is in my life. That includes you, dear Kirsten."

"What if I choose to not adore you?"

"Then I'll kill you too."

Kirsten nodded and pulled her hands back from Tamal's reach. "Good to know." She backed away from the table, quietly put the stack of papers in her briefcase, and shut the lid. She snapped the briefcase closed, stood up and went to the door. She pressed the button to be released.

Tamal started laughing then and said, "Good move, counselor. You are just a few inches out of my reach."

Kirsten shuddered and held her breath until the door opened and she could walk away from the vile woman who was her client.

CHAPTER FORTY-THREE

Kirsten sat in her father's law office. They sat, side-by-side, in deep leather chairs in his office, sharing a drink as they talked of her dilemma with her client. Wendall Holt observed his daughter as she told him of the interview with Tamal Chowdhury earlier in the afternoon. When she finished her tale he asked, "So what do you want to do?"

"My instinct is to run away fast and far."

"Do you have legal grounds to dismiss this client?"

She shook her head. "I don't think so. In fact, I'm not sure I'm doing the right thing discussing it with you."

"Well, I certainly won't discuss this conversation with anyone. I'm your personal attorney after all. If asked if we discussed this case, I would say only in very general terms. However, please don't gloss over the interview you had with her today. Your client threatened to kill you, Kirsten."

"Perhaps. But one could argue she was just saying she could if she really wanted to."

He nodded. "I see that point. What do you see as her best possible outcome?"

"That she admits to the murders of Simon Chowdhury and Heather Aldersen and not go to trial where I'm sure she'd be convicted of first-degree murder, two counts."

He pursed his lips, looked at the golden whiskey in his glass, swirled it a little, then said, "She implied she has killed others and that she intended to kill this Odetta Thomas woman as well. Is that correct?"

"Yes, but I stopped the interview before she could tell me who else she killed. I'm not sure I want to know."

"Let me think on this a bit, and you get home and sleep—as long as possible—if possible. Remember to take good care of yourself, please. I think I see a pathway of keeping her in prison for a long time, but maybe not indefinitely. There may be families out there without answers to their lost family members too."

"I agree, and that's sticking in my craw a bit, too." She sighed, drank the last of her cola and set the empty glass on the table between them. "Okay, Dad. I'll leave it with you and try to rest. But I doubt she'll go for any plea deal. She thinks she is justified in killing anyone who gets in her way. Then there are all the big-ticket items she's stolen."

"You didn't talk with her about those, did you?"

"No. I was too wigged out to even think of discussing them. I'm worried about the fact she admitted there were more dairies, but she wouldn't tell me where they are."

"My guess is a safe deposit box."

"Maybe. I might push her on that a bit too."

"Good," her father said. "There's bound to be a way to get her to admit her wrongdoings and keep her in prison. What you've tallied so far is a minimum of two life-time, non-concurrent stays in prison. This little darling won't be happy with those odds. She would hate coming out of prison a wizened old woman."

Kirsten smiled and chuckled softly. "Indeed, she would hate that outcome. Thanks for talking with me. This is the first time I've felt in over my head."

He chuckled and shook his head. "Just wait. It won't be your last."

She grinned, stood up and kissed her father on the cheek. "I love you, Dad."

He patted her hand. "And I you."

Stan texted the men of Old Man Coffee and said, *my wife and I are making donuts tomorrow morning. Bring your coffee mugs and hungry bellies. I'm starting the eating of donuts at seven a.m. on the dot. Simon deserves a donut send-off.*

The replies quickly dinged on his phone. The four remaining men of Old Man Coffee would celebrate their friend's life in the style to which they'd become accustomed. Coffee and donuts.

Odetta called Roger Cookson and asked, "You may not know who I am, but I'm Odetta Thomas. Hadar Hamal brought me to the states to work with Heather Aldersen at The Pacific Arts Gallery."

Roger smiled. "I've never met you, Ms. Thomas, but I've heard a lot about you."

"I hope it has all been good."

"It has. How can I help you?"

"Well," She said, "It's more how your mother-in-law can help me. I didn't know how to get in touch with her. Mr. Hamal had your number and suggested I try through you."

"She is sleeping right now. She's pretty tired with all the uproar of the past several days."

"I'm sure she is. I heard through the grapevine, known as Hadar Hamal, that she wanted to create a business of pastries and sweet treats. We had the pleasure of tasting her lemon cookies."

"I did too, and they are great. Were you wanting her to bake for a gallery event?"

Odetta smiled. "Yes, but more than that. I was wondering if she could come to the gallery tomorrow morning and visit with me."

"We had planned to go to Edmonds in the morning to get some of her things. She doesn't want to go back to her house yet. In fact, I'm not sure she wants to go back there ever."

"I understand and told Mr. Hamal, I felt she might not be comfortable there anymore. I've an idea that might be helpful for her and certainly helpful for me and the gallery."

"Sounds intriguing."

"Well, if you can bring her here, we could talk about the specifics."

Roger said, "I have a meeting with friends early in the morning. How would ten tomorrow morning be?"

"Perfect. I look forward to meeting you both."

Roger smiled as he hung up the phone. *My guess is with Hadar Hamal in the middle of things, the idea will be a splendid thing for Amma. I want her to move on with her life and create fresh ways of being. She isn't nearly old enough to give up yet.*

Tamal Chowdhury paced in her cell. The injustices she had been dealt kept her from being able to sleep. Her 'roomie' was snoring in the bottom bed of the bunk, which didn't help at all. So, she'd climbed out of her upper bunk and began pacing and thinking.

Her thoughts blazed and bounced through her mind. She was unaware when she began to verbalize aloud as she paced. At first it was just muttered whispers.

"Simon, if you hadn't been such a pompous shit, I wouldn't be here. You learned too well from Baba in his old beat-up Volvo. Darling, precious Heather. What a sniveling, driveling woman you were. If you'd continued teaching art at a small private college, you'd be alive today. You didn't give me a chance to show my skills to Hadar Hamal. Now there's a man who understands beauty. I know if he'd spent a bit more time with me, he would have seen and believed in my superior qualities."

Her voice was still quiet, but a little louder than a whisper.

"I feel a little bad killing the kid who smeared his chocolate ice cream on my favorite silk scarf. It was an Akris cashmere and silk beauty and cost nearly a thousand dollars. Besides, how was I to know the little shit was allergic to peanuts when I smeared my peanut butter and chocolate ice cream on his face. But still. I shouldn't have killed him in a public park. I could have followed him and given him a good sharp whack. That wouldn't have been difficult."

She smiled and even giggled a little.

"Oh, Tamal, control your temper! But why should I? Putting up with silly people, and stupid people, and nasty little kids is more than I should have to bear. I'm so relieved I'll have no children. My body is too perfect to let anything, especially a child, stretch it out of shape."

Now her voice became strident and even louder.

"But, no! Roger just had to have a baby! Amma had to beg for a grandchild, and Simon hounded me day after day after day. Well—at least week after week. If everyone had appreciated my beauty and superior qualities, they'd never have expected me to have a snot-nosed kid around. Certainly, I should never have to squeeze out a sniveling brat." She stomped her foot on the concrete floor. "None of this is my fault!"

The woman on the bottom bunk leaned out of the bed a little and said, "Hey, little Miss Prissy Pants, shut the fuck up!"

She turned to the woman who shared a cell with her. "I wasn't talking to you."

"I don't care if you were talking to the Blessed Virgin Mary, shut the fuck up."

Tamal swirled around and with the heel of her right foot, slammed the woman's nose into her brain. She smiled as the now dead woman flopped back onto her thin mattress. "No, dear. You shut the fuck up."

Tamal climbed up onto the top bunk, crawled under the covers and went to sleep. Her last thought before sleep took over was, *I feel better now.*

CHAPTER FORTY-FOUR

Out in his music studio, Stan decided to journey before the men arrived. His wife Renee, and their daughter Nina were putting the finishing touches on an assortment of donuts for them all.

He lay down on his yoga mat, turned on the journey drumming music, and went to The Tooth of Time at the Philmont Scout Ranch in New Mexico. Once he was in the Lower World, he looked around to see his Power Animal, the Elk named Nelson. As usual, Nelson was eating grass. When he heard Stan approaching, he looked up, grinning with long stems of ripe grass dangling from his mouth.

Stan laughed and waved at the goofy Elk. "Hey, Nelson, do you always have grass hanging out of your mouth?"

"Only until I lick it into my mouth." With a loud slurp, he did just that. Then he asked, "What's up, buddy? You have Old Man Coffee this morning?"

"Yes, I do. I just wanted to check in and see how Simon is doing."

"He's doing well, but he's a little sad this morning."

"Why is he sad?"

The Elk shook his head. "His sister killed a woman."

"Well, we all know about that, Nelson."

"No, you don't. Not this woman."

"Who is she?"

Nelson chewed the grass in his mouth and swallowed. "She's the one on the bottom bunk. I'm not sure what a bunk is, but she's on the bottom with a bloody nose."

"Ah. I bet the bunk is one of the beds in jail. Why is her nose bloody?"

"Simon's sister kicked her nose up into her brain."

Stan was shocked and felt tears starting. "Why would she do that?"

"Because the woman told her she wasn't the Blessed Virgin Mary, and to shut the fuck up." The Elk shook his head. "Everyone knows Tamal isn't the BVM."

Stan nodded. "Well, of course we do. Poor Basanti and Simon."

"Well, Simon said it was bound to happen."

"Why would he say that?"

"Simon said, she's out of control and no one should expect her to be any different. Simon says, that was his big mistake."

"I guess that's true. Did Simon have anything else to say?"

"Yeah, as a matter of fact, he did. He said to tell Roger, to tell Basanti there's a great kitchen and pretty apartment waiting for her. She doesn't even have to ask for it or pay for it."

Stan smiled and patted the Elk's head. "Well, that's good news. Tell Simon, Roger says they will release his body soon. He'll take it to the Recompose place in Seattle. It's where Simon said he wanted to go."

"I'll tell him. I think letting his body go is the only thing holding him back now that he knows his mother has a great place to go live and make a new life."

"Good. I will tell Roger. There's the call back."

"Yep. There's a cute little doe I want to chat with."

Stan laughed. "Good luck, buddy." Then Stan went back to Ordinary Reality. He sat up, took a drink of water, and wrote his journey in his journal. Just as he finished, there was a knock on the door.

He said, "Come in!"

Nina popped her head in the door. "Hey, Daddy! We've got lots of donuts ready for you."

"Good deal, I'll come get them. The fellas will be here soon."

"Except for Simon."

Stan nodded. "Yes, but he'll be here in our hearts. Always."

She smiled and took her father's hand. "Come on. Momma

won't let me eat any until you pick out the ones you want for Old Man Coffee."

"I'm with you!"

Roger, Harvey, and Jack joined Stan in his music studio. Harvey said, "You've done a fine job building this room, Stan."

"Thanks. I really appreciate your and Roger's help and advice."

"Hell, I did little but pontificate. Our buddy Roger here is the one who really knew what he was talking about."

Jack said, "I like how you've laid things out. Can't wait to get the gang in here and record some tunes."

"Me too," Stan said. "I've got a bit more trim work to do, then we'll be all set."

The men chatted. They all teased Harvey about his honeymoon and his response was, "You fellas are simply jealous. I have a beautiful wife who gave me a glorious holiday. She looks great in her little bikinis, which makes an old man sit up and take notice."

They all laughed, then Stan asked, "When do you go back to work?"

"Tomorrow, bright and early. The boss said he filled my schedule up for the next few weeks so to not get any more travel ideas in my pea brain."

The men laughed and teased him some more. Then Roger said, "I wanted to fill you guys in about Simon. His body will be released later today."

Harvey asked, "Is there going to be a funeral?"

"Basanti wants to wait until we have Simon's dirt."

Stan laughed when he saw the stunned faces on Harvey and Jack. Roger grinned, "Sorry. I'd already told Stan about this, but not you two. Simon's body will go to a place called Recompose."

"What's that?" Jack asked.

"It's a funeral home type of place. The medical examiner's

office will send his body there. He'll be placed in a long tube, where they will lay him on a pile of wood chips, alfalfa, and straw. Then they will cover Simon with more plant material. After about thirty days or so, Simon will be a nutrient rich soil. Basanti wants to wait until she has some of the soil. She wants to work it into her gardens at her home in Edmonds.

"You said 'some soil.' Does that mean she won't want all of it?"

Roger grinned. "Yeah, it turns out the average human body, when composted naturally results in about a pickup load of soil. She's donating most of it to Bell's Mountain in southern Washington. The soil will be used to revitalize the wetlands there and deforested parts of the mountain."

Harvey said, "I like it. I'll look it up for me too."

Stan asked, "When is Basanti wanting to have a funeral?"

"She's really not sure. Right now, with Tamal in prison, and me and Tamal getting a divorce, Basanti just isn't ready to say her final goodbye to her son."

Jack shook his head. "I'm so sorry for you, Roger, and all of Tamal's family. I can't imagine how awful all of this is."

"Thanks. It is awful. Right now, I can't see what my future holds, so I'm going to keep building homes, supporting Basanti and loving Pavlov."

Stan reached out and touched Roger's arm. "I went on a journey before you guys showed up today. I can share it with you privately or here with the group."

"Share the good bits now with us all. I think if there is anything awful, I want to hear it in private."

Stan nodded. "Well, I think this is a good thing. I told my goofball Elk, Nelson about Recompose. He said Simon knew and was happy you and Basanti are following through on his wishes. He also told me to tell you and your mother-in-law there is a place with a beautiful chef's kitchen and apartment. She doesn't have to pay a penny or even ask to be there."

Roger laughed. "I bet that is what Odetta, the new curator taking Heather's place, was talking about yesterday evening."

"There you go."

Harvey stood up and said, "I'm going to head home and enjoy my last vacation day before getting back to the grind."

"I'm heading out too," Jack said. "I'm going to look at a Djembe over on Vashon. It was made by Gordy Ryan. I learned a lot from him, and I'm looking forward to adding one of his drums to my collection. Besides, I'm wanting to add some African beats to our tunes."

Stan smiled, "I look forward to it."

After Jack and Harvey left, Stan said, "I hate like hell to pile on to your troubles, Roger, but maybe giving you a heads-up will help."

Roger sat back down and said, "I'd like to say I wouldn't be surprised at anything, but saying so wouldn't make it so."

Stan nodded. "I get that, buddy. Nelson told me that Tamal killed her cellmate last night."

"Holy shit. I haven't heard about it yet."

"Well, maybe he interpreted it wrong. He said she kicked the woman on the bottom bunk. She kicked the woman's nose into her brain."

Roger shuddered as tears rolled down his face. After a few minutes of quiet he said, "I can't say I'm surprised but, damn, I wish I couldn't believe she'd do such a thing." He stood up and sighed. "I will not tell Amma until we hear it from the police. She deserves, at least for this one morning, to have something good in her life."

Stan hugged Roger and said, "Keep on keeping on, buddy. I have faith in you and Amma."

"Your faith helps me—a lot." He left Stan's studio and walked the three blocks to Simon's home, which was now his. The sun was shining, the sky was blue, and the breeze was gentle and cool.

He found it difficult to believe his wife tainted this beautiful day with yet another murder.

CHAPTER FORTY-FIVE

Tamal was sleeping soundly when the klaxon sounded. She sat up too quickly and bumped her head on the ceiling. Before she could climb down out of the bed, one of the guards came in banging on the bed with his stick.

"Wakey, wakey, ladies!"

"I'm awake," Tamal groaned. "Now go away."

"That's not how things work around her darlin' and you know it. He banged on the bed again and tugged on the other woman's foot. "Come on, Mable. Time to get your raggedy ass out of bed."

When she didn't respond, he looked closer. He shook his head and hit the bed with his stick again. "Dammit all! Why does this shit happen on my watch?"

Tamal swung her feet over the edge of the bed. "What's up, Earl?"

He looked up and saw the blood on Tamal's heel. He jerked her down from the top bunk and threw her onto the floor. He put handcuffs on her behind her back.

Tamal shouted, "You idiot, Earl. What the fuck are you doing?"

He pressed a button on his shoulder mic and shouted. "Woman down! Woman down! I need assistance."

The klaxon sounded again as he backed out of the cell and waited for backup.

Tamal rolled over with her cuffed hands behind her back. She shook her head. "What are you screaming about, you slime bucket?"

Two more guards joined Earl, and he said, "See that blood on her heel?" He pointed to Tamal. "I think we'll learn it is Mable's blood."

One of the guards asked, "Why?"

"Mable's dead with a bloody nose. This little prissy pant has blood on her heel. My guess is she killed Mable."

"Of course, I didn't kill Mable, you idiot. I was asleep. She's probably not even dead." Tamal scooted closer to Mable's bed. She looked at her bunk mate. Mabel's face was covered with blood, and what wasn't covered in blood was blue. Her eyes were wide open and cloudy.

Tamal said, "Well, shit." She looked up at the guards. For once in her life, she had the good sense to say nothing.

Two of the guards came into the cell, picked Tamal up by the elbows, and quickly walked her out of the cell to a solitary confinement cell at the end of the row. They tossed her into the room, none too gently, and slammed the door.

A few minutes before ten in the morning, Roger and Basanti walked into The Pacific Arts Gallery. Odetta greeted them. "Thank you, Roger, for bringing Mrs. Chowdhury to visit with me."

Basanti smiled, "Please call me Basanti."

"Thank you, Basanti. I know you probably have been here several times and so are familiar with the Gallery."

Basanti said, "I was here only once when my daughter Tamal first started working here."

Odetta nodded. "I'm so sorry for the troubles you've been having. I'm sure it is very hard to deal with."

"It has been difficult, but I'm a strong woman."

Odetta turned and locked the front door. She left the *CLOSED* sign in the window. "I'm sure you are. I wanted to show you something upstairs and then chat a little if you have the time."

Basanti looked at Roger, who nodded. Basanti said, "We've the time. I am curious though. Roger told me you needed my help. I'm not sure there is anything I can do to help you but will do anything to make your life easier. I'm sure my daughter's activities have put stress on you."

"Please, don't worry about me. My aim is to help us both. Let's go upstairs. I want to show you some things and have a chat."

Once they were at the elevator behind the showroom, she opened the doors and invited them to join her. While the elevator took them to the third floor, Odetta said, "On this floor is what I wanted to speak with you about. I hope we will be able to help each other."

The door opened, and they stepped out into the main room of the event space.

Basanti said, "This is a lovely room. Is this where parties and gallery events are held?"

"Yes, that is exactly what happens in this room. Of course, since I'm new here, I've never hosted an event."

Basanti nodded. "I'm not sure how I can be of service to you, my dear."

"Come and let me show you the kitchen." Odetta led them to a full, commercial chef's kitchen with a twelve-burner stove, ovens, gleaming stainless-steel tables and much more.

Basanti looked around the room and smiled. She walked around and touched various things in the room. She opened the big oven doors, the walk-in freezer, the huge refrigerators with glass front doors and the large pantry. She smiled and said, "This is a big enough kitchen for many cooks."

Odetta nodded. "I'm not a skilled cook, but I've heard you are."

"Yes, I love to cook and bake."

"That's terrific, but it is only a small part of what I need you for."

"What else do you need me for?"

"I want to show you more of what is up here. There is a beautiful and comfortable place where we can sit. There, I can tell you, my ideas."

"More beautiful than these two rooms?"

"To my mind, yes. This is lovely, but just for show. Follow me to what I think of as a secret garden, a lovely place."

Roger said, "I wasn't aware you'd been here long enough to feel as you do about any part of the gallery."

She smiled. "You are right, but wrong, too."

He chuckled.

"Just wait. You'll understand in a few minutes."

She led them out of the kitchen and across the large gathering room. She pointed outside, "Later I'll show you how all the balconies work. There are terrific views from them. For now, let's go to the bookcase wall."

Roger and Basanti followed Odetta. When she stood in front of the end of the floor to ceiling bookcase, she said, "All we have to do is open this wall."

"How?" Roger asked.

"Like this." She went to the book Hadar had shown her and touched it. "This book, *The Secret Garden,* triggers a device that opens the wall."

Roger said, "So secret garden isn't just a feeling, then?"

"You're right, but you'll understand when you see what's next." She pulled the book forward and down. The wall quietly opened. She led them down the short hallway to a door. She unlocked the door, turned to Basanti, and said, "Please, you go first."

Basanti smiled and walked into the living room of the private apartment. Once again she touched various pieces of furniture, then turned to Odetta. "This *is* lovely, and you are right, it feels like a secret garden."

"I'm glad you like it. My friend Danny and I spent a few hours here yesterday, cleaning this apartment and making sure everything would be ready for you."

"For me?"

"Yes, for you. The details are this is a twelve hundred square foot two-bedroom apartment with a study, kitchen, pantry, laundry and balcony facing the sound."

"This is truly remarkable," Basanti said.

Odetta said, "I'd like for you to just walk through the apartment—every room—then come back here and sit with me for a chat."

Basanti smiled and nodded.

Roger asked, "Shall I wait with Odetta?"

"That will be fine. I'll let you know if I need help."

He smiled and sat in one of the overstuffed chairs by the fireplace. Odetta sat in a chair beside him. As Basanti left the room and walked through the apartment he asked, "Is this an apartment you are offering for Basanti to live in?"

"Yes, it is, but there are strings attached."

He smiled. "There always are."

After a few minutes of polite chatting, Basanti entered the living room. She said, "All right, young lady. Tell me your proposition."

Odetta grinned. "Happily. Will you join us?"

Basanti sat down on the sofa and said, "I've left my purse in the main bedroom assuming you want me to live here."

Odetta clapped her hands and laughed. "Yes, please! But. I want you to do much more than just live here. Mr. Hamal suggested I ask you to help me with the legal and financial side of the gallery. I'm from Jamaica, which you might have noticed from my accent."

"But, don't you want to live here?"

"No, I have a nice home here in town looking out on the sound."

"Ah. What are the terms of my employment?"

"You may create your culinary treats business using the big chef's kitchen as much as you wish. You'll be the planner and head chef for events held here a few times a year. You'll teach me the ins and outs of being a business owner. You'll keep all the gallery records, taxes, and accounts receivable—at least that's what Hadar called them. I call them bills that need to be paid. I'll pay you a reasonable salary for your work. How does forty thousand a year plus this apartment sound to you?"

Basanti smiled. "It is too much money, but I'll take it."

Roger laughed. "Good for you, Amma!"

Odetta shook her head, smiling. "What is Amma?"

"Amma, is an endearment for Mother from my Hindu culture."

"Ah. In my Jamaican culture we call our dear mothers Muma."

Basanti nodded. "Either will be fine for me."

Odetta grinned. "We are going to be lovely friends. I just know it."

CHAPTER FORTY-SIX

Darren called Sally into his office.

"What's up, boss?"

"Tamal murdered her cellmate last night."

"Holy shit, Darren. How did she do that?"

He smiled slightly, appreciating she'd used his name. "Apparently something happened in the cell to piss Tamal off, and with one quick kick of her heel, her cellmate's nose was plunged into her brain."

"Does her lawyer know?"

"I just got off the phone with the Prosecuting Attorney, Janice Sutton. She has informed Ms. Holt of her client's latest escapades."

"I actually feel sorry for her."

"Who? Kirsten Holt or Tamal Chowdhury?"

"Absolutely not Tamal, but her lawyer. It must be very hard to represent someone so very evil."

"Yes, I'm sure it is. It's one of the reasons I decided not to be a lawyer."

"Yes, and one of the reasons I do only legal aid work as a lawyer. What do you think will happen next?"

"Ms. Sutton said for us to continue working on our investigations, including the thefts, and any other possible crimes Tamal has committed. My best guess is there are more murders. Her only possible hope of getting out of prison, ever, is to make some sort of plea agreement. Later today, I'm to join the Prosecuting Attorney and Kirsten Holt. The three of us will interview Tamal."

"There are three murders we know for sure, then her father's murder, and her implied utterances that there have been more murders. If her prison terms aren't concurrent, she'll never get out of prison. We're talking a minimum of fifty years already."

"I know," Darren said. "It's mind-boggling to consider. What's with women being serial killers of late? This is our second one in two years."

"It's called equal opportunity."

Darren laughed, then shook his head. "I don't know about that."

"I do. The more women push for equality, the more things we used to be adept at hiding, are now in plain view."

"What do you mean?"

"I think women have done as much killing, serial or otherwise, as men throughout history. We aren't just pretty faces, you know."

He chuckled. "So I've heard."

She grinned. "Seriously though, I think women are less likely to be considered as killers and therefore get away with it more often than men."

"Maybe. I just hate to think in those terms."

"Well, I have zero proof of my conclusions. I've been researching the issue for several months now. There are some very notorious women serial killers, who are every bit as brutal as men, but still far fewer than men. But that's according only to the research with *known* serial killers."

"I'd heard 80 to 90% of all serial killers are men."

"Yeah, you're right on the stats. I simply don't believe it is that cut and dried. I don't think we know, for sure, how many women have been serial killers. Women are generally more quiet killers, using poisoning, drowning, or smothering as their main method. Therefore, they might never be discovered, which is usually the plan for women. They also kill longer."

"Well, our Tamal Chowdhury isn't a quiet killer, nor a gentle one."

"No, she is not. I think she is an emotional killer."

Darren looked up at Sally. "How so?"

"*If* she murdered her twin in utero, it was so she would be more loved by her mother. If she murdered her father, it was to get him to quit hounding her to marry and have children."

"But she married."

"Only after her father's death. I think she married because she wanted a beautiful home. Roger built a beautiful home. Roger was simply a means to an end. She killed Simon to get him to quit telling her what to do all the time. Then, she killed Heather Aldersen because she thought Heather was beneath her and she wanted the gallery all to herself. My guess is they argued. When that happened, Heather acceded to Hadar Hamal's suggestion that he found a replacement for her. Tamal simply couldn't tolerate being shoved aside."

"Is that why you gave me the research on sociopathic and personality disorders?"

She nodded. "It seems to me, understanding the why of the killing, is pivotal to whether someone will kill more than one time. Anyone might kill someone if they feel their lives are in danger or even when pushed too far. Not Tamal. She kills because she either isn't getting her perceived due, or because others push her to change. If she'd killed only once, no one would have noticed. Her ego demands she destroy anyone who doesn't adore her."

"I wonder why she didn't kill Roger or her mother, Basanti?"

Sally shrugged her shoulders. "I think she would have. Roger undermined her anger by agreeing to a divorce, and giving her the house, lock, stock and barrel. I think she loved her mother because her mother did special things for her. Also, Basanti agreed that both her husband and Simon nagged too much. But make no mistake, Darren. If Basanti had stood up to Tamal, or not done special things for her, she too would be dead."

"I hope they keep her in solitary after this."

"No shit."

Darren laughed. "Officer, you surprise me."

"Nah. Just stating the unvarnished truth."

"I guess the truth is best given raw."

"There's one more thing, Darren."

"What?"

"I think Tamal wants recognition of her skills as a killer. Her ego demands recognition of all her prowess in life. She *wants* to crow about the people she has killed."

"I hope you're right. In a way, hearing her story, directly from her would be a relief."

Sally shrugged her shoulders. "Maybe. Are you sure you can bear the truth?"

Darren sat back in his chair, nodded and said, "Oh. Maybe I should be careful what I wish for."

Sally nodded. "Just sayin'."

Roger took Basanti to her house and helped her with packing up her belongings and things she wished to keep. She left many things behind, which surprised Roger. "Amma, I'm surprised you are not taking more things with you."

She smiled and patted his cheek. "There is truly nothing I'm leaving behind that I'm emotionally attached to."

"You've left a lot of valuable jewelry, Amma. What shall we do with it all?"

"I've kept pieces that Simon or you or my dear husband gave me. There are a few pieces I bought for myself. The rest I want gone from my life. I suggest you box it all up and take it to that nice detective. I think most of the jewelry is stolen."

Roger shook his head. "You may be right, Amma, but it breaks my heart that Tamal has done so much harm."

"What she has done is not our burden to bear. We cannot undo what she has done, but we don't have to hang on to the ill-gotten gains either."

"I can understand how you feel, Amma. What are you going to do with the house?"

"I haven't decided yet, but I have a question about it. Do you want to live here?"

"I've never thought about it, Amma. Maybe. Can I think about it?"

"Certainly. What would you do with Simon's house?"

"I'd lease it out at a reasonable price for the right client, or maybe sell it."

Basanti smiled. "You are my only remaining son. I would like to have my son near me."

"Thanks, Amma. I'll think about moving here." He turned and looked through the large front window. "The sound and islands are beautiful to behold, Amma."

"You are a good man, Beta. You deserve beauty around you. I wonder what Tamal will do with the beautiful home you built for her?"

Roger shook his head. "I've no idea. I've been thinking about all the properties. Bottom line, it is just property, just stuff. I'd much rather that none of the evil we've endured had happened."

"Yes, my feelings are the same. It seems to me evil is always the greedy path. Sometimes the path is simple and sometimes not. But when we take the simple path without giving thanks for our blessings and good luck, we build more and more greed around ourselves. Then greed becomes the goal, which creates even more evil."

Roger nodded. "Sounds like Ganesh. Being able to see and understand before walking on a path is the only way to avoid evil."

"Yes, but the corollary is true as well. When a good path stands before us and we fear taking it, then my son, darkness compels us to evil and greed. We lament what we could have had—what was given to us and we didn't take. I'm taking all the good and lovely things life has given me. I hope in doing so I can make the world brighter. Everything else, I'm leaving behind."

"And you will create even more tasty delights for us all," Roger said and grinned.

"Of course! Now, do we need a big truck to haul my things to my new home or will yours suffice?"

Roger looked around the room filled with the boxes of

Basanti's life. He shook his head. "No Amma. I will count it a blessing to load your boxes into my truck and carry them for you." He grinned and scratched his head. "But it'll will take three or four loads."

"You're a wonderful son."

CHAPTER FORTY-SEVEN

Tamal's interview would take place in a larger room at the prison than the police department could provide. The room had glass windows all around.

When the guards took her to the room, she looked around and smiled. She knew behind one window, there would be other people watching the interview. They would listen to her every word and record both video and audio of the interview. She felt a little thrill at the idea of her words and beauty recorded for all eternity. She did love an audience.

She had been a little tired from the activities of last night, and all the bustle and hustle of today. Now she was excited.

The police, attorneys and guards thought they could add the murder of Mabel O'Bryant to Tamal's list. Such silly people. Regardless, she knew she should be released. It was difficult for her to think of mouthy Mable as a human being, much less a woman to be mourned. She'd done the world a favor. She smiled, remembering the speed and agility with which she dispatched a really loathsome woman from this plane of existence. She grinned, thinking, *they should give me a medal.*

Detective Darren Jordan sat diagonally across from Tamal Chowdhury. He felt the hair on the back of his neck rise as she smiled at him. He remembered his discussion with Sally about women serial killers. He found no comfort from their conversation in this moment.

Kirsten Holt sat beside Tamal Chowdhury. To Darren, Kirsten looked smaller today than previously. She held her arms close to her side. She clasped her hands on top of her open notebook and cast her eyes on her fingers.

Tamal smiled and pushed her shoulder into Kirsten's. "How nice to sit close to you, Kirsten."

Kirsten couldn't stop the involuntary shudder. To Darren's mind, she seemed to shrink and her face paled.

Janice Sutton, the prosecuting attorney, saw the shudder. She sat directly across from Tamal, and said, "Ms. Chowdhury you are in a lot of trouble. I suggest you not make more problems for yourself. Ms. Holt, would you be more comfortable if we traded places?"

"Yes, but it isn't necessary. I really don't think Tamal will try to kill me here in front of you. She does whatever she does for her own well-being."

Darren said nothing but thought, *she's done nothing I can see for her own well-being. Maybe for her ego, but certainly not for her own well-being.*

Ms. Sutton continued, "Let the record show we are in conference with Ms. Tamal Chowdhury, her attorney of record, Ms. Kirsten Holt and arresting officer Detective Darren Jordan. We will interview Ms. Tamal Chowdhury regarding recent events." She looked up and asked, "Does anyone present wish to say anything before we begin the formal questions?"

No one answered, but Tamal wiggled a little in her chair and stretched her neck to hold her head high, looking down on the rest of the participants.

"Good," Ms. Sutton said. "Let's begin. Ms. Chowdhury, have you been apprised of your rights under the laws of Washington State?"

"Oh, my goodness, yes." She smiled at Darren and licked her lips. "Detective Jordan has read me my rights several times. Boring stuff every damned time he read them."

"Do you understand your right to an attorney?"

"Yes, and I have my dear little attorney right here beside me." She smirked a little, but the Prosecuting Attorney ignored her.

"Do you understand your right to not answer questions we ask you?"

She glared at Ms. Sutton. "Of course, I do. I'm not a simpleton."

"Do you understand you have a right to stop any questioning at any time?"

"Yeah, yeah, yeah. *And* I understand all the rest of the drivel, including anything I say will be held against me in court."

"Good. Now, Ms. Chowdhury, do you know why you're here today?"

Tamal laughed. "You all think I've done *terrible* things. You want to lock me up and throw away the keys."

"Do you know what those terrible things are?"

"Well, I think it is a matter of opinion whether they are terrible."

"Then I'll tell you why you are here."

"So kind of you to do so," Tamal responded but continued to glare at the Prosecuting Attorney. She envisioned the attorney with her eyes gouged out and blood pouring down her face. The vision helped her to calm down a little.

"You are charged with murdering Heather Aldersen, owner of The Pacific Arts Gallery on the 17th of December of last year. You are charged with forcing her body into a large suitcase, boarding a plane with her body in the luggage compartment of the same plane at the SeaTac Airport. You flew to Paris, France, and used Ms. Aldersen's passport for the trip. You are charged for using a passport that was not your own. You are charged with leaving her body in the suitcase on the luggage carousel in the Paris, France airport. You are charged with embezzlement of four thousand dollars from The Pacific Arts Gallery. Part of that money was to pay for your trip and that of Ms. Aldersen's body to Paris, France. You are charged with murdering your brother, Simon Chowdhury, early in the morning of December 31st of last year on Little Si Mountain in North Bend, Washington. You are charged with stealing your brother's car, then hiding it behind the Sallal Grange in North Bend, Washington. You are charged with the murder of Mable O'Bryant, an inmate at the King County Detention Center sometime after midnight this morning. Do you understand these charges?"

"Yes. I'm not a simpleton. However, you make it sound like I just go around killing people, willy-nilly, for no good reason."

"How would you make it sound, Ms. Chowdhury? How could these killings have good reasons?"

"Well, in the first place Heather Aldersen was a snippy bitch. She didn't appreciate my skill or beauty. She was going to go along with Hadar Hamal's suggestion she should fire me. The plan was to bring in a little Jamaican urchin to replace me. She earned her death. After all, she got to go to Paris."

"What about your brother?"

Tamal rolled her eyes and sighed. "He was lucky he lived as long as he did. He just *would not* shut up! Simon says! Simon says! He bossed me around constantly. I tired of his bossiness and thinking he had a right to tell me what to do with my life. Head of the family, my ass! He had his head *up* his ass."

"And the killing of Mable O'Bryant?"

"Well, she is certainly no loss to society. Surely, even you see that. She never brushed her teeth, never bathed, and stank to high heaven. Then last night I couldn't sleep. I was trying to sort out, in my mind, how to handle this little kerfuffle I'm in." She shrugged her shoulders. "You know, talking it through. The disgusting woman told me to shut the fuck up. I had a better idea. I made her shut the fuck up. She was useless anyway. Now the state doesn't have to feed her."

"Do you enjoy killing people, Ms. Chowdhury?"

"I wouldn't say *enjoy*. I simply do what needs to be done. However, I take pride and pleasure in a job well done."

Janice Sutton kept things friendly, though deep inside she felt revulsion for the woman sitting across from her. "So when you kill someone it is because it needs to be done?"

"Yes. There's no other reason for killing."

The attorney nodded. "You seem to be a lovely woman with a lot going for you in life."

"Well, I am beautiful. Even so, there are many things I want to achieve in life."

"I see. Does it ever bother you that other people might not

agree with your views on killing people?"

"No. I've never worried about what anyone thinks about me *or* the people I've killed."

"Do you know how many people you've killed?"

Tamal shook her head and looked up at the ceiling. "Whew. I'd have to think about that to know for sure. There are so many."

"Take your time."

The Prosecuting Attorney looked at Kirsten Holt. She was pale and there was a sheen of perspiration above her upper lip. "Ms. Holt, are you okay?"

Kirsten shook her head, but before anyone else could say anything, Tamal said, "She's fine. She's just a little queasy with all of this. She couldn't do what I've done. She's just not woman enough."

Kirsten said, "You are right, Ms. Chowdhury. I'm not sure I could do what you've done even once."

"Oh, it's no big deal. It gets easier and easier as time goes on."

"How long have you been killing people?" Darren Jordan asked.

"All my life, little man. From my infancy onward. All my life."

Janice Sutton said, "Let's halt the interview. I need a break."

Everyone but Tamal stood up. She smiled at them. "I'm only guilty of doing what I have to do for me. I'm so sorry if you can't take the truth."

Ms. Sutton pushed the button by the door. A guard came immediately and asked, "Everything all right in here?"

"Depends on who you ask. We're taking a break. Please take Ms. Chowdhury back to her cell."

"But don't you want to hear what else I have to say?"

"I do, but I need a break. We'll talk again soon."

Tamal's laughter felt like fingernails on a chalkboard to Darren. *I'm sure it felt that way to everyone except Tamal.*

CHAPTER FORTY-EIGHT

After Roger unloaded the first truckload of Basanti's belongings, he let Darren know about his mother-in-law's feelings about the jewelry. He called the detective's private number. Darren answered almost before the first ring tone finished.

"This is Detective Jordan. How may I help you?"

"This is Roger Cookson, Tamal's soon to be ex-husband."

Darren chuckled. "Lucky man. What's up?"

"I'll be relieved to no longer be married to her. I'm helping Basanti move into the apartment above the gallery here in Edmonds."

"She doesn't want to stay in her home?"

"No, she doesn't. I think she is ready to build a new life and has a great opportunity to do so."

"I'm glad. She is a lovely woman and makes incredible cookies."

Roger laughed. "That she does, but the reason I'm calling you is to alert you about something Basanti is worried about."

"What?"

"She fears a lot of very fashionable and expensive jewelry Tamal gave her is actually stolen."

"We've been wondering about that as well."

"Good," Roger said. "Basanti doesn't want to keep any of the jewelry. Some she has worn, but many pieces she has not. Some I think I may have paid for but don't remember. A few, really high dollar items still have the price tags on them. I never paid more than a hundred dollars for any jewelry other than Tamal's engagement ring. Anyway, Basanti wanted me to call you and get the jewelry to you."

"I would appreciate getting the jewelry. I'm at the detention center right now and will go in to continue interviewing Tamal with the Prosecuting Attorney. Could you take photos of the jewelry and send them to me?"

"Absolutely. I'll ask Odetta to keep the jewelry in the safe at the Gallery."

"Perfect. I'll call Sally to come pick them up later today. We'll compare the jewelry to our theft reports. But I want the photos to use as we continue questioning Tamal."

"I'll have the photos to you in the next five to ten minutes."

Odetta and Danny helped Basanti with unpacking her things. Basanti said, "I'd been thinking of selling my big old home. I wanted to start a new life. I didn't expect a new life to fall into my lap."

Danny said, "My momma always told me that if I do the right things in the right way, things will always turn out right."

"You have a wise mother."

"Yes, I do, and I'm very grateful for her presence in my life."

Odetta said, "I'm so sorry all this evil has come into your life, Basanti."

"Thank you. I'm going to work very hard to make up for the evil my daughter has done. I've known all along she was egocentric and thought only of herself. I never realized how deep her selfishness ran though."

"My Muma always said, 'There is love and evil in the world. To conquer evil, love must stay alert to all the possibilities because evil always cheats.'"

"Your mother was a wise woman. I've never thought of it that way, though. I wish love could truly conquer all. Obviously, it does not."

Odetta said, "Love is a blessing and helps us get through life, but we have to watch out for evil. I think Muma was right."

"I think so too, Odetta," Basanti said. "However, I think we must always work to keep evil at bay. Some say love conquers all. Some say light will always win. I disagree with both ideas. We must not let evil enter our hearts and minds, for evil always lies, cheats and glorifies pain and destruction. We must hold on to light and love."

Danny chuckled and shook her head, "Love, and even light, has a big job to do. Evil is a sneaky bastard."

The three women laughed together, forming new bonds of love.

Darren showed the photos of the jewelry Basanti thought might be stolen to the Prosecuting Attorney. "I have a police officer, checking these photos against the open theft cases right now. So far, we know the emerald earrings, the diamond bracelet, the amber beads, and jade pendant are on the list. These items alone are worth about twenty thousand dollars."

She smiled. "Thank you, detective. Let's print out all the photos before we go back in to talk with Ms. Chowdhury."

Back in the interview room, the Prosecuting Attorney handed the stack of photos to Tamal. She didn't ask a question or say anything. She just watched Tamal.

Tamal took the photos, looked at the top one. She smiled, "I gave these earrings to Amma. She would only wear them when I asked. Finally, I told her they cost five thousand dollars and she could be at least grateful for them. The diamond in each earring is nearly a whole carat and the emeralds are all real. No fake lab shit. Who wouldn't love these earrings?"

Janice Sutton said, "They are beautiful. You must truly love your mother to spend that much money on a pair of earrings."

"Silly woman. I never use *my* money for these baubles."

"Whose money do you use?"

"No one's mostly. I fall in love with this beautiful jewelry, and then it is mine."

The attorney tapped the stack of photos. "All of them?"

Tamal raised an eyebrow. "Let me look at them and I'll tell you." She looked at each photo and placed each photo in one of two stacks. The photo of the earrings was in a stack of several photos. The other stack was only two photos. She smiled and said, "These two items Roger and I bought together for Amma. They were both less than a hundred dollars. Trinkets, really. The rest, the superb pieces, I got for her."

"So, the two you and your husband bought were not stolen."

She shook her head. "No, they weren't stolen. Roger paid for them."

"Who paid for the rest of these?"

Tamal shrugged her shoulders.

The Prosecuting Attorney took the two photos of the jewelry that Tamal's husband had paid for and handed them to Darren. "These Mrs. Chowdhury can keep."

Tamal leaned forward and tapped her fingers on the table. "They all belong to Amma."

"Stolen property belongs with the person who owned the property before it was stolen, Ms. Chowdhury."

Tamal sat back in the chair and said, "Once they are mine, it is my choice where they go."

The attorney picked up the taller stack of photos and said to Tamal's attorney, "We'll give you copies of these photos when we charge Ms. Chowdhury for theft of these items."

Kirsten Holt nodded but before she could answer Tamal said, "You don't get it, do you? The jewelry is my property. I saw them, I loved them, they are mine."

Darren asked, "Did you pay money for them?"

Tamal glared at him. "No comment."

The Prosecuting Attorney, in a quiet, soothing voice, said, "Let's talk about these items later. I know you must be tired, Tamal."

Darren glanced at Tamal's face, which softened immediately.

It was amazing and creepy at the same time how quickly she changed her face when she didn't feel trapped.

Tamal sighed. "Yes, I am tired. I've been working very hard lately."

"I understand," Janice said. "You really need a break from everything. Is there anything else you want to discuss before we take a short break?"

"I do. Has Roger filed for divorce yet?"

"I don't know. Do you know, Ms. Holt?"

Kirsten nodded. "Yes. He filed three days ago. I have the papers here with me and thought we could talk about the divorce later."

"What does he want from me?"

"Just your signature."

"Really?"

"Yes."

"What about the house?"

"He signed the deed to your home over to you. He also has paid all the insurance and taxes on the house for this year."

Tamal smiled. "Good. It would have been a shame to kill him, to get what is really mine."

Darren shuddered a little bit but tried to not let it show. He wasn't successful. Tamal laughed. "Poor little detective. I promise not to kill you unnecessarily."

He nodded. "Thank you, I guess."

Kirsten bit her lower lip.

Tamal looked at the Prosecuting Attorney. "What else do you want to talk about?"

"What's the earliest time you remember killing someone?"

"You mean other than my twin brother when I was being born?"

It impressed Darren that the Prosecuting Attorney kept a straight face and even breathing. Tamal's defense attorney turned pale again, and Darren was sure his face showed horror.

"Yes, after that," Janice said.

"Well, when I was three years old, a little boy at daycare

wouldn't let me play with a truck. He was a selfish little shit."

"How did you kill him?"

"I followed him to the bathroom, closed and locked the door, and put his head in the toilet. I flushed and flushed and flushed until he quit kicking. Then, I dried my hands, left the bathroom, and closed the door."

"What happened next?"

"I went outside and played on the swing. I always loved swinging as high as I could."

"When did the teachers discover what had happened?"

"I don't know. It was longer than I thought it would be. They were both talking about sex and boyfriends while we were playing outside."

"Are there more children you killed?"

"Just one more until high school."

Kirsten Holt stood up and said, "I need to go to the bathroom right now."

Darren stood up and pressed the button for the guard and helped Kirsten to get to the bathroom. She didn't make it before she was vomiting in the hallway.

In the examination room, the Prosecuting Attorney, Janice Sutton said, "Interview over."

She stood up, picked up all her papers and told the guard, "Please take Ms. Chowdhury back to her cell."

"Wait," Tamal said. "Don't you want to hear the rest?"

"Yes, I do, but for now we are out of time."

Tamal laughed and laughed, but before Janice was out of hearing range, the laughter took on a loud, cackling, macabre tone.

She, too, went quickly to the bathroom.

CHAPTER FORTY-NINE

Janice Sutton could hear Kirsten Holt vomiting in a stall. She took a handkerchief from her purse and ran cold water over the cloth. She smiled and thought, *thank you mom for telling me tissues were fine, but you never know when a nice handkerchief will be exactly what you need.*

She squeezed the excess water out and went to help Kirsten. She handed her the cool cloth and said, "I'd give you some water, but there are no cups in here."

"This is marvelous. Thank you so much. I'm sorry to have interrupted the process. My stomach just couldn't take it anymore."

"Don't worry about it. My stomach was churning too."

Kirsten said, "I'm pregnant and have had only one episode of morning sickness. I thought it was past."

"Trust me, it was harrowing to hear her, and I've heard a lot of horrible things."

"Me too," Kirsten flushed the toilet and stepped out into the room. "I think it was the image of that poor little boy being killed by a three-year-old girl." Tears flowed down her face. "Next week we have our ultrasound and will learn our baby's gender."

Janice put an arm around Kirsten's shoulder. "Don't beat yourself up over this. I won't tell a soul you're not the Iron Maiden you're made out to be."

Kirsten chuckled. "Thanks. I have learned to be tough when dealing with clients and prosecutors. You being willing to protect my rep helps a lot."

"Don't think that means I won't remember."

"I know you will, but in this moment I'm glad you're on my side."

Janice said, "I'm going back out. We'll talk just you, me and the detective whenever you are ready."

Back in the interview, without Tamal present, the lawyers and the detective talked about the case and how to move forward.

Kirsten said, "I don't think an insanity plea will work in this case. However, I think Tamal is bat shit crazy."

Darren chuckled. "I agree. I'm sure there could and probably should be a psychiatric diagnosis for Tamal. She needs help in a big way."

"I agree," the Prosecuting Attorney said. "The question is how to move forward. Detective, have you heard any more about the stolen items?"

"Yes, all the items other than the two Roger bought with Tamal, are on the list of stolen jewelry. I've got a team at Tamal's house right now, comparing some high dollar items on the lists from the burglary team. I remember seeing many things with price tags still on them. Lots of purses, shoes, boots and silk scarves look as if they've never been used."

Kirsten said, "She could spend many years in prison for the thefts alone. We are unclear about how many murders she has committed. I don't know if she'll take a plea deal, but it is her only path forward."

Janice nodded. "Well, certainly a jury trial would be distressing for everyone involved, but I will charge her for every offense, and take her to court if she doesn't accept a plea bargain. My gut level right now is she won't take a plea. She loves the limelight and wants to tell us about every murder and all the details. I don't think she has an ounce of regret in any of the murders."

"Regardless, she can't be allowed in the general prison population and must be confined to a single bed cell," Darren said. "I know she'll hate that, but after the death of Mable O'Bryant this morning, the prison system can't take a chance with her."

Kirsten Holt sighed. "Let me know what deal you will make. My hope is we can learn about all her murders and give those families some relief."

Janice agreed. "I want to get a psychiatrist working with her. I don't think there will be any way the courts would allow an insanity plea, but I must cover the bases. Regardless, she is going to prison for a long time. There may be a plea deal, but her incarceration will be at a maximum-security prison where she will be watched all day, every day for the rest of her life."

Kirsten nodded and stood up. "If there are going to be more interviews, let me know. My father has offered to take over the case. I'm inclined to let him."

Janice stood up and said, "Let's do nothing more today. Talk with your father and then your client. We can set up video conferencing with her, so you don't have to be in the same room with her."

"Thanks. I'll let you and my client know how I'm going to proceed."

Darren said, "I'll walk you out, Ms. Holt. Ms. Sutton, I'll send you our report on the thefts. I'll also see if I can find out more about the boy she says she murdered."

The Prosecuting Attorney watched the detective and lawyer leave. She blew out a sigh and muttered, "What an unholy mess." She picked up her bags and went to her office.

She called her aide to come into her office.

"Okay, Brian, let's see if we can come up with a plea deal, we can stomach with this mess."

"You've got her dead to rights on her brother's and employer's murder. Why would you bargain on this case?"

"Sit down and hear the rest of the story."

He sat down then asked, "Is there a story that exonerates her?"

"Only in her gold-plated ego."

CHAPTER FIFTY

Odetta asked Basanti, "Is there anything else we can help you with before we go home?"

"No. I'm really excited to be in such a beautiful and safe place. This feels like a new beginning for me."

Danny said, "I feel a little weird leaving you up here all by yourself."

"I'll be fine. Very few people know where I am. With all the security features in the gallery and apartment, I'm safe. Remember, I've been living by myself for a few years now. This is a lovely place to be."

Roger leaned over and kissed her on the cheek. "I love you Amma."

"And I you, Beta. Have you decided yet about moving into my old house?"

"Yes. I think Pavlov and I will move this week. We both need a fresh start and to get started on living our lives again."

"Good, boy. Let me know if you need my help."

"I will, Amma."

When the young people finally left, Basanti went to the kitchen and cooked herself her favorite dinner. A hamburger on a soft bun with caramelized onions and mushrooms, fried potatoes, and a chocolate milkshake. She was pleased that Roger went to the grocery store for her without questioning the grocery list. She loved American food nearly as much as the Indian foods she was raised with. Tonight, was a celebration of freedom though, and she was going American all the way, including watching television. There were several new series she hadn't seen yet. The only difficulty for her this evening was which one to choose.

Tomorrow she would set up her office and start helping Odetta with the gallery. She was looking forward to building her new life.

Odetta and Danny sat on the big soft sofa in the large sunroom, watching the sunset on Puget Sound. Danny said, "I don't know what to do next."

"I have an idea."

"Good. I'm feeling lazy and unsure."

Odetta scooted closer to Danny and took her hand. "Do you love where you live?"

"Not particularly. It's nice enough, but it's just a place to live. It's a studio apartment about halfway between here and downtown Seattle. The view of Mt. Ranier is good, but otherwise not much to write home about."

"How about you stay the night here with me?"

Danny smiled and turned to look at Odetta. "I might be interested. Would we be in the same bed?"

"Unless you have a better idea."

"Kiss me and we'll see."

Roger sat with Pavlov on the reclining sofa watching Expedition Unknown and eating dinner. He'd stopped and bought his guilty secret for dinner. A hamburger from Zippy's. Onion rings and a root beer float topped off his dining pleasure. He and Simon had watched every show of every season of Expedition Unknown together. He missed Simon more than he could believe. In fact, he missed Simon more than he missed Tamal. Thinking of Tamal made him sad, but also made him furious.

He told Pavlov, "Even if she gets off scot free, I don't want to see her ever again. I'm not sure I can ever forgive her."

Pavlov looked up at him and whined with a bit of drool coming out of his mouth. Roger wiped the drool away with a napkin and said, "I think you just want more of my hamburger."

Pavlov licked his lips and Roger said, "Okay, one more bite, then the rest is mine." He broke off a sizable chunk of his hamburger and gave it to the dog. He quickly finished the hamburger and Pavlov whined again. "That's it buddy, it's all gone."

When the television show finished, he said, "Let's go for a walk." Pavlov jumped down and went to get his leash. Roger laughed and said, "What a dog!"

He called Stan and asked, "Do you have a few minutes to walk and meet Pavlov and I at the park."

"Sure. I'll meet you there in a jiffy."

Pavlov and Roger were at Highland Park about five minutes before Stan. Roger tossed a stick for Pavlov, who thought this was the best thing in the world to do. The air was brisk, but the sky was clear. Stan walked up and asked, "What's up, buddy?"

"I wanted to talk with you and tell you, my plans."

"You're moving, right?"

Roger chuckled. "How did you know?"

"I didn't but Renee and I talked about how hard it would be for you to stay in the neighborhood. Lots of heartbreak and misery for you to deal with here."

"Yeah, that's it exactly. Plus, Basanti is my only family now."

Stan nodded. "I'm grateful every day to have my parents still alive and close by. Family is a big deal for me."

"Me too. When I first met Tamal a month or two after her father's death, I thought, now—now, I get to make a family. Simon was my best friend before I met her. Her mother was a jewel and reminded me of my mom. I thought my life was set. I jumped in with both feet."

"I'm sorry it turned out so awful."

"It's not all awful. Simon was a gem, and I can't quit thinking about him when I'm in his house. I don't want to be in the house I rebuilt for Tamal. It all just feels creepy and sad."

"Where are you going to live? And before you answer, Renee

and I have a bet on this so be sure I don't lose five bucks to my wife."

Roger laughed. "Okay, here it is. I'm going to move into Basanti's house. She is going to live in the apartment over the gallery and help Odetta with the gallery."

"Dammit. There's five dollars gone, Roger. Plus, I'll miss you a lot."

"I know and I'll miss you too. However, I'm pretty sure I can line up a gig for your group when there are doings at the gallery."

"Well, that will be nice, but what about Old Man Coffee?"

Roger stopped walking and turned to Stan. "That's the only thing I'll really miss. But, hey, it's only an hour or less away. I figure when I have work closer to here, I'll let you guys know and you'll let me horn in."

"Always. When are you moving?"

"In a few days."

"Good, then let's have an Old Man Coffee before you go."

Roger nodded. "I'd like that a lot."

"What are you going to do with Simon's house?"

"I was thinking to lease it out, but maybe I'll sell it."

"Either way, let me know. My sister and her new hubby are talking about moving from Renton back here."

"Really?"

"Yeah, her husband works in Seattle. It would be a simple trip for him on the bus. One stops right in front of his office. A three-block walk from Simon's house to get on the bus. A short trip and he's at work. My sister's been offered a teaching position here at Highland Park Elementary starting this semester. One teacher had to take long-term sick leave and boom—Carol had a job."

Roger grinned. "Now isn't that something. They want to buy or lease?"

"Buy."

"Good. Let them know about the house and we'll see what we can work out. Give them my phone number and email too. I'll make them an offer they can't refuse—within reason."

Stan grinned. "My sister's name is Carol, and her husband is Edward Hilyard. They'll be really excited."

The two men walked a few blocks more, chatting about life, the Universe and everything. Finally, Stan said, "I'm freezing my nuts off out here."

"Me too. I'm ready for winter to get out of town and let us have a little nicer weather."

They stood, both looking up at the sky. Finally, Roger said, "Give me a hug and let me know when the next Old Man Coffee is."

They hugged and Stan said, "I promise we'll keep in touch. And, just so you know, I think you're doing the right thing."

"Even though it cost you five dollars?"

"Yep. Even then."

CHAPTER FIFTY-ONE

Darren and Martin sat side-by-side on the sofa, watching the last episode of Wallander.

Martin said, "Damn. I was hoping his mental lapses were just fatigue and over-work. I feel really bad for him."

Darren said, "You are aware he is a fictional character, right?"

"Oh, sure, but I found myself really worried about him. He seemed to have difficulty with the important parts of his life. He let his work consume him to the point of not being human."

"I agree. It's hard when we're in the middle of a big case not to let it consume us. When I was watching the show, I had to remind myself all his cases weren't back-to-back without ceasing. But, when we watched the shows, one a night until we watched them all, I too felt bad for him. It was like, 'is he the only detective in all of Sweden?' Then I'd have to remind myself he is a fictional character."

Martin chuckled. "Well, sometimes when you're in the thick of a big, important case, I feel that way too."

"Really?"

"Yeah. I know I'm the most important person in your life, but when a case drags on you seem consumed. I worry you'll burn out. I also worry I'll start taking it personally."

Darren took his hand. "One issue Sally pointed out in this case is that the perp of all the murder and mayhem kept secrets. We both have been feeling a need to talk about secrets with our spouses."

"Really?"

"Yeah. I've been trying to think if I have any big secrets from you."

"Well, I wouldn't know since they are secrets, but I know I don't have any big secrets from you."

"Well, Sally and I realized that the big secrets often started as little secrets and grew."

Martin nodded. "I can see that happening. Do you have any little secrets from me?"

"I haven't come up with any yet except the bit about having secrets."

Martin laughed and elbowed Darren gently. "Okay. Here's a little secret of mine."

"You don't have to tell me if you don't want to."

"I promise its nothing terrible. I know you *think* you don't like mushrooms."

"I don't. They are just nasty."

"I think you think they are nasty because they are fungi."

"Yeah, I've heard the old *there's a fungus among us* and all I can think of is smelly nasty feet. What do mushrooms have to do with secrets?"

"You know my meatloaf you adore?"

"Yes…"

"I chop mushrooms up very fine because I think my meatloaf tastes lots better with mushrooms."

Darren looked at his husband with raised eyebrows. "Are you telling me that all these years I've been eating mushrooms?"

"Yes, I am."

Darren shook his head. "What else are you keeping from me?"

"Not much of anything. How about you?"

"Well, I know you think eating at fast-food places is awful, but I can't help myself. When you're not around, I head straight to McDonald's and buy a Mc Muffin with Sausage."

"Really? I've never seen a McDonald's bag in the trash bin."

"Of course not. I'm a detective. I know how to bury evidence."

Martin hooted with laughter, then said, "And I know how to bury mushrooms."

Both men laughed at the other, then Darren said, "Okay. I

don't know how I'll tolerate it, but I can't deny your meatloaf is the best I've ever had. Do *not* tell my mother that."

"Ah, another secret, but one we can share."

Darren grinned. "So, I'll quit saying I don't like mushrooms, but I will say I don't like the idea of eating fungus."

"Fair enough. I won't fuss when you eat fast food as long as you don't expect me to like it or partake of it."

"Deal," Darren said. "What other secrets do you have?"

"I can't think of any, but I know now I won't feel guilty when I make meatloaf."

"Good, and I won't feel guilty when I eat fast-food."

"I want to talk about Basanti Chowdhury though," Martin said. "I know she is going to be working at the gallery in Edmonds. Is she going to give up creating pastries to sell?"

"No, in fact she has free rein to use the commercial kitchen there to build her business."

"Good. Will you ask her to call me? I want to discuss seasonal variations for desserts and hopefully incorporate more apples into the desserts."

"I've already given her your number. She'll call you in a few days. She wants to have things a bit more settled over her daughter before she moves full steam ahead."

Martin shook his head. "It all seems too gruesome and awful. I don't know how you can deal with the sorrow and pain."

"Today was hard. Really hard. I won't tell you about it because it just gets worse every time we talk with her. Each interview is more gruesome and grueling than the last."

"Did she reveal more murders?"

"Yes, and thefts too. She's been murdering all her life."

"All her life?"

Darren nodded. "Since childhood and according to her since infancy."

Martin shuddered. "Okay, let's watch something fun on television. There's another season of The Voice starting up, and I've got it all recorded. I'd prefer to go to bed with music and fun in my brain."

"Excellent choice," Darren said. He sat next to his husband, watching television, and hoping his own dreams wouldn't be too haunted.

Meanwhile, at the King County Detention Center, Tamal lay on her bed going over and over in her mind about her life. She was pleased with how things had gone earlier in the day with the Prosecuting Attorney, her lawyer, and the silly detective. He was too nice a man for the job he had, at least so she thought.

She began playing back her life and enjoying every moment of every time she defended herself by simply taking the lives of people she didn't feel deserved to live. She thought, *I'm sure Ms. Sutton will offer me a plea deal. No way am I staying in jail a moment more than necessary. I've got a feeling Little Miss Holt isn't up to the task though. There are more lawyers with fewer scruples than hers. Regardless, it's important to me to be sure they understand I'm the one with power and they are simply the supporting cast. Surely, they know the supporting cast are all disposable.*

She giggled, planning exactly how she would *dispose* of anyone who stood in her way.

Since I'm just dreaming about the how's and where's, let's get exotic, especially with little Ms. Holt.

Nelson shuddered and joined Stan in his dreams. "Hey buddy, be sure you don't go anywhere near Tamal."

"I won't. Besides, she is in jail. I think she might spend most of the rest of her life in jail."

"Don't count on it. She certainly isn't counting on it."

"Yeah, but she doesn't know enough about me to hurt me."

"All the same, she is making plans for all the people, including Roger and Darren, who she calls the supporting cast. I'm worried she has set something in motion."

Stan chuckled. "This isn't a stage production."

Nelson said, "No, it is real life. And real death."

Kirsten Holt was happy to be driving home. She needed to be with her husband Steve and in her own space. Her father agreed to take over the case, which was a great relief. They'd have a few legal hoops to jump through, but she well and truly didn't want to be near Tamal Chowdhury ever again in her life. She shuddered, remembering the gleeful way Tamal had told them about the all the murders she'd committed and the thefts.

I've never seen a client behave as she did. Kirsten shook her head and touched the brakes on her car as she exited Interstate 5, merging onto Interstate 90, ready to be home in her own comfortable space with her husband on Mercer Island. She smiled a little, knowing she was privileged to live on the island. She tapped the brakes again, surprised that they seemed a little soft.

Her phone rang, and she touched the Bluetooth phone icon on her steering wheel. She said, "Hi, honey. I'm just entering I-90 and heading home."

"Great. I'm relieved. I've been worried about you all day."

Kirsten looked in her rearview mirror, glad no one was behind her. She turned on her left turn signal to merge into the heavy traffic heading east. A car was close on her left rear side and she decided not to push it but slow down and then merge behind him. She tapped her brakes again and her foot went all the way to the floor. She shouted, "Steve, my brakes aren't working."

"Honey! Downshift if you can but don't speed up under any circumstances. Get to the shoulder and let the car coast to a stop."

"The traffic is crazy." She quit trying to merge and gradually could get close to the shoulder, but a lot of cars were surrounding her. She turned on her emergency blinkers, trying to get to the shoulder. The tunnel across to Lake Washington was looming ahead. Kirsten shouted, "Steve! Steve!"

Her husband yelled back, "Slow down!" He heard the sounds of metal-on-metal crashing together. A car horn blared. Screams and cries sounded loud and then suddenly quieted. He screamed, "Kirsten!"

Kirsten did not answer.

Author's Notes

I first met Gordy Ryan over 15 years ago in Norman, Oklahoma. Marial Martyn and her husband Wiley Harwell invited David and I to a weekend of drumming. Wow! What a terrific weekend. We learned to play djembe drums with about thirty or forty other people. Once we got rolling together, beating on goat skins, we were hooked! For several years while we lived in Norman, we went to the drumming event. We even joined a drumming circle hosted by Marial and Wiley.

I bought a rather inexpensive drum that was smaller than many but fit my short torso just right. I still love the sound of my drum. By the end of the first weekend, David wanted a Gordy Ryan built djembe. His drum is taller than mine and a beautiful maple base with a higher, sharper tone than mine—a lovely sound too. We both still have our drums although we don't play them much anymore. They are a source of intrigue and fun for the grandchildren though.

Gordy and his wife Zoe were an inspiration to us. What we learned and experienced in those weekend workshops still resides in us today. They are based out of Hollyhock on Cortes Island which is about 100 miles north of Vancouver, British Columbia. Click on the link to see what they are all about—it is MUCH more than drumming although drumming is still a part of the experience.

Recompose is a public benefit organization working to change how we deal with death and how we can help our planet. They work hard to allow people to have a dignified passing from this body back to our planet. Each body is treated with natural reverence as detailed in the story. Once the process is complete, the human body has become about a pickup load of dirt. Now that's a return to Mother Earth!

The company is working to help all humans across the country become again a part of Mother Earth after we die. There are legal hoops they are jumping through and hopefully someday this will be available to every person in our country. I'm excited that this is the pathway David, and I will take when our bodies give out, years and years from now.

We didn't kill off the villain this time. At first, I was having difficulty deciding how Tamal could leave this earth. Neither David nor I had a good answer. I wrote the rough draft and just left it all hanging. I wasn't clear about my ambivalence to it all. Certainly, if any woman needed killing, Tamal did. But I just couldn't in good conscience do it.

Then, I remembered the story of Abraham and Isaac. Their story has become a cornerstone for much of literary writing and is called 'The Horns of a Moral Dilemma'. The question is: Do you kill your son to appease your god, or do you tell you god to beat feet away from you? It seems either choice is dire.

When we were talking about this with our son Ray (who provides a lot of inspiration for our work) he asked, "So, it's like the streetcar story." We didn't know what he was talking about, but he shared the concept as he'd learned it.

A streetcar in San Francisco is careening down a hill out of control. Ahead is a man tied to the tracks who will surely be killed by the streetcar. The streetcar driver has mere moments to decide whether or not to save the man's life by taking the emergency ramp exit. Taking the ramp very probably will kill the streetcar driver and all the passengers on the streetcar.

That's the 'Horns of a Moral Dilemma' in a nutshell. Do we kill Tamal as a society or do we risk her killing more people if she ever gets out of prison—or even does more killing in prison. She is obviously skilled enough to wreak more havoc.

As a nation, from time-to-time we've grappled with the death penalty. In Washington State there is no death penalty anymore. One could argue, Tamal is a woman in need of dying—but who are we to do the killing? I couldn't do it.

In 1981 as a young mother and wife, who was raised in a repressive and abusive home, I was faced with a moral dilemma. I could have killed my father and that would have made the world a safer place. BUT. I'd at the very least spend most of my life in prison or been executed. I could have done nothing and put my children, myself, and my marriage at risk. I chose, instead of the first two options, to isolate myself and my children from my birth family. It was a hard thing to do. But. I think it was the right choice. When my father was in his early 80s, he died a natural death. For me, it was 60 years too late to be of any good use for me.

So, in this book, I decided to leave it hanging. My brilliant son, Ray, said, "While she's in prison, maybe something needs to happen to create the suspense that maybe the world isn't safe from her even in prison." Thus, something goes wrong with Kirsten's brakes.

Is this caused by Tamal? Is it caused by someone else? Is it just Kirsten's bad luck? I have no idea, dear reader.

THANKS, DEAR READER!!

Thank you for reading our book.

We hope you enjoyed reading or listening to our story as much as we enjoyed writing and recording it. If you enjoyed this book, please leave an honest review on Audible.com, Amazon.com, or Goodreads. As independently published authors, the only way we become known to readers, is through your reviews and your sharing of our stories.

Glenda has written seven novels in The Paradigm Books series. They are available on Amazon and Audible as well.

The Paradigm Books are:
1. The Gloriana Paradigm
2. The Mother Paradigm
3. The Belle Paradigm
4. The Father Paradigm
5. The Cora Paradigm
6. The Dakota Paradigm
7. The Adoption Paradigm

She also has written the Shaman Chronicle series:
1. Buffalo Dreams
2. Salmon Dreams
3. Bobcat Dreams
4. Sparrow Dreams
5. Crawdad Dreams
6. Elk Dreams

Glenda and our granddaughter Marti have written Nobody's Home, a children's book about spending spring break at Grandma and Granddad's house during the COVID times.

They are available on Amazon as e-books, Kindle, or paperback books. They are also available as audio books on Audible.

You can follow Glenda and David Clemens on their website, Facebook, Amazon, or Goodreads.

Made in the USA
Columbia, SC
04 July 2021